Imagine A New World

Judgment In Time Series Book II

IMAGINE A NEW WORLD

New People Publishing

Follow us on Facebook and Twitter to keep up with
Judgment In Time Series conversations and updates

Facebook: Search for Judgment In Time Series
Twitter: @JITSeries

Available in Hardcover, Paperback, and
eBook as ePub, Kindle, and Nook

Fiction: Action and Adventure, Political Intrigue, Alternative History, Romance, Mystery, Thriller, Historical Fiction, Military Fiction, Science Fiction, Naval Battles

Judgment In Time Series
    Book I: Judgment In Time
    Book II: Imagine A New World
    Book III: Another Fine Mess
    Book IV: Another Side of Armageddon
    Book V: Title Coming
    Book VI: Judgment of the Gods

New People Publishing
www.NewPeoplePublishing.com

Editor: Robert Allen Fisher
Cover Art and Full Page Illustrations: Jennifer Cole
Production Design and Illustrations: Tom Hultgren

ISBN-13: 978-0-9835020-9-8
Advance Edition: Trade Paperback

Printed in the United States of America by:
Lightning Source

10 9 8 7 6 5 4 3 2 1

About the Author

Kevin Klesert, a successful independent businessman, has experienced firsthand how small businesses all over the country carried a disproportionate amount of the burden to meet their legal obligations. The steady erosion of Main Street USA under mountains of onerous regulations, licenses, taxes, and fees from Federal, State, and Local Governments have all but destroyed their ability to succeed and turn a reasonable profit.

His intense study of historical trends brought to him the correlation between the downfall of dominant societies of the past and the current struggle to maintain the most noble and ambitious political experiment in human history, the United States of America. He discovered the seeds of ruin were planted within the very generation that launched the United States to world preeminence.

Kevin Klesert's desire to shed light on this dire situation through the means of a thrilling adventure has produced a story worthy of the fight against these negative forces. The ideas for the Judgment In Time Series percolated in his adventurous imagination while he raised his four children and ran an award-winning design and construction company. A 3rd generation native of Southern California, Kevin Klesert imbues his writing with his passion for history, adventure, and fantasy.

Table of Contents

Characters

Main Characters

Rear Admiral UH Sean Phillips – Commander, Enterprise Task Force
Captain Anthony Knox – Chief of Staff to Admiral Sean Phillips
Rear Admiral UH Retired Alicia Calhoun – Secretary of Defense
Captain Renée Aslan – Naval Attaché to Alicia Calhoun

Secondary Main Characters

Dr. William Safire, PhD – Comstock Technologies Chief Specter Engineer
Dr. Rebecca Cutler, PhD – Comstock Technologies Lead Specter Engineer
Dr. Forrest Phelps, PhD – Comstock   Computer Specialist
Commander Carl Eddington – First Officer, USS Missouri
Commander Logan Barrish – First Officer, USS Enterprise
Lt. Commander Daniel Osaka – Information Warfare Officer,
    USS Missouri
Captain *Dash* Nelson – Air Wing Commander [CAG], USS Enterprise
Commander Michael *Thorny* Thornton – Task Force SEAL Commander
Lt. Commander Edwin T. Layton – Codebreaker
Lt. W. J. Jasper Holmes – Codebreaker

Support Characters

Chief Warrant Officer Mark Brunel – Chief Engineer, USS Missouri
Chief Warrant Officer Brad Sanders – Chief Engineer, USS Enterprise
Chief Warrant Officer Patrick Callahan – Chief Engineer, USS Decatur
Lt. Commander Harold Ramis – P-3 Orion reconnaissance pilot
Lt Franklin Morris – SEAL Squad Leader
Lt. Anatoly Ginsberg – Russian Language Interpreter
Ensign Gloria Layworth – Bridge Communications Officer, USS Missouri

Enterprise Task Force Captains and Their Ships

Captain Charles Folger – Commanding Officer, battleship USS Missouri
Captain Steven Brewster – Commanding Officer, carrier USS Enterprise
Captain Frederick Johnson – cruiser USS Chancellorsville
Captain Gordon Lincoln – cruiser USS Princeton
Commander Regis Goddard – destroyer USS John Paul Jones
Commander Steven Holmes – destroyer USS Decatur
Captain Mark Daily – attack submarine USS Seawolf
Captain Marlowe Turner – attack submarine USS Hampton
Commander Andy Gable – cargo ship USNS Amelia Earhart
Lt. Commander James Peck – fleet oiler USNS Laramie

x

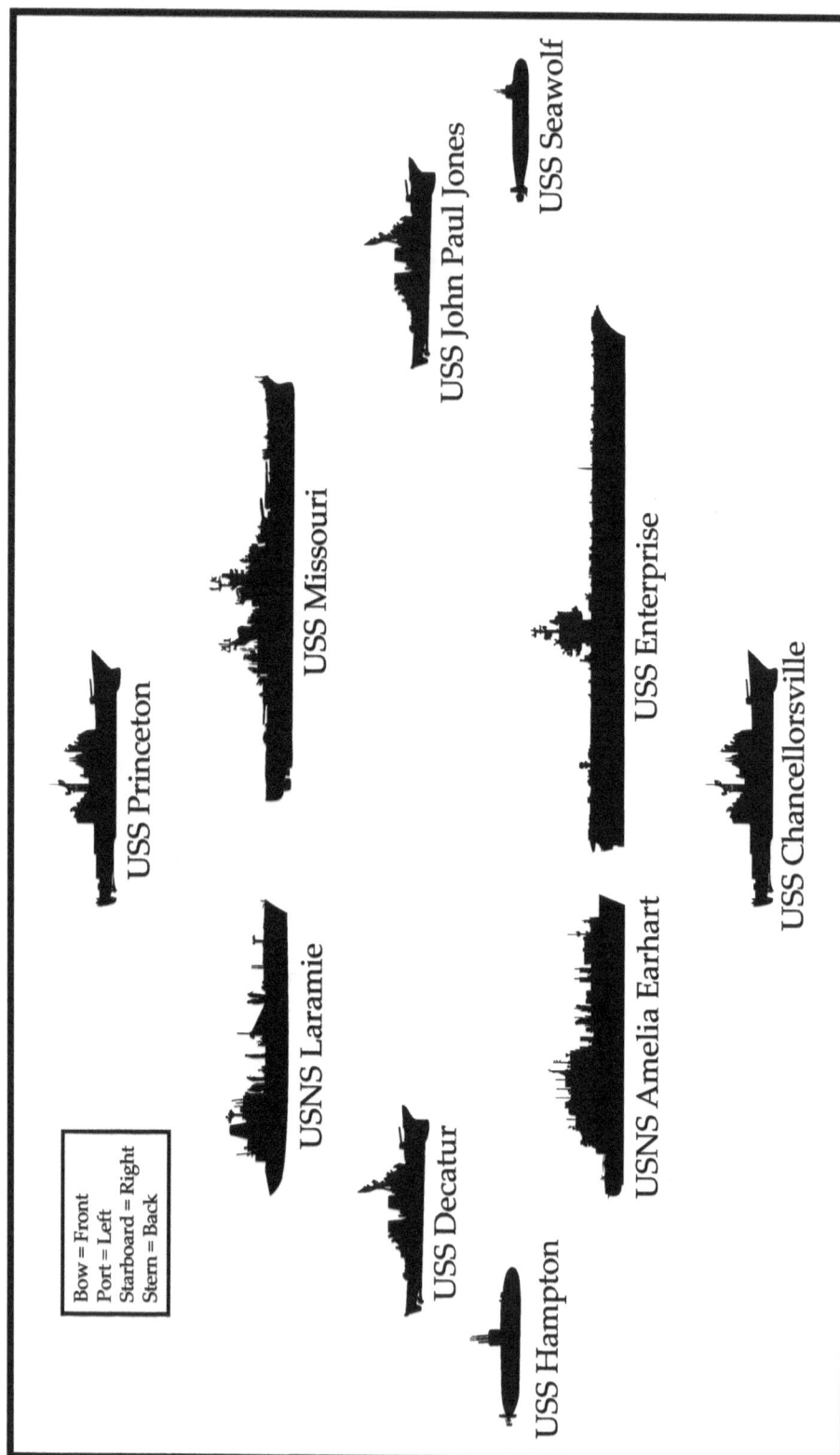

Bow = Front
Port = Left
Starboard = Right
Stern = Back

USS Princeton

USS Missouri

USS John Paul Jones

USS Seawolf

USNS Laramie

USS Enterprise

USS Decatur

USNS Amelia Earhart

USS Chancellorsville

USS Hampton

Chapter One

Convoy

When the aircraft carrier USS Enterprise cleared the Panama Canal locks on the Atlantic side, the task force reformed around her. Seahawk helicopters landed on the flight deck with the last of the SEAL squads who had kept the United States Army units from trapping the ships in the locks. With Specter engaged, they passed invisible under the silent gun emplacements at Fort Sherman on Toro Point. Contact with the supply ships still on the Pacific side of the canal established they would arrive at Panama Bay in six hours.

Lt. Daniel Osaka handed Sean a transcript.

After reading it, Sean laughed and turned to Tony with a sly grin. "Osaka intercepted communications between General Andrews and the Admiral in command of the task force headed our way."

"Who'd they send?"

Intentionally ignoring Tony, Sean issued orders to the CIC Officer. "Change course to intercept the approaching task force."

"Aye Aye Admiral."

Unable to stand it, Tony asked again, "Who did the President send?"

"It's Halsey," Sean deadpanned. "And based on the radio intercepts, he's every bit as confused as the commanders in the

Canal Zone. It's obvious that Roosevelt didn't feel obligated to explain much when he gave his orders."

"From what we learned at Annapolis of Halsey's aggressive command style," Tony recalled, "as his Commander-In Chief, all the President had to do was tell him we are a threat.

Sean agreed. "That's why the president chose him. Anyway, I think it is time to find out if Alicia can convince him to keep his dick in his pants."

"So you don't think it would be a good idea for me to make the introductions?" Tony asked with a wry smile.

"Not unless our only other option was Sarah Palin." Alicia laughed at the absurdity that someone so vacuous would ever have this kind of power.

Tony feigned shock. "I am deeply offended by your assumption that you don't have any faith that I can be fair and balanced."

Though enjoyable watching the two go at it, Sean turned his attention to Lt. Commander Daniel Osaka. "Let's get this over with. Contact Admiral Halsey."

"Yes Sir."

Osaka had already coached his 21st Century digital colleagues on how to communicate through 1941 naval analog communications. After five minutes of repeated transmissions, a gruff voice boomed out over the CIC speakers. "Who the hell is this?"

"Good morning Admiral. This is Secretary of the Defense Alicia Calhoun. I would like to verify the reports you have received from the garrisons on both Fort Sherman and Quarry Heights regarding their failure to keep us in the locks."

Halsey was completely mystified with what was happening. One minute he commanded Task Force 8 from the USS Enterprise CV-6 in the Pacific, then orders from Washington sent him halfway around the world to command a 6th Fleet task force centered on the aircraft carrier USS Wasp CV-7 in the Atlantic.

That his orders were to confront an unknown naval threat trapped by Panama Canal forces on Gatun Lake only added to his confusion. Now he found himself addressed by a woman asking him to confirm news that he had only received minutes ago.

In the Enterprise CIC, they heard a conversation in the background before Admiral Halsey returned. "I ask again, why am I addressing a woman and what the hell is a Secretary of Defense?" This mystery on the high seas so soon after the Japanese threat miraculously ended was not suited to Halsey's temperament. He hated unknowns.

His abrupt manner didn't faze Alicia. "It appears that President Roosevelt decided to keep you in the dark about our existence, Admiral."

Halsey completely lost it. "I repeat, what the hell is a Secretary of Defense, and why am I talking to a woman?"

"If you could give me a moment to explain Admiral, I'm sure I can clear up some of your confusion." From all of her years of dealing with a misogynist military, Alicia knew how to deal with the very definition of a man's man in 1941. "First off, I need you to suspend your beliefs about how the world works and listen with an open mind to what I am about to tell you. Please understand we are not a threat to you, the President, or the interests of the United States. In fact, we are a United States 7th Fleet Naval Task Force deployed out of San Diego."

It dawned on Halsey that the woman sounded American. He also knew General Andrews had included in his report statements from his soldiers who told of Southern accents and oblique references that only Americans would use. Regardless, he had his orders. "The only thing I care to know Missy, is when we make contact is that you will heave to, and surrender your ships."

"I'm sorry I will have to decline your offer Admiral. We didn't come all this way to play Anthony to your Augustus. The next time you hear from me is when we are cruising right through the middle of your task force." Alicia made a neck slicing motion with her hand to cut off communications. "It's not like we didn't already know he would need a push."

Sean agreed. "Let the show begin. Launch the F-35s."

Halsey turned in frustration to his Chief of Staff. "Any word from our reconnaissance planes?"

"Nothing but the usual local water traffic Sir."

"Get a squadron of Wildcats in the air to cover the fleet, and have the Dauntless and Helldivers readied for action."

"Aye Aye Admiral."

With his task force at battle stations, Admiral Halsey sat in the Admirals Chair on the bridge of the carrier Wasp. Minutes later, two F-35s appeared out of nowhere and screamed across the flight deck at the height of twenty feet, blasting a shock wave that shook the bridge. The next second they went vertical and disappeared as fast as they had appeared.

"What the hell was that?" an astonished Halsey shouted when two more of the alien looking craft appeared from the opposite direction to repeat the same maneuver, forcing the flight deck personnel to fall flat on the deck in panic.

"What the hell are we dealing with here?" Admiral Halsey's heart raced right along with the rest of the sailors watching the spectacle of the 21st Century war machines blazing through their propeller driven world.

With Halsey's fleet now only two miles northeast of the cloaked task force, Captain Charles Folger had a front row seat to the spectacle from the bridge of the Enterprise. Looking through a set of binoculars he smiled at the disruption the F-35s created on Halsey's carrier.

Charles reported to Tony in the CIC. "The F-35's had the desired effect Sir."

"Thank you Captain," Tony replied.

"Let's see if he's willing to talk now," Sean said as he turned to Osaka. "Re-establish contact with Halsey."

This time his response was immediate. "You've got my attention."

"This is Admiral Sean Phillips, Commander of the Enterprise

Task Force. The aircraft buzzing your carrier have the capacity to blow your ships out of the water. Along with that unpleasant fact, we are sitting two miles off your port quarter, and if I choose to, I can pump 16-inch armor piercing shells right though the bridge you are standing on." Sean then recited Halsey's exact coordinates to him.

Though Sean gave the correct coordinates on Halsey's location, he lied to Halsey about their position. He was curious to see if the response from the aggressive Admiral would fit the man who left the entire invasion fleet under his command in Leyte Gulf exposed, while he chased after the carrier bait the Japanese dangled in front of him in 1944.

Tony reversed their roles and knew he would be climbing the walls if confronted with such an insane situation. He almost felt bad for him – almost. He was about to suggest toning the rhetoric down, when the CIC Officer reported.

"Sir, Alpha Whiskey reports the contacts are firing weapons into the empty ocean about two miles off their port side."

On the bridge of the Enterprise, Commander Logan Barrish's voice came over the CIC loudspeakers, "There are flashes along the length of every one of their warships. The 14-inch guns on the battleships, the 12- and 8-inch guns on the cruisers, and a hail of 5-inch fire from the destroyers. Wait, they've stopped. Hold on—, now their Helldivers are dive bombing the same area."

While his narrative played out, they watched video footage of the misdirected attack. Tony was impressed. "How long do you think the stubborn fool will continue to tear up empty ocean?"

Just then, reconnaissance video came into the CIC from the cloaked F-35s circling Halsey's fleet.

Sean didn't hesitate as he focused on the CIC Officer. "Flank speed! Hard to port! Order Captain Aslan to have the Missouri simultaneously lay a 16-inch barrage two hundred yards off the bow of the lead escorts, and another two hundred yards aft the trailing destroyer as soon as we are far enough off for the gunners to make the trajectory."

After The CIC Officer relayed the orders, Sean added, "When the Missouri fires swing aft of Halsey's fleet to his port side five miles out, and then match his course and speed."

"Yes Sir," the CIC Officer acknowledged.

Tony smiled at the action. "It is nice to operate without the two supply ships slowing us down."

Over on the Missouri, Commander Eddington got off the phone and reported to Renée. "The Gun Captains report loaded and the trajectory laid in. They are ready when you are, Captain.

Captain Aslan didn't hesitate. "Fire!"

All at once, 12,000 pounds of metal exited the six 16-inch rifled gun barrels. The simultaneous blast, combined with the concussion, sounded as impressive as two freight trains colliding. Renée stood in stunned silence for a moment letting her emotions ride along with the shells. When they exploded right on target, the sensation was as close to an orgasm without sex that she would ever experience.

Renée had difficulty gathering her thoughts. She turned to a grinning Commander Eddington. "Now I understand what Tony was trying to explain. What a rush."

In the Enterprise CIC, Captain Aslan's excited voice burst out from the overhead speakers. "Six shells – right on target!"

Alicia placed a call to the Missouri to share her excitement with her friend. "You did good Renée."

Tony then took the phone from Alicia. "You got to unleash the big dogs. Welcome to the elite group of Captains."

When Admiral Halsey heard the whistle of the 16-inch shells, and then witnessed the enormous and precisely positioned explosions fore and aft of his fleet, he let loose with a stream of profanities. After the last of these, he came to the realization that he didn't have the means to deal with this invisible enemy.

"Admiral, they're back on the radio."

"Son of a Bitch!" He hesitated long enough to get his anger under control before grabbing the phone out of the operator's hand. "Just who the hell are you?"

After he breathed a sigh of relief, Sean jumped to take advantage of Halsey's frustration. He calmly replied over the radio. "Do you feel better now?"

"Look, you've made your point. I repeat, who the hell are you and what exactly are your intentions?"

"We are Americans just like you, and I can tell you with absolute certainty that we are not the threat the President ordered you to neutralize. Our reluctance to return fire should inform you that we do not have any interest in killing American sailors. If you could expand your thinking and listen to our position, we could turn our attention to our real problem; the orders President Roosevelt gave you."

"How do you know anything about my orders?"

"You'd be surprised what I know Admiral Halsey. If you would allow me to come aboard the Wasp, I can supply you with all the proof you need that we are not your enemy. Have you asked yourself who you think was responsible for Japan's sudden decapitation?"

Sean then took the next few minutes to explain how they had neutralized Japan and the subsequent conference with Roosevelt and Churchill. He finished with the President's betrayal. "So as you can see Admiral, all I want to do is carry out our mission, and if you'll agree to allow my supply ships safe passage through the canal, we both can continue to Norfolk."

"My orders are clear about the threat you pose, and to keep you from clearing the canal. But since you've rendered that part of my mission moot, and I can't see you to hit you, it seems those supply ships are the only leverage I have." The radio was silent for a few seconds before he continued. "What assurances do I have of your intentions if I allow your ships through the canal?"

"I don't know how many times you want me to repeat the same thing before we can move on."

The line went quiet again, as Halsey weighed the offer. "What do you need from me to prepare my ship to bring your craft aboard?"

Sean smiled and answered Halsey. "The mode of my transport will not require any efforts from your deck crew. This will be self-explanatory when you see it approach, so please resist any instinct to shoot it down. Thank you for your patience, Admiral."

"As long as you don't do anything to give me a reason, there won't be a problem."

"Good. What I do need is for you to recover all of your planes. Don't worry about our planes; the ones you experienced earlier are flying CAP."

"Agreed." Then under his breath, he added, "It's not like my planes are doing me any good anyway."

After they broke off contact, Sean explained to a horrified Alicia and a perplexed Tony his reasoning for the risky meet. "I think the only way to convince him is Admiral to Admiral. It also wouldn't hurt to make an impression on the sailors onboard his ship. I'll bring along my laptop to show him the documents both Roosevelt and Churchill signed, along with the video of our meeting. Should be a piece of cake."

Tony and Alicia looked at each other and realized it didn't matter what they said, he was going.

"This is something we should have done a long time ago. We need to ally ourselves with other sources to protect ourselves from any further attempts to spread misinformation about us. The President already has proven to be untrustworthy, so it's time to take our case to our naval counterparts."

Alicia felt it was necessary to remind Sean of one little snag in his argument. "I seem to recall an earlier conversation where we agreed I would be the one to handle negotiations."

"Nice try. The agreement stated civilian negotiations; this is Admiral to Admiral. Halsey needs a sit down with someone who is his equal."

Wrong choice of words. "So now I'm not your equal?"

Sean locked eyes with Tony. "Don't look at me. You dug your own hole."

Everyone else in the CIC kept their head down and waited. A weak smile preceded Sean's attempt at a mea culpa. He leaned close to Alicia so no one else could hear. "What I meant to say is that as someone Halsey would recognize as his equal, not that you are not mine. Let's give the dinosaur some time to adjust to our modern sensibilities before springing your genius on him."

Alicia smiled as she subtly reached down and tapped his manhood. "You mean until I can grow one of these?"

Sean's eyes narrowed. "Honey, not around the children."

She removed her hand and reached into her jacket pocket to pull out an envelope that she handed to Sean. "Since there isn't anything neither Tony or I can say to stop you, you might as well take the letter I wanted sent to Roosevelt with you."

"That's a good idea," Sean happily acknowledged.

Sean immediately returned to the matter at hand. "Position the fleet two miles off Halsey's port Tony, and wait until you hear from me." Sean wasn't going to leave anything to chance.

"That's a smart idea, but I think it would also be even better to bring some backup with you."

"All right, see to it."

"I'll be on the bridge when your plan blows up in your face and I have to come to your rescue," Tony quipped.

Sean rolled his eyes. "Thanks for your vote of confidence."

Sean boarded a Seahawk with a four-member SEAL squad and was surprised to see Commander Thornton was one of them.

When he saw the look on Sean's face, Thorny laughed. "You

thought I would miss out on this?"

"Glad to have you aboard Commander. When we land on the Wasp, I want to see weapons holstered."

"Not a problem, Sir."

"Captain, as soon as we are clear, I want you to return to the Enterprise. I don't want Halsey's curiosity to get the better of him and attempt something stupid."

"Yes Sir Admiral," the pilot acknowledged as he lifted off the carrier's deck.

On the bridge of the Wasp, Halsey scanned the ocean for any sign of his invisible opponents. "God Damn it! How am I supposed to carry out an order against an enemy that I can't see?" He dropped the useless binoculars unceremoniously onto the counter. "I'm going down to the flight deck."

Before he could reach the door, one of the spotters yelled out. "Strange craft off our starboard quarter two miles out. About one-thousand feet off the deck and closing fast Sir."

The Seahawk carrying Sean rapidly closed in on Halsey's carrier. When it reached the Wasp, Sean ordered the pilot to hover twenty feet above. "Let's see who comes to greet us before putting down."

With all of the dignity he could muster, Halsey slowly made his way off the bridge. Once he stepped out onto the flight deck, he couldn't take his eyes off the craft that stayed perfectly still above his ship. "That bird has got one hell of a lot of technology none of us have ever seen built into it." Halsey looked up to see his ship's photographer frantically attempting to set up his movie camera to document the scene.

When Sean could see that neither Halsey nor any of the men accompanying him appeared armed, he signaled to land the Seahawk. Ten seconds after touching down, and its passengers safely off, the craft took off and headed back toward the Enterprise, where it continued to circle just within Specter's screen.

For a brief moment, the five stood alone as the stunned sailors on the flight deck stared at Sean and the all Black SEAL squad as if they were demons. That their uniforms matched those of the ones they were used to saluting only added to their confusion.

Sean could see the sailors who stood in front of the ship's island were moving out of the way to let Halsey through. As soon as he was visible to the deck hands, all came to attention. "Stand easy." The sailors not involved with the strangers reluctantly resumed their duties upon hearing the booming command.

He quickly strode up to Sean and reached out his hand. "You said nothing about bringing armed Marines along with you." Halsey made it clear he was not pleased Sean brought along the SEAL squad. "Admiral Phillips, have your men..." After taking a closer look, he found it difficult to find the right words. "And a woman?"

"Yes Admiral, we have women serving in every aspect of the modern Navy."

Halsey didn't have the time to digest the color of the skin of the SEAL team, as he was still trying to digest the idea of woman in the ranks. "What I was trying to say is I need your escorts to surrender their arms."

As he made his request sound more like a demand, a group of Marines moved out of the crowd of sailors toward the SEALs.

Commander Thornton stepped up to block their approach and requested of Sean, "Is this what you want Admiral? If not, I don't see a problem keeping these jarheads off our backs until the Seahawk returns."

The Marine's reaction to Thorny's challenge made Sean stifle a laugh as they stepped backwards, one of them tripping.

"I'm sorry Admiral Halsey, but I promised my Chief of Staff nothing would come between me and the SEAL squad. Either you don't worry about them, or I return to my ship."

After a few moments to think it through, Halsey decided not to push it for now.

"Stand down Marines," Halsey ordered.

"Why don't we have a seat Admiral?" He motioned Sean to a table set up on the flight deck in the shadow of the superstructure.

Commander Thornton and the SEAL squad followed their charge, the Marines relaxed, and all eyes focused on the Admirals.

Sean sat down, opened his laptop, and turned it on. "I understand you're a man who likes things straight up, so let's get to it. Before I try to give you a lengthy explanation, I think this will help move things along in a more useful manner."

Admiral Halsey did his best to hide his reaction to the bright color LCD clarity of President Roosevelt and Churchill surrounded by naval officers and one attractive well-dressed woman coming out of the thin metallic box.

He remained quiet for the next thirty minutes, intently watching the video play out. After the meeting portion of the video ended, the sinking of the Japanese carriers in the waters north of Oahu followed, which included the brutal destruction of the two Japanese battleships by the USS Missouri.

Though Halsey had to believe his eyes and ears, he would be disobeying direct orders from his Commander in Chief if he let Sean go unchallenged. "With everything I've witnessed so far, I understand there isn't much I can do, however, I have been ordered to stop you."

"What the hell am I in the middle of?" Halsey thought, as his mind raced through all of the implications the man in front of him represented. The Naval Academy hadn't prepared him for anything such as this. Hell, how could it? "I could hold on to you to see if your companions would surrender to get you back, but we both know that will never work. So what do you suggest we do Admiral? What's your name anyway?'

"I am Rear Admiral Sean Phillips, Sir. In addition, what I recommend is that you stop treating me as an adversary. Our goals are one in the same."

Halsey leaned back in his chair and sighed. "It's like if me and my ships suddenly showed up off the Thames in the fifteenth century. Your planes are right out of Buck Rodgers, while in comparison I have Wright Flyers. I suppose even if I wanted to stop you, all I would accomplish is getting many of my people killed and my ships sunk. If what you say is true, I refuse to be responsible for that after what you just showed me."

Halsey then turned to his Chief of Staff. "Contact Admiral King and report our situation. Also inform him that the Admiral in charge of the mystery force is with me, and ask for orders."

"Yes Sir."

"Looks like we've got some time," Halsey stated. "It would be helpful to understand more about where you came from."

"Unfortunately your curiosity is going to have to remain unquenched for now."

They spent the next twenty minutes in uncomfortable small talk, until his Chief of Staff returned.

"What have you got Greg?"

Halsey took the communiqué and quickly scanned its contents while shaking his head. "It looks like you were right Admiral. The President has given me new orders. I'm to escort you to Norfolk."

"As I said, win, win," Sean replied with a smile.

"I'll have your ships cleared through the locks."

He nodded to his Chief of Staff, who left to make is so.

"Thank you, Admiral."

They spent the next hour over breakfast, while they waited for news of the supply ships.

This time an Ensign reported to Halsey.

"Admiral Phillips, your supply ships are moving through the Miraflores Locks and should be through the Gatun Locks within the next five hours."

"Thank you Admiral." Sean answered with a polite smile as he relaxed in his chair.

14

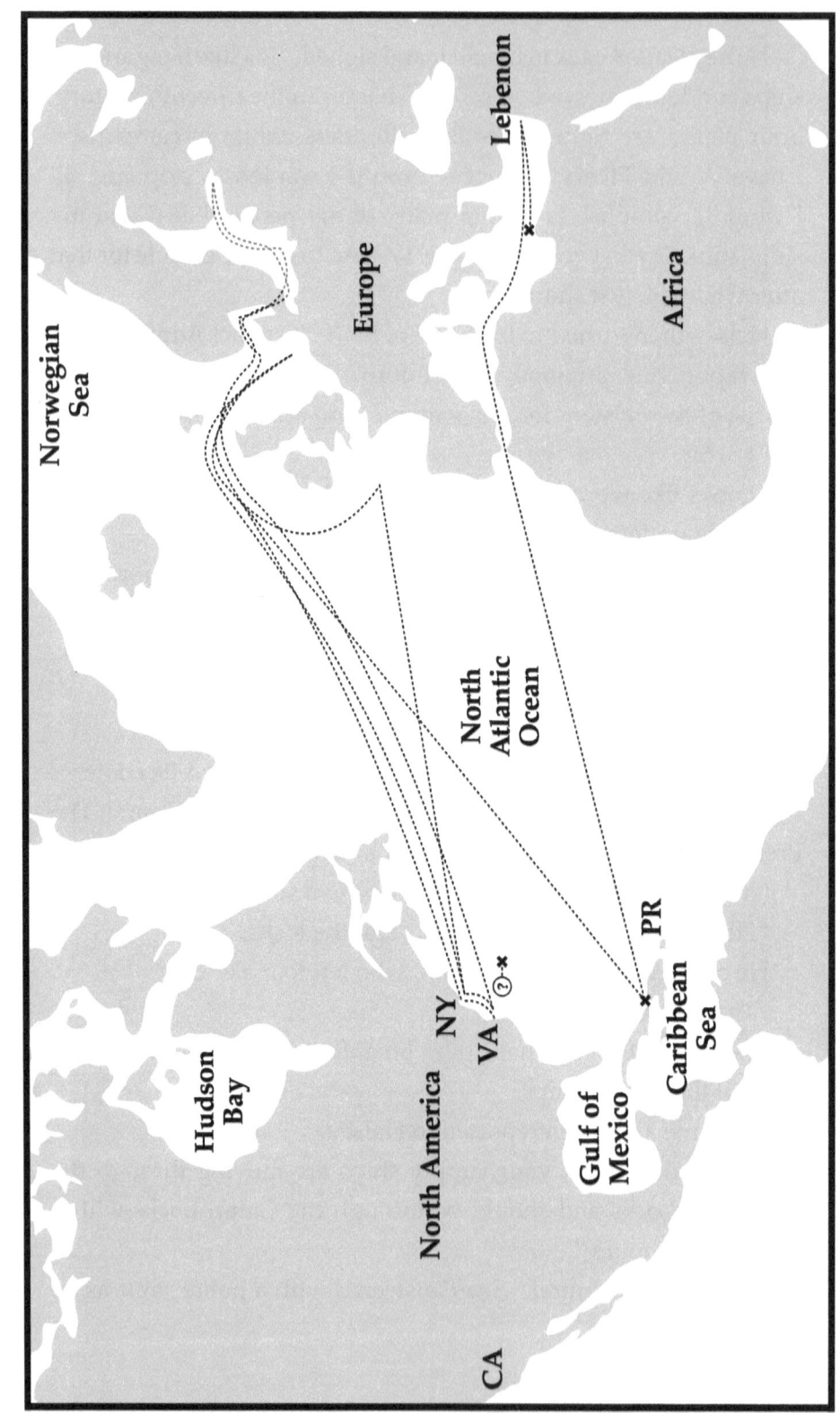

"Is there anything I can say to convince you to at least let my men see your ships?" Halsey asked. "I understand your reluctance, but what could it harm?"

Sizing up the man, Sean understood the benefits of gaining his trust. "Commander Thornton, get Tony on the horn."

Thorny unclipped his radio from his belt and keyed the mic. "This is Commander Thornton. The Admiral wants Captain Knox."

After a brief moment, he handed the radio to Sean. "Captain Knox, show the fleet." Sean ended the conversation before a confused Tony could question the order.

Moments later the Enterprise Task Force appeared two miles to port of Halsey's battle group; exactly where Sean had said they were when Halsey attacked the empty ocean.

Sean watched as Halsey surveyed the ships. Sean could also see the Missouri's 16-inch guns trained directly on the battleships USS Texas BB-35 and New Mexico BB-40 astern of the Wasp. He knew Tony would not hesitate to unleash their firepower with the slightest provocation.

"That's one hell of a carrier you've got, Admiral Phillips."

Sean imagined the sight of the pre-World War I HMS Dreadnaught appearing out of nowhere alongside Admiral Rodney's HMS Victory, a 19th Century wooden ship of the line. He smiled at the image of sailors abandoning their ships in horror and was grateful they were in a more enlightened era.

"All of your ships have smoke coming from their stacks, but I see the carrier is not only clear of smoke, I don't see a smokestack. You're not exactly burning oil to power her, are you."

Sean laughed at the common observation. "As I keep repeating, there's much I'd like to tell you Admiral, but let me say you're better off without that knowledge for now. What I can offer you is the same berth aboard my ship I offered to Admiral Nimitz."

Sean waited while Halsey weighed the tempting offer. "Sounds good Admiral, but my responsibility is here with my ships. Halsey took off his cap and scratched his head. "What say we get this show on the road. Based on what I've seen so far, I sure wish I were a fly on the wall when you meet with the President."

"I'll make sure the President is aware there wasn't anything you or anyone could have done to stop us.

"One more thing Admiral." Sean reached into his coat pocket and handed Halsey the envelope containing the letter Alicia gave Sean before he left the Enterprise. "Could you see this is transmitted to President Roosevelt? I don't mind if you read it."

Halsey took the letter, opened it, and began to read.

Mr. President,

You have not only returned our trust with deceit, but also forced your will on servants who only wish to act in our country's best interests. After saving America from four years of bloody war against the Japanese Empire, and with the promise to remove Hitler, you choose instead to make enemies of us.

Therefore, instead of negotiating for your support, I now demand it. The consequences of your refusal will result in parking the ships of this force right off the Potomac.

We will then broadcast to the world who we are and when we came from. We will also broadcast the covert conversations you had with the Prime Minister over the last two years. Let's see how long it takes Congress to begin impeachment proceedings when they find out how you manipulated the Constitution.

We will be off the coast of the Potomac three days from now and expect you to live up to our agreement. If you refuse, we will find those in the government who will deal with us with honesty.
Alicia Calhoun
United States Secretary of Defense
Civilian Authority aboard the USS Enterprise CVN-65

Halsey chuckled at the lack of respect the letter showed toward the President. "Sounds like I might have to square off with you again," he added with a smile.

Sean decided there wasn't any more to accomplish by hanging around, so he stood up and reached out his hand. "Thank you for your time, Admiral Halsey."

Halsey stood up and shook it. "Well, I can't say it was boring. I sure hope you are shooting straight because I wouldn't look forward to matching arms with you."

The sound of the Seahawk landing made further communication difficult. With Sean's attachment standing at attention, they and Sean snapped off a sharp salute, which Halsey returned.

When they returned to the Enterprise, Sean immediately went to the bridge, removed the ear bug, and handed it to Commander Barrish. "Make sure this gets back to where it belongs."

"Yes Sir."

Tony, pleased he didn't need to fire on the USS Texas nor the USS New Mexico, was feeling expansive. "You know how cool it would have been if we arrived in, oh let's say the 15th Century, where the natives would have worshipped us as Gods."

Sean shook his head. "Is that something that appeals to you?"

"Not really. With our luck, they would eat us to gain our powers."

The reward for Sean's trip appeared at 1400 when the Amelia Earhart and Laramie steamed into view. After they formed up, the group engaged Specter and turned northeast for the three-day cruise to Norfolk, with Halsey's battle group trailing behind.

That evening Sean broadcast the results of his discussion with Admiral Halsey to the fleet. He also took the time to express his gratitude to the SEAL squads, Marines, and the aircrews who flew the covering missions when they forced the Canal. He finished his speech with the promise that if his sailors continued to perform at this high standard, the rewards of a thankful nation would follow.

Meanwhile, five sailors from one of the plane crews failed to show up for duty. The only time they could have left the Enterprise was while they were in the locks. When the news reached Captain Folger, he immediately reported the AWOL sailors to Sean.

"I'll report their disappearance to Admiral Halsey," Sean replied. "It shouldn't be too difficult for the authorities to track them down. Fortunately, they picked a stupid location to exercise their opinion of shipboard life."

With the cooperation of the local military, two hours later the five sailors were in chains and waiting for a Seahawk to pick them up, which created quite the stir when it landed in the middle of the base.

Once in custody aboard the Enterprise, MPs brought them to Captain Charles Folger, along with the belongings they had taken with them. It wasn't difficult to ferret out the leader. After a quick read of Seaman Richard Harris' performance ratings, Charles discovered this was his first deployment. All five were pampered suburbanites under the age of 21 and weren't in the Navy long enough to commit any other offense that required severe discipline.

With years of command experience, this wasn't the first time Charles needed to deal with a breach of honor. "Miss your mommy do you Seaman Harris, and the way she made excuses for your inability to stand up on your own?" Charles picked up one of the laptops and slammed it to the deck. "So you and your buddies thought you could profit from our misfortune?"

Charles watched as the sailor's face started to turn red in anger. "What's the matter Seaman Harris? Did I just destroy your only reason for living? I don't care if you and your buddies spend the rest of this deployment in chains, which is exactly where I will put you if you disrupt this ship one more time. When you are off duty, you are restricted to your berths for the next 60 days and prohibited from accessing any of the technologies you so selfishly attempted to profit from."

Captain Folger turned to the Marine escorts. "Return these men to duty. Now get them out of my sight."

"Yes Sir, Captain."

When they left, Charles knew from experience their shipmates would see to it they got the message, and if they did not, the brig would become their permanent home. That only five inexperienced sailors jumped ship after three weeks in this alien reality proved the trust most felt toward their Commanders.

While Captain Folger dealt with the deserters, at the White House President Roosevelt was on the phone with Churchill. "It is obvious by their early arrival in the locks they saw through your plan. I had no choice but to let them proceed when I received the news Admiral Phillips was with Admiral Halsey aboard the Wasp. Based on the reports I received from General Andrews, they blew through his forces like butter in the middle of the night without inflicting casualties. According to his Commanders on the ground, not only are their ships and weapons years beyond ours, but their night fighting abilities are incredible as well."

Always quick to recover from miscalculations, Churchill reached his own conclusion. "That they went out of their way to avoid casualties showed great restraint."

Roosevelt was incensed at their lack of foresight. "Not only did we piss them off, there is the disaster we could have prevented if we had listened to their warnings. Close to forty merchant ships were sunk over the last week by prowling U-Boats all along our entire eastern seaboard."

Even this did not ruffle the Prime Minister's feathers. "Since they are still proceeding to Norfolk, hopefully they will keep their agreement to escort the convoy to England. We are down to 45 days of supplies before both our military operations and our ability to feed the nation will suffer. We need that convoy to sail as soon as possible."

Roosevelt looked at his watch and noticed he was running late. "I hope you're right, because if they do retaliate directly against the United States, there isn't a hell of a lot we can do to stop them. I will release the convoy to sail on the appointed date, with or without their help."

"Let me know the minute you find out their intentions."

Turning his attention from Churchill, Roosevelt opened his top drawer and pulled out some paperwork. These outlined the plans to integrate the US military, as spelled out in the agreement. The President knew he had only two days to announce this controversial idea to Congress before their arrival.

Conflicted with what he should do, he called his secretary to send for General Marshal and his adviser Harry Hopkins. He wanted their advice to help write what the President feared would be his political swan song. He knew to push this would splinter the Democratic coalition as soon as it hit the desk of the first Senator from below the Mason-Dixon line.

"You can't be serious Franklin. Do you want a second Civil War?" Harry Hopkins saw this as the political suicide it was. "How do you propose to support England Mr. President, when we're going to need to send the Army to keep the Southern States from trying to secede from the Union again?"

This was the reason Roosevelt wanted to hear from these two men. General Marshal a native of Virginia, and Harry Hopkins, the political realist of the President's brain trust represented exactly the obstacles he would have to overcome if there was any hope to drive the civil rights agenda forward.

Roosevelt wasn't convinced. "I don't know. When you consider the Japanese are no longer a threat in the Pacific, our plans for a military buildup might be a moot point. If they can accomplish the same magic against Germany they did against Japan, this should gain us enough political capital.

"In regards to your argument Harry, you're right. It will be political suicide for the Democratic Party the minute I announce we want to give equal rights to the Negroes. However, if this will end the conflict in Europe, the savings in lives and capital should help to minimize the fallout at home."

"How can anything be minimalized, when we haven't even gotten into the war yet," Harry retorted. "No one has had to suffer, so exactly what benefit will you receive from a war that fizzled out?"

General Marshall didn't even bother with this obvious fact when he threw in his strong objection. "Mr. President, it isn't my place to offer an opinion on how the Prime Minister chooses to answer their offer and the strings they attached to this support. I do know the American population is not ready for radical social experiments with the Negroes. I agree with Mr. Hopkins. It will violently split the country."

Though known as the US Army Chief of Staff during WWII and the face of the Truman Doctrine that saved Europe afterward, the pragmatic General did not want to see his Army used as an experiment in social change. The man's culturally ingrained bigotries are in the Congressional record.

Harry Hopkin's pragmatism kicked in. "It also doesn't address how to deal with the threat these people pose to this government. If their ultimate goal is to use their power to overthrow the government and replace it with a military dictatorship, how do you propose we stop them? We might exchange an enemy we know, for one we clearly have nothing to counter."

"They'll be off the Potomac on the 2nd, and we need to make a decision by then," the President concluded. "I have already informed Admiral Halsey I will be aboard the battleship New York, and with luck I'll be able to convince Miss Calhoun to place their forces under government control after the mission to Europe. We have nothing to lose by supplying their ships as long as they bring about the defeat of Germany. In the meantime, we need to bring in the leaders from the hill and tell them of our need to see this civil rights legislation through." With the same smile the American people had grown to love, the President began the process that could potentially rearrange the political map for decades to come.

The next day, 1 January 1942, took the Enterprise Task Force into the heart of a storm that hit them straight on and forced Sean to order a reduction in speed to minimize the battering to his screening force and the supply ships.

As the Enterprise rose and fell to the rhythm of the thirty-foot swells, Tony noticed Sean, who had arrived in the CIC, looked every one of his fifty plus years. "You look a little green in the gills. Maybe you should head to your quarters and get some more rest."

Ignoring his friend's concern, Sean pulled Tony aside. "I need to speak with you for a moment in your cabin."

When they arrived at Tony's cabin, he could see Sean was in one of his conflicted moods. "What's the matter? You look like I did after an afternoon in front of the Senate committee."

"We are having trouble figuring out our options when we return from Europe. Alicia wants to allow a team from the State Department to come aboard to act as onboard liaison with the government to begin our integration back into the chain of command. She thinks it would mitigate the threat that precipitated their attempt in the canal. I tried to convince her their deception only proved our need to remain autonomous for the safety of the crew, but she feels the longer we wait, the more desperate they'll become to take us out. Alicia is rightfully worried that another situation will arise where we might have to use deadly force to defend ourselves."

Tony had been thinking along similar lines. "I see her point. Our first priority should be the disposition of our personnel."

Convoy

Sean looked at his watch to see it was 1130. "We have less than a day before we reach Norfolk and the only thing we've agreed on is, regardless of what happens, we still head to Europe to finish what we started.

"She now thinks it was a mistake to try to force the President to bite off so much until after we dealt with Hitler and Stalin. I argued we would lose our leverage if we can't get guarantees before we take action. We need to have a secure means to resupply our ships, preferably with the cooperation of the United States Government. If they refuse, then we can threaten to share our technology with foreign interests and hope they don't see this as the bluff it would be."

The ring of the phone interrupted their conversation. Tony answered, and after he listened for a moment, he handed it to Sean. "Captain Daily has reported. They're in position outside New York Harbor."

"Put him through." After a short conversation verifying a smooth cruise under the Arctic cap, Sean filled him in on the turn of events. He ordered Captain Daily to new coordinates that would have the two attack submarines forming up with the task force outside Norfolk the next day.

Tony stood up to leave. "I might as well keep track of what is going on in the CIC. Why don't you take the opportunity to get some rest?"

"If Alicia will let me. She is determined to have all of the world's ills solved by the time we reach New York."

"Well good luck with that. It must suck to be you."

Sean picked up the nearest object and threw it at Tony. "Sometimes I think you enjoy yourself at my expense a little too much."

"Only a crazy person would spend their entire professional career climbing the ladder to reach your exalted state of bullshit. I'm just a reminder for you to stay humble."

"More like a blowtorch to the eye."

"Seriously, get some rest."

Sean waved him off and then made his way to his quarters, where surely enough Alicia stood waiting to hammer twenty new ideas into his head. They spent the rest of the day and late into the night debating the best way to minimize the chances of armed conflict with their own government. They finally reached consensus and dropped off to sleep at 0200.

When Sean woke up six hours later, he came out of a dream in which he was sitting cross-legged in front of an elaborate teepee across from a faceless man dressed in buckskins. Sean instinctively knew him to be a shaman.

The spiritual leader intently laid out a series of disasters set in the future, a future where he spoke of invaders who laid waste to his people and lands. He then told how Tony was the one chosen to change this horrible future. The shaman began to fade from view as he continued to speak.

Moments later Sean stood alone on a windswept beach staring out at three small sailing ships coming into view. His last memory of the dream before it faded was a soothing voice. "Isn't this fun?" As hard as Sean tried to hold on to the dream, it was quickly lost, leaving him to feel a sense of disconnectedness that followed him through the rest of the morning as they approached Norfolk.

The Seawolf and Hampton rejoined at 0915 and took up stations fore and aft of the task force. Soon after, the Enterprise CIC Officer reported to Sean that the Hampton had made contact with a U-boat on the outer edge of their sonar.

"Tell Alpha Whiskey to get a Seahawk in the air to pinpoint it only. Then get me Admiral Halsey." Sean preferred to have Halsey's screening destroyers attack the U-boat.

"Yes Sir."

Moments later, the operator reported. "I have Admiral Halsey

Sir."

Sean took the phone from the sailor. "Admiral, there's a U-boat off your starboard bow, about sixty-five hundred yards out. If you'd like to send your tin cans over to intercept, one of our Seahawks will direct them to the contact."

"You can see it from sixty-five hundred yards?"

"Besides the point Admiral. Will you send out your destroyers?"

"Affirmative."

A minute later, the two forward screening destroyers from Halsey's task force broke off at high speed and raced to the coordinates, and within ten minutes depth charges were rolling off their stern racks.

Now fifty miles east of Norfolk, this was the fourth contact with Hitler's undersea assassins, though the only one unlucky enough to be a hazard to the ships. They identified the previous contacts early enough for Sean to recommend course changes to Halsey.

Alicia had something else on her mind and brought it up to Sean. "I think it's time to reach out to the President."

Sean thought for a moment. "Let's take the Missouri to the meeting with the Seawolf as her only screening vessel. This will leave the task force without Specter's cloak, so I will order the rest of the task force to lie to in deep waters in case Roosevelt has planned any further surprises."

Alicia nodded her approval. "I will notify Renée we are coming aboard."

As they finished a loud explosion lifted up the ocean in the direction of the U-boat contact. "Scratch one U-boat."

At 1300, the USS Missouri steamed within sight of the battleship USS New York BB-34, which lay at anchor about a mile from the mouth of the Potomac. They had silently passed a screen of five destroyers in the outer harbor on patrol against any lurking U-boats. Sean could feel the eyes of the hundreds of sailors on those ships as they passed by.

Halsey's task force continued up the coast to New York to join the merchant convoy and transfer command to Admiral Chester Nimitz. Admiral Halsey would then fly back to the Pacific and *his* Enterprise Task Force 8.

Sean and Alicia boarded a Seahawk to take them over to the USS New York. As they rose above the flight deck, the sight of the Missouri's sailors lining the rails to honor the President put a lump in Sean's throat. The President and his party were waiting for them when they landed, and within ten minutes, they were in the Admirals Ready Room.

"It's good to see you again Admiral Phillips, Miss Calhoun." Roosevelt greeted his guests with his biggest smile as he motioned for them to sit. Accompanying the President was a man in a rumpled suit, hitting hard on a cigarette without a filter. "This is my good friend, Harry Hopkins. I asked him here to this meeting so I could get his impression of you."

Ignoring the introduction, Alicia did not waste any time getting down to business. "That was a nasty surprise you played on us in Panama Mr. President."

"You'll have to excuse my rash decision Miss Calhoun. You of all people should understand these are perilous times, and frankly, your mere existence has caused great concern among those of us aware of your actions in the Pacific. Add to this your demand to change American domestic policy at the point of a gun, and well, we had to try to protect our interests."

Alicia was not going to let the President off the hook. "At no time did we threaten to use force against the United States. The demand you refer to would have been resolved in 1865 if it had not been for the assassination of President Lincoln. That history holds him in such high regard is ironic considering how long it took the nation to finish what he started.

"Though there isn't any doubt the events taking place are

horrific, they pale in comparison to the world we left behind. Where your generation believed with certainty that they fought to preserve freedoms threatened by despots, self-serving corruption drained the nation's soul in the name of democracy."

Alicia shrugged her shoulders. "Mr. President, I don't understand why you find it so difficult to take advantage of the fantastic opportunity we represent. But on the other hand, if you continue to fight against us, we can always turn to others if we must."

Mr. Hopkins weighed what Alicia said for a moment before responding. "What you're asking for is not at all out of line, Miss Calhoun."

He leaned back in his chair, crossed his legs, and relit his cigarette before he continued. "Two days ago I met with the leadership of both parties to discuss this very issue. It was made clear by members of the Southern Democratic Coalition they would bolt the party if we proceed with Civil Rights legislation." Hopkins looked directly at Alicia. "You do know what these people represent, don't you?"

It took a moment for it to register to her as a question. When she realized his intent, she didn't mind showing her anger at his trying to school her. "Throwing away your party's principles to appease racial bigots is one hell of a way to run a government Mr. Hopkins. You can't tell me the price of doing business with them is worth selling the President's soul."

Roosevelt was impressed. It was rare for Harry Hopkins to underestimate his opponent.

Sean decided this was a good time to enter the fray. "I'll tell you what Mr. Hopkins, I understand the situation you are in, and I have a compromise that I think might buy us all some time.

"We will escort the cargo ships safely to England as promised. After they are safely in port, we will continue on to the North Sea and mount our assault on the leadership in Berlin, *before* you announce your civil rights initiative. We then return to the States with the war over, and you with the political capital to give *all* Americans all of the rights promised under the Constitution.

"If you are wise, you will use this time to think about how to regain our trust, because this is the only way we will share any of our technology." Both Sean and Alicia could see he had hit the mark.

Harry leaned forward, throwing all attempts to maintain his poker face out the door. He wanted all the cards on the table. "Admiral Phillips, when you say share your technology, let's be clear about whom you intend to share with. Are your interests with the United States Government or the world at large?"

This problem had kept Sean and Alicia up through the night working out the balancing act they hoped would ensure their objectives. Alicia answered.

"We guarantee we won't share anything with any foreign government or individual that threatens the national security of the United States. What I will not guarantee is to allow the United States Government to have complete control of the commercial applications they represent. We will preserve control of any licensing of these technologies to companies that agree with us about how they will use them ad what products they will produce. We worked out a timeline not to exceed ten years, after which we will place our ships and personnel back under United States civilian authority. This agreement could be finalized when we return from Europe, *if* you meet your end of the bargain."

Roosevelt looked at his chain-smoking adviser, who begrudgingly nodded his approval to the idea. "Your plan sounds well thought out, though I can't guarantee every aspect of your offer. However, seeing how Mr. Churchill has promised dire consequences if we do not get him supplies by the end of next week, I don't see any reason not to accept your offer of support for the war effort. When you return, we will need to bring other members of the government into our discussions if you want your proposal to succeed. I'm sure you're aware this is a republic, and I'll need their support as well."

Sean had one more request that was part of Tony's strategy to take out Hitler. "Mr. President. We would like you to convince Churchill to halt the bombing of Berlin. Our plans will have a greater chance of success if Hitler's military command believes it is safe to stay above ground."

"I'll see what I can do."

The rest of the meeting revolved around questions from the President, most of which Alicia and Sean deftly avoided answering. "It is obvious you will not talk about anything significant from your history, so would you mind if I ask if you know why you are here?"

Sean didn't hesitate. "I don't mind if you ask Sir, but I'm afraid we have not come far enough to trust you or anyone else with too much information about our past future. This will remain so until trust has been regained."

This put a bit of a chill in the air, with even the President's smile disappearing at Sean's rebuke. He motioned to Harry Hopkins, as if to ask if he had anything else. After a nod in the negative, Roosevelt wrapped up the meeting with a curt statement. "We have covered everything for now, so we will get out of your way. I know you have much to do to get ready."

"Once again Sir, it has been an honor to meet with you." Alicia had one more thing to add. "But please refrain from trying to provoke us. It would be a real tragedy for all of us if you ever force us into a corner."

The President's famous smile returned as if he had forgotten all that had happened. "I'm sure there's nothing but sunny skies ahead, my dear lady."

Alicia returned the smile as she rose from her seat and shook his hand. "I pray you're right."

Captain Renée Aslan was there to greet them upon their return to the USS Missouri. "Well, how did it go?"

"All is forgiven for the moment. The President thinks he got the better end of the deal, thanks to Alicia's expert understanding of the man's ego. I think he and Mr. Hopkins are still salivating over our offer to share our technology."

"Did you hear anything to make you believe we can trust him?" Renée asked.

"It isn't a question if we can trust him, or anyone else from here on out," Alicia answered. "It is completely on us to make sure we don't put ourselves in a position where we have to."

"Sounds like a lonely place to be in," Renée acknowledged.

"Amen to that," Sean added.

While Sean and Alicia met with the President, Tony was already working out the details of their role to protect the convoy. His plan called for the Enterprise Task Force to cruise ahead of the convoy under the cover of Specter to clear a path through the voracious Wolf Packs. Nimitz's forces would patrol the flanks and aft of the merchant ships picking off any contacts the Enterprise Task Force might not have finished off.

Nimitz' screening force of naval warships included two battleships, the USS Arkansas BB-33 and the USS Idaho BB-42, with ten heavy and light cruisers, and fifteen destroyers, plus the elements of Halsey's Task Force. Destroyers had been busy during the previous two days, trying to find the U-boats that continued to sink merchant ships before they could reach New York.

On the early morning of 4 January 1942, the Enterprise Task Force was twenty miles outside of New York harbor. Tony was on the bridge scanning the early morning horizon looking for the surface contacts ahead of the task force the Sea Wolf had reported ten minutes earlier. He watched as the first crack of light exposed numerous silhouettes dotting the ocean. The convoy had formed and spread out as far as he could see through his binoculars.

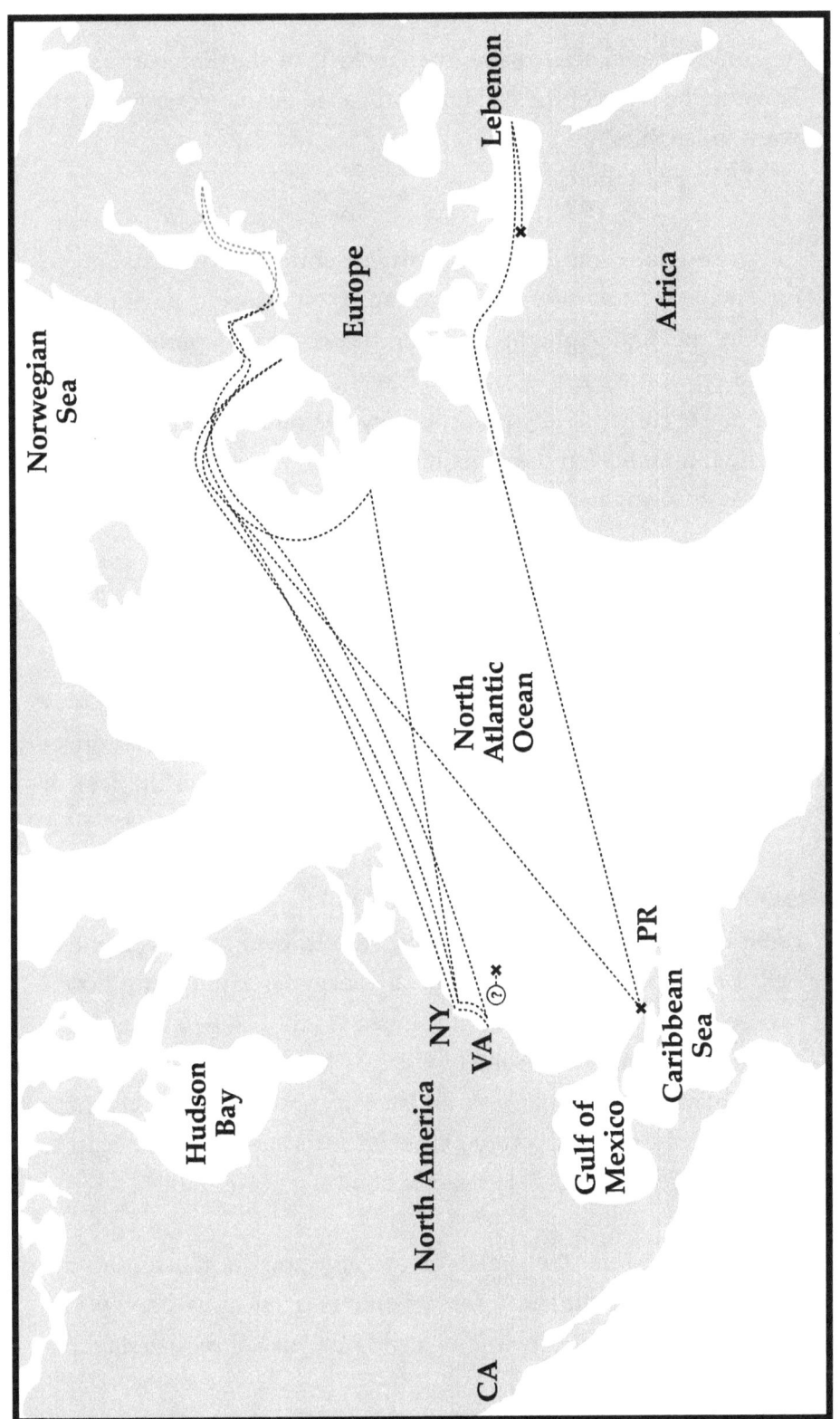

Tony ordered the course change to take the Enterprise Task Force to the front of the convoy, and called Sean. "You're going to want to see this."

"I'll be right there."

An hour later, the Sea Wolf reported submerged contacts spread out like a net intersecting where the convoy would have to sail. Within the first eight hours after the convoy departed, Alpha Whiskey on the Chancellorsville directed Nimitz' destroyers with pinpoint accuracy to ten contacts. They destruction of eight U-boats in under an hour left the remaining two survivors no other choice than to go silent and let the convoy pass unharmed.

In London, Churchill was initially opposed to suspending the bombing campaign, even when informed by Roosevelt that the Enterprise Task Force would take its place in the convoy screening force. "I think it would be wise after the fiasco at Panama to give them a little leeway Winston. Let's face it, how many other offers do you have to destroy Hitler that does not involve the loss of hundreds of thousands of our fellow citizens?"

The Prime Minister relented, though not without his usual petulance when having to accept someone else's idea. "If the request came from anyone other than you, I'd tell them to go straight to hell. I am offended that a group of renegades is dictating how I prosecute the war after standing alone over the last two years. I will take the idea under advisement with my War Ministry."

Both men knew this was all bluster, and sure enough three hours later he ordered a very pissed off Air Marshal *Bomber* Harris, Commander of the RAF, to halt the bombing of Germany.

Back in Berlin, the smell of sweat hung in the air at the Kriegsmarine Command Center. Panic had set in as one by one they lost contact with their U-boats. By the end of the 7th day, the total climbed to thirty boats unaccounted for, with the successful sinking of enemy ships at zero.

Admiral Dönitz, the Commander of the U-boat service was beside himself. He couldn't explain the abject failure of his command to his irate boss, Grand Admiral Erich Rader. The Kriegsmarine lost more U-boats in a week than the enemy had destroyed in the first two years of the Battle of the Atlantic. Before this convoy, their wolf packs had sunk twenty percent of all enemy supply ships headed for England.

It only took two hours after the dismal news reached Hitler before Admiral Rader received another shock. Hitler, after a blistering tirade, ordered him to deploy his surface fleet in Brest, France to intercept the convoy. In his rage, Hitler had decided to throw every available resource to stop the convoy.

The force at Rader's disposal consisted of two of his most successful raiders, the battleships Scharnhorst and Gneisenau, supplemented by the heavy cruiser Prinz Eugen, the ship that had accompanied the Bismarck on its fatal maiden voyage in June 1941.

Rader then ordered Dönitz to withdraw all but one of the U-boats tasked to attack the convoy. The remaining U-boat was to maintain contact with the convoy to send its course and speed to the surface fleet.

Outside the range of *known* detection methods, four of the retreating U-boats surfaced to speed away. Unfortunately for them, Alpha Whiskey picked up their radar return the second they surfaced. An hour later in Berlin, four more U-boats were classified as lost. Admiral Dönitz and his command were shocked. Over the course of a week, they had lost 45 percent of the U-boats deployed in the Atlantic, along with their over 800 officers and crew.

In the Enterprise CIC, Osaka read the intercept that a surface force was on the way and immediately called the Admirals Quarters. Five minutes later Sean and Alicia joined Tony in the CIC. He had already plotted the direction the German task force would need to travel from Brest to reach them.

"It looks like we can expect them right about here." He pointed to an area about 500 miles west of Ireland.

"As I see it, under the cover of Specter we cruise to within two miles of the German battlegroup and pump a few rounds from the Missouri's forward 16" guns into the battleship Gneisenau, while the mid turret takes care of the battleship Scharnhorst, and the aft turret hits the cruiser Prinz Eugen. That will leave their escorts to help them limp home." He then pointed to a location on the plot map. "Let's say we give them two days to reach here, approximately two hundred miles south of our track."

The ease with which Tony swatted a major offensive force out of their way impressed Sean. However, this new threat gave him an idea. "I think our duty to this convoy has been fulfilled."

Alicia and Tony looked at Sean as if to say, this is news to us.

"Think about it," Sean continued. "The U-boat threat has been removed and with them sending out the only other threat to the convoy, we can go to meet it head on."

"I'm not going to disagree. If there is anything more boring than convoy duty, I hope never to experience it." Tony was happy with the idea. "I'll inform Admiral Nimitz."

In the Sickbay on the USS Missouri, Dr. Safire violently sawed on the leather restraints around his wrist with a worn down plastic knife. In a silent rage, his fractured mind swung back and forth between images of arcane coding and flying monkeys with masks that bore the face of a leering Dr. Rebecca Cutler. She had robbed him of his freedom, and while he slowly moved the worn out knife back and forth, his mind focused on how if he killed her his nightmare would be over.

"Chop off the head and kill the body." It was funny how he remembered hearing this somewhere before. Maybe they had stolen this thought from his mind, but he had forgotten. "Yes, kill her and all would return to the way it used to be, with me on top, reunited with my creation."

Meanwhile, Captain Brewster spent his time wisely in the ship's chapel in fellowship with those he felt burned brightest in their shared vision of God. He never overtly questioned the actions of those in command, but instead subtly exploited those whose fear drove them to question the direction Sean and Alicia chose to lead them.

He decided on the six men he felt trustworthy enough to ask to join him in his mission to restore God's will to return them to where they belonged. He meticulously laid out the role his new acolytes would play. One of these men was a Corpsman on duty in Sickbay the day Brewster faked an illness, which gave him unfettered access to Dr. Safire.

"Good morning Dr. Safire. My name is Captain Steven Brewster." He decided before going in that the tone for this first meeting would be one of subservience. "I cannot believe they would treat a great man such as you like a shackled mad dog. Is there anything I can get you to help ease your pain, Sir?"

The doctor was suspicious of this stranger's overtures. Was he in league with the evil monkeys who wanted to trick him into revealing more of the genius hidden deeply in his head? Nevertheless, Dr. Safire had lain in one place for so long, with only brief guarded walks on the deck, any situation was better than the one he was now stuck with.

From the manner in which this monkey spoke, it was obvious in Safire's addled mind that Brewster needed something from him. Maybe he could manipulate this monkey to his advantage. This prompted yet another internal dialogue. "Yes, I can manipulate him. Yes, I have to take a chance and gain his trust."

"You could bring me a laptop if you really want to help me,

Captain Brewster."

Brewster was unprepared for this coherent response from the supposedly heavily sedated man who had been unable to string together a sensible sentence for weeks. "What would you do with it if I could get you one?"

"Why do you care, monkey boy?"

Dr. Safire's queer response made Brewster pause to think. "Monkey boy? What is he talking about? I better be careful, this man is delusional."

"The only reason I ask, is a mind as great as yours must be going crazy with nothing to work on."

"Does that mean you need me to work on something for you, monkey boy?"

"No, no, there is nothing I want from you but to help, no strings attached."

In his fractured state of mind Dr. Safire thought, "This is one of the dumbest monkeys I have ever met. He will be easy to manipulate. When I get the computer, it will be easy to interface with the ship's systems and gain access to one of the back doors I planted in Specter's operating code."

"If it will make you happy, go ahead and bring me your computer, though I'm sure it will be a piece of shit." Dr. Safire looked straight into Brewster's eyes with the look a tiger gives its prey before it sinks its teeth into its throat. "If you want to make my life easier, I could also use a real knife to cut my food. The plastic ones they give me are worthless."

Unnerved by the Doctor's cold glare, Brewster worked to control his speech. "I think I can get you the computer, and I also think I can get you to a place where you can use it to get back into Specter's program."

Brewster's eyes traveled up to where the shackles attached to the bed, and spied the frayed edges those who treated him failed to notice. Then gaining back a little of his composure, he took back some control. "As far as the knife goes, let's get to know each other a little better before you finish freeing yourself from those restraints."

With the knowledge he had cornered his prey, Dr. Safire softened his attitude. "So, what do you want from me in return, monkey boy?"

"I want the same thing you do. Get you back in control of Specter so you can take us back to where we belong in time. It may take a little while, but I'll get you your computer, and when you're ready, I have other people willing to help get you out of here."

Safire's splintered mind began to race. "This monkey is not making any sense. Get us back to where, from when? What does that mean? This monkey is not only a dumb shit, he is crazy as well. He did say he would get me a computer, but then he can track my movements. That's good. I can trick them. It doesn't matter. Get the computer."

Safire's eyes raced from focused to unfocused, finally settling back on Brewster. "Get me the computer and I'll help you get back to where you want to go, and then we'll talk some more about that knife."

Though Dr. Safire's deranged behavior unsettled Brewster, the scientist was all he had. "It's been a pleasure meeting you, and I know with my help we'll have you back where you belong, standing tall as the greatest mind in American science today." Captain Brewster was now sure the man was evil, and he knew science was at the root of it. However, he figured with God's grace, he could make it work.

Two days later in the Enterprise CIC, Sean listened to the pilot of a Specter equipped F-35 radio the position of the German Naval forces, now two hundred and seventy miles southeast of them.

Tony was on the phone with the CAG, and after confirmation reported to Sean. "Ready to launch."

"You made sure it was clear they were to only target the battle cruisers and heavy cruisers?"

Tony shook his head in the affirmative and added, "And to make sure they cripple propulsion and rudder control. They've got it. A well-placed two thousand pound laser guided bomb apiece should take care of business. But I really wish you had agreed with broadsides from the Missouri instead."

"And easier for them to hit us with a lucky shot? Let me think, a one-hundred thousand ton carrier or an F-35 flying three times faster than their tracking radar can follow. Give the order."

Forty-five minutes later, the three F-35s tasked for the attack found the German strike force. As flight leader, Captain *Dash* Nelson waited for the other two in his flight to peel off before he broke hard left.

He dropped down to five thousand feet and leveled off when his search radar picked up his target, the battle cruiser Scharnhorst. "Lining up for my run – ten miles to target."

In the Enterprise CIC, the audio from the pilots played out on the overhead speakers. "Have acquired target, coordinates loaded, bombs away!" This was repeated two more times before the speakers went quite.

The pilots watched as the first bomb struck the battleship Scharnhorst in the stern, followed by the cruiser Prinz Eugen, and then the battleship Gneisenau. In the case of the Prinz Eugen, the two thousand pound laser guided bomb blew the stern completely off. Moments later, the pilots could see the battleships slowing to a stop, crews battling the flames.

In the Enterprise CIC, Osaka reported, "Sir, radio intercepts confirm the Germans are attempting to tow their damaged warships back to Brest."

"Thank you Commander. Don't report their location to the British Admiralty. I don't see the point of sinking these ships. If everything goes as planned, the Germans won't have enough time to repair them before the war is over and I don't see the need to lose over three thousand lives for no reason."

Sean then turned to the CIC Officer. "Set course to the North Sea. We have twelve hundred miles to cover before we can reach out to the Führer."

"Aye Aye Admiral."

Back in the Missouri's aft hanger, Dr. Cutler was working herself and everybody else to death. "We can now successfully track any intrusions into Specter's operating system. However, I still believe there is some serious shit lying dormant just waiting to launch."

Dr. Phelps pushed himself away from his workstation. "And if that were true, there is nothing even in this weird reality that will help us find it. That is at least unless we had a year or two, but by the way you're driving everyone, we don't. We've already planted enough tracer programs in Specter's operating system that everything is noted right here as soon as it is launched." Forrest pointed to his monitor where a constant list scrolled rapidly down the page.

"All I know is I would feel much better if we could take it offline until we could completely scrub the coding." Without an answer to solve the immediate needs of the task force with certainty, Rebecca could not stand down. She also knew if she didn't, her mind would start to scatter. "All right. I'm going to try to get some rest. Contact me the minute there are any outside attempts to commandeer its operation.

The team had done everything they could. Now they had to see if they could maintain secure control of Specter.

After six hours and still too wound up to sleep, Rebecca went to the coffee maker and loaded it. "How many people do I know that like a cup to relax with?" She laughed at herself. "Screw it. If I'm going to be awake, I might as well work." She waited long enough to get a full cup brewed and then headed back aft.

Though her work kept her too busy to think about it much, Dr. Rebecca Cutler hadn't been happy since they left New York Harbor, and the current stormy conditions was making this voyage to England a living hell. Her only previous experience on blue water was an afternoon spent on the ocean whale watching. She couldn't understand how anyone would be drawn to the endless sight of, well nothing. Unlike the officers and sailors who were used to months at sea, Rebecca, more than the rest of the other civilian lab rats, felt lost.

With all her time wrapped up chasing ghosts in Specter's program, it was only now that she began to think about what she had left behind. She missed her trips to Whole Foods to find the perfect cut of swordfish to eat while she watched the latest Blue Bloods on her DVR. She couldn't get enough of their folksy moralizing, no matter how much she disagreed with their conservative messages.

In one of those epiphanies that always seem to show up without ant rhyme or reason, she sadly realized there would be little mystery as the world retraced all the wonderful discoveries in Cosmology. She angrily railed at herself. "For God's sake, I actually wore the same clothes twice in one week. I'm totally losing my edge."

In a fit of anger, she shook her head and decided there was no way in hell Dr. Rebecca Cutler would allow her future to become so average. With this realization, a smile of self-satisfaction turned up the right corner of her mouth. Anyone who had witnessed this manic display would have come away with a warped impression of the young scientist.

While most professionals enjoyed the pomp and circumstance their PhDs entailed, long flowing evening dresses, or elaborate tuxedoes, in her free time she was more at home at 6,000 feet surrounded by a forest in a pair of jeans and a T-shirt.

"Damn it. I'll never get to build my dream house on the piece of property I purchased in the Rockies." This brought the anger back, but the rational thinker in her quickly soothed her. "Wait a minute, I could always buy it again, and this time God knows I'll probably be able to afford ten times the land. Okay, so there are some advantages."

Her thoughts ricocheted into her biological needs. All she had done since they left San Diego was work and sleep. Rebecca noticed she was more frustrated and short tempered than usual. After one particularly nasty tongue-lashing directed at Dr. Phelps, it finally dawned on her why. In all of the chaos that was now a part of her daily life, she had neglected the one thing that made her totally relax.

She looked into the angry face of the man she had just dressed down, and to his amazement, she smiled. Rebecca leaned close to the young engineer and said, "Forrest, don't ask any questions, and come with me."

"Where are…"

"I said no questions."

Dr. Forrest Phelps was an attractive man, but he was not what Rebecca normally gravitated to. She preferred her men more like Commander Eddington, though she had no idea of where that attraction came from. However, Forrest was in the right place at the right time. Fortunately, for both of them, the sex lacked the spark that could have complicated their lives and left it for what it was. She made sure to spread out any further encounters in case either one of them made the mistake of imagining it was anything more.

Thirteen days after they left New York, all 120 merchant ships arrived off the coast of Ireland where the convoy split into smaller groups and headed toward their assigned ports throughout England. Every one of the merchant ships arrived safely at their destinations, while the German U-boat service tallied a devastating loss of thirty-five U-boats.

In Berlin, the news of this debacle added to the stress of keeping half a million soldiers supplied at the siege of Leningrad. Unbalanced by this sudden reversal of fortune, the Führer, isolated as he was in his East Prussian forest complex Wolfsschanze, began to issue a stream of conflicting orders to the German General Staff in Berlin.

Like his counterpart in Russia, he decided a mass conspiracy was underway to seize his power over the Reich. His erratic response was to order the arrests of Air Marshal Hermann Goring and his staff for their treasonous actions in the German defeat in the air battle over England the previous year. Hitler followed Goring's arrest with Ambassador Ribbentrop, the man who negotiated the non-aggression treaty with Russia, which guaranteed their neutrality when Hitler invaded Poland. Admiral Dönitz, whom Hitler held responsible for the debacle in the Atlantic, resigned and fled Berlin on the same day the convoy reached England.

The British decision to cease their strategic bombing of Berlin was in stark contrast to the U-boat losses and only added to the mystery. After fruitless hours of debate over the reasons, the majority opinion of the German High Command attributed the pause to the high attrition rates the English bombers were paying in the nightly raids.

An obsessed Hitler spent twenty hours of each day pouring over maps to regain control over the tactical chaos. Even with all of the evidence to the contrary, the lunatic chose to see the bombing cessation as a sign of England's weakness and decided to increase the pressure against the Soviet Union. He ordered another Army group consisting of four divisions to transfer from France to the Russian front.

Meanwhile in Berlin, the citizens of the city felt safe enough for the first time in a year to travel openly throughout the city, and military leaders left their underground bunkers to return to their above ground offices.

Convoy

Captain Charles Folger had his own set of problems to deal with, issue number one being the escalation of disobedience amongst the crew. He decided to go belowdecks to find out why, but before he left the bridge, he picked up the mic to the ship's intercom. "Chief Warrant Officer Brad Sanders report to the enlisted mess hall immediately." Not only was Sanders the Enterprise Chief Engineer, he also performed the role of COB [Chief of the Boat].

Five minutes later, he approached the hatch to the mess hall to see Captain Folger already there and waiting. "Not bad, but also not good. Five minutes?"

Rather than give his perfectly acceptable explanation that from where he started, five minutes was pretty damn good, his reply was simple. He snapped off a crisp salute. "I'll do better next time Sir."

Captain Folger and he both knew this was all part of the game, and better yet, both men enjoyed playing the game. It only took a second for a sailor to yell out, "Attention!" when they entered the hall, bringing the rest of the room to their feet.

"As you were."

After he got a cup of coffee, Charles walked over and sat down across from the COB. "Hell of a situation, Brad."

Anyone who mistook Chief Warrant Officer Brad Sanders' small size as an indication he would be a pushover, instantly regretted the assumption. His aggressive style permeated every one of the Petty Officers under his command.

"Hell of a situation would be an understatement. Do you have any idea how crazy the scuttlebutt has been belowdecks? I feel like I'm babysitting a bunch of housewives who spent the day seeing whose story can top the others. For example, did you know we have aliens in the Missouri's hangar and they have mind control over all of the senior officers?"

"Maybe that's why Captain Brewster is such an idiot. Speaking of which, I have noticed an alarming increase in sailors on report. What's up with that?"

Chief Sanders took a drink of his coffee before he answered. "Some of it is what you would expect under the circumstances. The uptick started last week when a couple of bible thumpers tried to push their criticism of how we are meddling with forces beyond our simple-minded abilities. Eyewitnesses claimed the Christians showed unchristian-like behavior and threw the first punch in the fight that broke out. Apparently, they didn't get to the part where Jesus preached turning the other cheek."

"How many share this opinion and have been willing to express it freely?"

"I'm guessing 20 to 30 of them are hardcore. I've put the ring leaders to work in the laundry where their opinions can't do any harm. The rest are first timers at sea and are scared shitless by something none of us can explain to them."

"Outside of those who believe the Devil is responsible, have you picked up any other scuttlebutt?"

"No Sir."

Satisfied, Charles shared another cup of coffee with the Chief, who had served under his command on other deployments. "I know if anyone can keep a lid on the crew, it's you. Let me know if there is anything you need, Brad."

The Chief smiled. "How about you find a way to spin back my age instead of the age we're in. It would be nice to be thirty again. I knew this little…"

"I got it. I'll see what our space aliens in the hangar can conjure up for you."

After Captain Folger left the mess hall, he decided to get some air. When he reached the flight deck, the chill in the air portended the approach to their most northern position, the Orkney Islands above the coast of Scotland. The weather there in February made the hardiest of seaman yearn for the comforts of home.

Seas were running between twenty and thirty feet, with sleet whipped up by fifty mile per hour winds. This made life miserable for anyone with the bad luck to have to stand a watch outside. Charles felt for the crews of the destroyers who felt every plunge their ship took into the next trough. That anyone would still want to go to sea after weather like this increased his admiration for the mettle of the average sailor.

Charles noticed Tony standing near the port side rail and walked over to him.

Tony spoke first. "What can I do for you Captain?"

"I spoke with the COB about the morale problems the more radical crew members are creating belowdecks. He assured me that he already has a handle on the problem."

Captain Folger then laughed. "It seems the ring leaders will be too busy sorting laundry for the foreseeable future to find time to stir up any more trouble."

Tony smiled remembering his own preferred punishment for malcontents. "If that doesn't do the trick there is always cleaning out the bilge tanks."

"I'll keep that in mind," Charles chuckled.

"Anyway, make sure to keep your COB close. He's a good man and with three thousand sailors under your command, it doesn't take much for things to turn sour, especially under our current situation." Tony turned to leave, but had one more thing to add. "Report to me if the problem persists."

"Yes Sir."

After he reached the Admirals Ready Room, Tony removed his layers of weather gear and grabbed the cup of coffee Sean held out. "It's especially good to be the Admiral's pet on a night like this."

Tony told both Sean and Alicia about his conversation with Captain Folger and the mood of the crew.

While she typed away on her computer, Alicia changed the subject. "I don't mean to interrupt, but I believe Osaka and I have found all the information we need about where the German leadership will be. It won't be very precise considering we have changed so much history, but with confirmation by way of radio intercepts, Hitler, Goring, Hess, and Goebbels shouldn't be too difficult to target."

Tony wanted to discuss the discipline problem a little further, but decided it was more important to see the information, as it was vital to his plan to strike the Nazi leadership. "I must say I'm impressed that without the aid of the internet you found such mundane data."

"Believe it or not, I found it because there are way too many Tom Cruise fans among the crew."

Alicia's comment caught both Sean and Tony off guard. Almost in unison, they turned and stared at her, waiting for an explanation.

"You'd be amazed at the content the crew downloaded before the time jump. I've seen enough pornography to keep a frat house happy for decades."

"And this has what to do with Hitler's location and Tom Cruise?" Tony wasn't used to Alicia acting loopy, and expressed this by twirling his finger in the air and whistling the Twilight Zone theme.

"The connection, smart ass, is Cruise did a movie about the 1944 assassination attempt on Hitler. This led some of the more curious crewmembers to research his stays at his Wolfsschanze complex, near the town of Kętrzyn in Eastern Prussia, now 2014 Poland. They even have detailed maps of the complex."

Sean's head was also somewhere else. Without any regard to what was being said, he clinically stated, "I think it's fascinating that in the middle of this insanity how our reactions to it have maintained a level of normalcy. No one has mentioned once during the last two weeks a single word about who is yanking our chains."

Tony now looked at both of them as if they lost their minds. "Okay, I see you two need to be alone with your thoughts, so why don't you print up those maps, and I'll get out of here."

Alicia laughed. "Poor Tony, usually it's you that drives everyone out of the room. Here, I already printed them out."

"Thanks." He opened the door to leave, hesitated, and turned around. "Why don't you let me give you a hand sorting out all that disgusting porno? I know it must be highly disturbing to one as sensitive as you."

"Goodnight Tony."

He made to leave and instead slapped himself on the forehead. "I almost forgot to tell you why I was here in the first place. I talked to the meteorologist a little earlier. We're in for another twelve hours of this foul weather, followed by two days of clearing. I also wanted to let you know we have a small problem with some fundamentalists upset because we might delay Armageddon. I think we know who is stirring that pot."

Sean was already ahead of Tony. "After the attack, I want you to get someone close to Brewster and find out what the good Captain is up to."

"Why don't we find an excuse to throw him in the brig until, oh I don't know, he slips on a bar of soap and breaks his neck?"

Once again, Alicia ignored Tony's comment. "You think Captain Brewster could be planning trouble? What could he possibly do without any access to critical spaces?"

"It only takes a spark to start a fire."

"My God Sean, you sound like my grandfather." Alicia winced for added effect.

Tony's only comment was only a sad shake of his head as he walked out the door.

After he left, Alicia yawned and fifteen minutes later she was sound asleep wrapped in Sean's arms.

On the bridge the next morning, 17 January, Tony was pleased to see the meteorologist had correctly assessed the weather change. He looked out to see the sky was now a beautiful mix of clear blue, highlighted by a grand procession of clouds lit up in shades of scarlet and purple. The other ships looked like they were dancing on a field of stars. With temperatures in the low twenties, it was perfect football weather as he fondly remembered from his college days. He was so mesmerized by it all, he didn't notice the Communications Officer had walked up to stand next to him.

After a few moments, unsure if she should interrupt Tony's thoughts, she broke the silence. "Commander Osaka needs you in the CIC Captain."

"Thank you Ensign."

When he entered the CIC, he noticed Osaka with ear buds on, surrounded by what Tony could only describe as chaos.

Oblivious of Tony's presence, Osaka stayed focused on what was coming through the ear buds.

As Tony approached from behind, the sight and smells emanating from Osaka's workstation assaulted his senses. It was obvious that lately Osaka had apparently lacked the necessary time to keep his personal hygiene up to date.

Tony pulled the ear buds out of Osaka's ears. "It is starting to look like a frat house in here – *Mister* Osaka. I hope your report is a little more organized than your appearance." Tony was serious. Contrary to his image as man's man, he loathed any mess aboard ship.

"Sorry Sir," He scrambled to organize the mess, while at the same time trying to explain. "I've been listening to German radio traffic for the last two days, and I've got to tell you, they're all scrambling to cover their asses after we tore the heart out of their U-Boats and crippled their surface force." He picked up a handful of papers and handed them to Tony. "These might be of interest to you and the Admiral."

Tony took a minute to glance through the documents, while Osaka finished policing his workstation. "Looks like a repeat of the Tokyo mission. The German High Command has been chasing after ghosts. Nice work Commander."

"I have one other thing, Captain. We picked up a lot of chatter on the German military communication bands. Apparently, Hitler has ordered the arrests of most of his top leadership, including Herman Goring and Admiral Dönitz."

"Once again, great work Commander." As he spoke, he looked around the room with obvious disdain. "But if I ever come in to see this mess again, I'll have you detailed to swabbing the heads for a month. Now go take a shower and burn the uniform you're wearing."

"Yes Sir. Sorry Sir." Osaka knew from the tone of Tony's voice this was more than an idle threat.

When Tony finished berating Daniel, he walked over the CIC Officer. "What is our course and speed, and when will we arrive at our launch coordinates?"

"Yes Sir. We are 170 miles southeast of the Orkney Islands, 360 miles from Bremerhaven, and we have been cruising at the increased speed you ordered last night of twenty knots. We'll be arriving at our launch coordinates at 1950 hours this evening, Sir."

Tony flashed a smile of satisfaction. "We get to kill the most despicable human beings of the 20th Century. Hell, even if none of this turns out to be real, what a kick in the ass."

Chapter Two

Betrayal

Throughout the rest of the day, the flight crews who would take part in the raid studied their attack profiles in the Enterprise Pilot Ready Room. Once again, they would utilize the F-35s to carry out the mission. The entire ship's complement, from Admiral Sean Phillips down to the mess hall cooks, moved with a heightened sense of awareness now that they were hunting the man who embodied evil in the 20th Century, Adolph Hitler.

As they drew near the coast of Germany, a now clean Osaka weaved together intercepts that gave a comprehensive overview of the current German war effort. He matched up the intercepts with the time and was able to pin down where the targets in Berlin would be.

Hitler was another story. One of the reasons for his survival against assassination attempts was his propensity to take off without notifying anyone until his Folke-Wulf FW 200 Condor was in the air to points unknown. The only person he truly trusted was Hans Baur, the same man who flew him from city to city in 1933 in what became the first modern political campaign. There was a good chance the political upheaval going on in Berlin might prompt

Hitler to return to the German capital.

Tony was less concerned about the rest of the Nazi leadership, as Osaka's work had discovered Himmler worked out of his headquarters in a building just north of the center of Berlin. They also planned an attack on the Reich Air Ministry, located on the Wilhelmstrasse to disrupt the Germans air defenses during the duration of the mission.

Based on this wealth of information, three strike packages of two cloaked F-35s each would carry out the missions. As in Japan, Tony kept three of the four uncloaked F-35s in reserve for follow up attacks, if necessary.

The Enterprise Task Force arrived at the launch coordinates at 2005; within fifteen minutes of the estimate Barrish had supplied Tony earlier in the day. Throughout the rest of the night, the aircraft were prepared while their flight crews rested and the task force kept watch on the surrounding seas. German naval activity was light, because the German naval command had deployed the balance of the German Naval surface fleet to its French and Norwegian ports to better access the Allied Atlantic convoys.

The pilots received their final orders early the next morning, 18 January 1942, with 1000 set as zero hour to launch the attack. Throughout the task force, conversations centered on debates about what lay in store for the sailors after the attack. Opinions ran heavily in favor of returning to the States to the reward of weeks of shore leave with appreciative beauties hanging on their arms for their efforts.

Sean was in the CIC where Osaka updated him about the latest radio traffic intercepted out of the Third Reich. The news was good.

Earlier at 0700, Tony had ordered one of the four reserve F-35s with an electronics pod on a high altitude reconnaissance mission over Kętrzyn. It was now sending information back to the Enterprise CIC. Osaka was able to compare this with radio intercepts out of Berlin that confirmed Hitler was still operating out of Wolfsschanze.

Based on this real time information, Sean gave the final orders to launch at 1000.

As the last F-35 catapulted off the Enterprise, Alpha Whiskey immediately ordered four F/A-18Fs to ready alert to protect the ships if Specter malfunctioned. The two aircraft tasked for the strike against Hitler, launched a half hour ahead of the Berlin strike. Flying at over 1000 miles an hour, the plan called for simultaneous strikes on the Air Ministry, the SS, and Wolfsschanze. Now they waited anxiously for the strike force to begin their bomb runs.

With everyone else focused on the mission, on the Missouri Captain Brewster arrived at Sickbay with a small case in hand and walked right by the Corpsman on duty with a wink. He went straight to Dr. Safire's bed, withdrew a knife from his pocket, and sliced the restraints from his wrists. "Here is the computer you asked for. Now put these clothes on. We have to hurry."

When his eyes took in the computer, Safire decided it didn't matter what this monkey wanted from him, because once he accessed the computer, he would no longer need him. Freed from his restraints, he quickly put on the Ensign's uniform Brewster brought so he could get past the Marine guards. They left Sickbay with Brewster leading him further into the bowels of the battleship.

The flight of F-35s tasked to Wolfsschanze slowed their aircraft and turned off Specter as they approached Kętrzyn using the town to line up on their target. The flight leader went into a shallow dive, leading the other two F-35s into their bombing run. The other strike force, with Specter turned off, repeated this maneuver over the city of Berlin. At five thousand feet and eyes focused on their laser designators, the pilots counted down silently to their release points.

Captain Brewster picked up two of his acolytes on the way down to what turned out to be a storage locker no bigger than the size of a prison cell and closed the door.

"We are amidships right below the CIC, so connectivity shouldn't be a problem. I'll leave you here while I go topside so no one misses me. Good luck Doctor."

With his fingers shaking, Dr. Safire opened the laptop and with nervous excitement stoked by the need to destroy his enemies, began to type.

Dr. Rebecca Cutler was at her workstation along with Dr. Forrest Phelps who monitored communications to the subsystems on the other ships. When he looked back at the Enterprise monitor, one of the tracer programs they had installed began to flash, warning of a breach.

He shouted in excitement, "Someone is trying to override Specter's operating system from somewhere on this ship!"

Pointing to one of the Marines in the room, Rebecca yelled, "Inform Captain Aslan we have a security breach, NOW!" When she turned back to the monitor, what the screen showed horrified her. "Whoever it is, is trying to activate one of the Harpoon targeting systems on the Princeton." Rebecca could see she did not have time to close the breach. "Shut down Specter and all its subsystems. We don't have time to neutralize whoever is sending the commands."

While frantically typing on her keyboard and without looking up, she added, "Tell the Captain I've isolated the wireless signal to amidships and it is transmitting right below the CIC."

At Wolfsschanze, Hitler was busy giving orders to his Field Commanders that further guaranteed the defeat of his German 6th Army Group fighting on the Russian Front. After six months of bloody fighting for Stalingrad, Soviet forces now encircled the German Army. Despite the advice from his generals to withdraw, Hitler demanded they stay and fight to the death. Having already tasted defeat in the Battle of Britain, the loss of his Japanese allies, the sudden elimination of his U-boats, and now dealing with generals who suddenly lost the will to fight, Hitler issued a stream of orders, oblivious to the impending threat from above.

The pilot leading the attack on Hitler released his laser guided two thousand pound bomb and the computers took over the job of guiding it along the laser's path. The bomb arced its way over the forest toward its target, as the second F-35 released its bomb.

The first bomb cut through the twelve-foot thick roof that protected Hitler's bunker. When it exploded, there wasn't enough left of the Führer to stick in an envelope. The second bomb arrived seconds later, redundant and unnecessary.

F-35s repeated this in the skies above Berlin. Without warning, bombs ripped through the SS Headquarters, killing Heinrich Himmler and the General Staff of the Waffen SS.

Moments later, the newly installed leadership in the Air Ministry met the same fate. The F-35s held in reserve, dropped their bombs on the Reichstag to complete the decapitation of the Nazi leadership.

As Sean and Tony listened to the pilot chatter over Berlin and Wolfsschanze, one of the CIC radio operators broke in. "Admiral, I have an emergency communication from Captain Lincoln. He reports his aft Harpoon launcher has activated and is trying to acquire a target. All attempts to disengage the system so far have failed." As they received this report, another message came in from the Missouri. "Captain Aslan has an emergency message for you Admiral."

Sean rushed to grab the phone. "Has what you've got to report involve the Princeton's weapons system?"

"Dr. Cutler reported someone hacked into Specter's program to activate the Princeton's weapons systems and is overriding our commands. She has tracked the signal to somewhere below our CIC. I've sent Commander Eddington with a Marine detachment to locate the source."

With Specter's past issues, it would have been easy to chock this one up to pre-existing commands, but because it was a real-time hack, Sean believed this was something more sinister. "Dr. Safire must have gotten free and has access to a computer, which would have required help. Track down Captain Brewster. There's a good chance Dr. Safire is the one hacking into Specter's program and Brewster is behind it."

"Aye Aye Admiral."

It was already too late when the Princeton responded to general quarters. From the bridge, Captain Gordon Lincoln was horrified to see the Harpoon missile leave its launcher and arc its way toward the destroyer Decatur. Seconds later a second missile launched.

The Decatur's Phalanx in-close Gatling guns opened at two thousand rounds a minute and spewed uranium enriched projectiles in an attempt to bring down the Harpoon missile before it hit the ship.

"What the hell is going on?" Tony asked.

"Grab your coat; we are going to the flight deck."

They were too late to see the missile's four hundred and eighty eight pound warhead explode at the base of the ship's superstructure. The force of the blast killed thirty-eight of the ship's crew, including Commander Steven Holmes and everyone on the bridge. Immediately after the explosion ripped through the superstructure, emergency crews sprang into action to battle the fires on the devastated destroyer.

The Enterprise was the target of the second Harpoon launched from the Princeton. Captain Folger had given orders to turn the carrier away from the Princeton to lower her massive profile. He followed the tracers from his Gatling guns right into the missile at four hundred yards and watched it explode.

Commander Eddington felt the blast as he and armed Marines

searched the lower decks for Dr. Safire. While checking several storage lockers, they came upon a door with a shattered lock. The Marines took up firing positions and threw open the door. They found a laptop sitting on a storage shelf with a schematic scrolling across its monitor.

Commander Eddington grabbed his radio. "Connect me to Dr. Cutler in the hangar." When she answered, he calmly relayed the news of his find. "I've got a laptop and it's scrolling through some programming. What should I do?"

"Disable the Wireless Network Connection."

"Done."

"Excellent! Leave the laptop running and bring it to me."

"Will do."

With all the confusion and everyone looking outward at the burning Decatur, no one, including the Marines guarding the entrance to the hangar, noticed the smallish Ensign slip through the door. After he looked around at the personnel absorbed with trying to regain control of Specter, he calmly walked over to some tools lying on a workbench and picked up a large screwdriver. With his eyes focused on his prey and with the screwdriver at his side, he quickened his pace, which got Dr. Phelps attention from the other side of the room.

"Rebecca, look out!"

When she turned around, the charging Dr. Safire was five feet away with an expression of pure hatred on his face. He raised the screwdriver to stab her while he screamed, "Die, you devil monkey."

Rebecca lunged to get inside his thrust and succeeded in throwing him off balance, but he kept enough control to drive the screwdriver through her shoulder. He tried to withdraw the screwdriver to stab her again, when Rebecca, fighting through the excruciating pain, managed to ram her knee straight into his groin.

The butt of a Marine's rifle struck the side of his head and Dr. Safire collapsed to the floor unconscious.

While Sean and Tony watched the Decatur burn, Sean's radio crackled with a report from the CIC Officer. "Admiral, Captain Lincoln reported they regained control of the Harpoon system on the Princeton. Alpha Whiskey has ordered all warplanes launched and the task force to change course north at the supply ship's top speed. Seahawks are ferrying Corpsmen over to the Decatur."

With Specter down, Sean knew the burning Decatur would be a beacon to any German air defenses in the area, and was pleased with Alpha Whiskey's rapid response.

With the view of the Decatur burned into his brain, Sean took a moment to reflect on the dedication to duty his sailors displayed. Their attention to precision amazed him, especially knowing that a couple of hundred of them were now fighting a life or death battle to save their ship.

"Tony, I'm heading back to the CIC. I want you on the bridge with Captain Folger."

Without a need to acknowledge the orders, Tony headed to the bridge.

More bad news arrived when the E2D Advanced Hawkeye [airborne early warning (AEW) aircraft] flying east toward the coast reported a group of planes 25 miles inland flying on a course toward their position. In response to the attacks on Hitler and his command in Berlin, every fighter the Luftwaffe had in the area scrambled to enact revenge on the attackers.

From the bridge, Tony called Sean in the CIC with an idea about how to deal with the threat. "Why don't we see if we can get them to turn around?"

Sean didn't have time for a debate. "Convince me quick."

"With the over-whelming advantage in speed and maneuverability we possess, let's see if we can cause enough disruption to make them forget their mission. Besides, down the road it might be a good idea to have those German pilots around to fight Stalin."

"Good idea. Work it out with Alpha Whiskey."

"Will do."

Tony called Captain Johnson who was holding Alpha-Whiskey on the Chancellorsville. "Order the flight leaders to focus first on disrupting their formations. Hopefully a Mach 2 fly by will make them shit their flight suits. Have you sent up the Prowler [Advanced Capability EA-6B Prowler electronic warfare aircraft] to jam their communications?"

"Part of the package Captain." Johnson was miffed Tony felt the need to ask. "Between the F-35s and the Nazis not being able to communicate plane to plane, they would have to be brain dead to want to press on."

"Let's hope so. However, if that doesn't have the desired effect, target the German flight leaders. We want the Germans to disengage, not get slaughtered."

As he talked to Captain Johnson Tony could see the F-35 raiders sent to Berlin and Wolfsschanze lining up to land. On the other end of the flight deck, aircrews refueled and loaded armaments onto the planes that would aid fleet defense.

Renée had just finished getting an update from Dr. Phelps, when she heard a commotion outside the starboard side of the bridge, punctuated by the sound of gunfire. Wisely, she didn't immediately rush out to see; instead she drew her side arm and brusquely ordered the bridge personnel, "Get to the port side now!" Then to the Marine who had un-shouldered her rifle she commanded, "Cover the door, I've got them."

The Marine took a firing position to the front and side of Renée, crouched down, and pointed her weapon at the door. As the last sailor cleared the area, the door burst open, and two armed sailors rushed in, their weapons raised to fire. Before they could level their weapons, the Marine emptied her clip into their upper bodies, dropping one and driving the other back through the door. The assailant's undirected fire bounced off the steel ceiling, ricocheted around the bridge, and struck the navigator.

Just as the Marine was slamming a new clip into her rifle, Brewster lunged through the door and wounded her. His adrenaline had pumped him up so much, he didn't see the weapon Renée had lowered to help out the injured navigator as he walked up to her. "Now it's your turn, bitch."

Renée dropped her head feigning resignation, and as Brewster lowered his rifle, she rolled to her left and fired three rounds in a tight pattern into his chest. The nightmare lasted less than thirty seconds, but to everyone on the bridge the brief firefight felt like an eternity.

Renée, who now battled her own overdose of adrenaline, caught the sight of someone pushing the door open and was about to fire when a voice yelled out, "Cease fire!" It was Commander Carl Eddington.

Renée lowered her weapon and yelled, "All clear in here, but we need Corpsmen immediately."

He rushed in and reached down to help her to her feet.

"I'm fine Commander. I thought you were headed to the hangar."

He answered her only after he made sure Renée wasn't injured and the wounded were seen to. "I figured you didn't need your XO and two Marines to take the computer to the techies, so I headed back. Unfortunately, I wasn't close enough to stop Captain Brewster when I saw him rush through the door." Eddington looked over at the bullet-riddled body. "The Marine shoot him?"

"No. I need you to go to the hangar to check on Specter," Renée said as she picked up the phone to report to Tony.

Yes ma'am, on my way," Eddington acknowledged, as he headed out the door.

Renée waited for Tony to calm down before she reported. "I have everything under control on the bridge, and yes we are at General Quarters. I can't understand what they hoped to accomplish by committing suicide."

Though he was still concerned, Tony managed to reign in his emotions. "The only thing that makes any sense is Brewster expected Safire would create a hell of a lot more damage than he did."

"What do you want me to do with Brewster's body?"

Tony didn't give it a second thought. "Weigh his body down with the other traitors and throw them overboard. Make sure the crew sees you throw the trash out."

"I couldn't agree more."

The first thing Commander Eddington noticed when he arrived was the blood on the floor of the hangar. As soon as he saw a Corpsmen standing over Rebecca stabilizing her for the trip to Sickbay, he rushed to her side. "Is she going to be all right?"

The Corpsman shook his head in the affirmative. "The wound is deep, but it looks like her decision to close on her attacker saved her life. According to the Marines she gave as good as she got, and judging by her attacker's condition, he'll be lucky to keep both of his balls. With your permission, I'll withhold painkillers from him when he wakes up so he can fully experience her gift." The Corpsman was smiling as he looked over at Dr. Safire laying in a fetal position.

"Get her to Sickbay and take those two Marines with you to stand guard." The XO motioned to the Marines who nodded in acknowledgment. "It's obvious someone working there looked the other way for Dr. Safire to get as far as he did.

"Dr. Phelps, have you had a chance to see if the laptop is any help?"

"The only thing we know for sure is the Princeton was the

only ship affected. Apparently, Dr. Safire planted the code on the Princeton during the early tests of Specter. I have disabled it, but there is no doubt that there are other subroutines. Because we have the running program on his laptop, we now have a better idea what to look for. I should have more for you in an hour or two."

"Do your best. We don't have much time before we will have the entire Luftwaffe on top of us, and we can't be fighting our own weapons systems while fending them off."

Without Rebecca to lead the search, Dr. Phelps didn't feel confident that he could find anything in the short term that would be of use. "We're doing everything we can Commander, but this isn't like in the movies where I can come up with some obscure epiphany that cracks the secret code. It doesn't work that way, and to tell you the truth there is a chance that our only solution could be to dump the whole program."

Instead of anger, Dr. Phelps was surprised to see Commander Eddington smile. "Trust me Forrest, Specter will be just fine. Besides don't sell yourself short, I'm sure you're more than capable of an epiphany every now and then."

Eddington walked out of the hangar without waiting for a reply. He headed starboard where a group of sailors were watching the rescue efforts, which now included the cargo ship Amelia Earhart traveling alongside the Decatur. For all of the destruction to the ship's super-structure, the propulsion system still drove the damaged ship defiantly forward with enough power to keep up with the task force.

The smoke from the fires on the Decatur had died down and this gave Carl hope the crew was gaining control. He could also see a helicopter take off from her aft pad, while another one waited to take its place to recover the wounded to the Enterprise for treatment. "It's times like this that I sense there is some hope for humanity," Commander Eddington thought. "Too bad it always takes something horrific to happen before people rise to the occasion."

Seated in the Enterprise CIC, Sean listened as the squadron of F/A-18Fs closed in at twenty thousand feet above what they identified as a group of twenty-four propeller driven Messerschmitt Bf 109s at fifteen thousand feet. When they were ten miles out from the approaching fighters, the flight leader called out, "Let's break 'em up."

The only reason Lt. Herman Graf led this flight of German Me 109s was because he had been in Berlin to receive the Iron Cross for his 45 kills in the European theater. The orders for the transfer were strange to say the least. The attack on Berlin couldn't have come from anywhere but England, so why was he off searching a thousand miles away for an enemy fleet off the German coast. So far, there wasn't anything to contradict the obvious, and his anger grew the further away they flew from any action.

That was right up until a blaze of metal and fire blasted not more than fifteen feet off his left wing. The Me 109 shook violently from the turbulence, forcing Graf to focus all of his strength and energy to regain control. The moment he succeeded and was able to look around frantically for the source, a second flash drove his fighter into a steep spin.

This time it took the Lieutenant every bit of strength to wrestle the plane level a mere two hundred feet from the ground and on a heading back to Berlin. Furious and determined to find out what the hell happened, he kicked the rudder over hard to bank back to his original heading. It was then he discovered the sky ahead of him completely empty.

Every attempt he made to contact his flight only resulted in the sound of static, which prompted the hair on the back of his neck to stand up. This moment of discomfort turned to outright horror when the most evil incarnation from hell appeared out of nowhere, a quarter mile in front of him. In the time it took for his terror to register, the apparition swept over the top of his plane, which forced the Me 109 to flip over on its back as the force of the close encounter ripped strips of sheet metal from the fuselage.

This time the Lieutenant was not so fortunate. The fact that he managed to crash land the plane into a field with his wings level was a testament to Lt. Graf's flying skills. He quickly unhooked his flying harness and stumbled out of the cockpit before the plane burst into flames.

The F-35 pilot who brought him down, Air Wing Commander Captain *Dash* Nelson, with Specter still disengaged made a slow low-level pass over the downed plane and dipped his wing in salute. "That ought to give him an incredible story to tell well into old age."

In the CIC, the flood of confused commands from both the Luftwaffe and Kriegsmarine gave Sean a clear picture of how to arrange his defenses. Because the majority of the German Navy lay at anchor in France and the fjords of Norway and they could easily handle any U-boats in the vicinity, the threat of a surface engagement was minimal. To Sean, the only real threat they faced right now was their own computer operated weapon systems on the warships.

Alicia listened quietly in the CIC throughout the confusing actions precipitated by the cyber-attack and their defensive counterstrikes. She watched with pride as the task force personnel focused on the defense of their ships.

Miraculously Dr. Phelps managed to restore control of Specter's program on the Princeton when the solution appeared on his monitor out of the blue. His first thought was, "God must have a strange sense of humor." Then, "Epiphany my ass. More like blind luck."

Betrayal

If he had more of Rebecca's curiosity, he would have delved further only to discover an even deeper mystery. However, in the hustle and bustle of the task force pilots successfully fending off two hundred and sixty German fighters and bombers without a single enemy plane closing to visual range of the task force, small details went unresolved.

In the Enterprise CIC, the Communications Officer reported to Sean. "We have re-established contact with the Decatur Sir."

"Put it on the overhead."

After the Communications Officer complied, Sean addressed the ship's Captain. "This is Admiral Phillips. Will you be able to save your ship Commander Holmes?"

"Admiral, this is Chief Warrant Officer Patrick Callahan. I'm sorry to report that Commander Holmes and all of the ship's officers were killed in the blast. I am the most senior rating left alive."

This shocked Sean, who took a few seconds to digest the news. "How's your crew holding up Pat?" He knew the Chief Engineer from a few of his former commands.

"They're fighting like demons to save the ship Sir. With the bridge all blown to hell, we are manning the ship from the aft steerage. With the help you sent over, we have managed to get the fires under control. Our weapons systems are operational, but as of yet we don't have the means to direct them."

"As soon as I'm sure the task force is safe, we'll remove all unnecessary personnel to the Enterprise. Keep Captain Knox appraised of your progress and anything else we can help you with."

"Thank you Sir."

Later that day in the Admirals Ready Room, Sean, Tony, and Alicia read the after action reports of the battle.

"Tony, how many did we lose on the Decatur?" Alicia asked.

"As of the last report, forty-two killed, including Commander Holmes, with another twenty-seven injured, ten seriously. We've evacuated most of the casualties to the Enterprise."

Sean appeared to be in a trance as he stared at nothing. After the intensity of the unexpected internal attacks and drained by the sudden death of so many in his command, he retreated into his mind to play back the sequence of events.

Sean's mood concerned Alicia. "There wasn't anything you could have done differently. If you had acted against Brewster without any direct evidence, it would have proved we were persecuting Christianity. You would have made his case."

"It doesn't change that I saw it coming and did nothing to stop him."

Alicia had heard enough. "You're right. It was a failure of command. A failure on all our parts for sure, but ultimately the responsibility is yours. In addition, as far as not having enough time to think through all of your actions, what makes you think you're so much better than any other theatre commander who has to make split second decisions while the bullets are flying. We are in a deadly business where people die, and there is nothing you can do about it. Let it go before your second-guessing does get someone killed."

Tony figured it was a good time to break out the booze. "I couldn't agree with you more. We knew we signed up for a dangerous business. To think that none of us would die after Safire had Specter turn on us, would be naïve. Look where we are for God's sake. True, Brewster gave Safire the access to Specter, but I'll bet you your Admiral's Flag Rebecca will discover the program didn't need him to activate it. Think about it. The program was already there and waiting.

"Though it doesn't make up for our losses on the Decatur, the deaths of Brewster and his acolytes should put an end to the friction belowdecks."

He handed the drinks to Sean and Alicia. "So let's give a toast to the honorable men and women on the Decatur who gave their lives to their country."

They raised their glasses and drained them.

Although Alicia was grateful for Tony's thoughts, she turned her attention to their current needs. "I know one sure way to take your mind off this mess. Don't you think it's time we talked to Berlin?"

Sean pushed through his angst and gave her a smile. "Yes it is."

He called Osaka in the CIC. "Contact Berlin, and tell them the people who took out their government want a few words with whomever is in charge. Secretary Calhoun and I are on our way to the CIC."

Osaka was ready for the request. He had been monitoring transmissions between the German High Command and the German Army. He sent Sean's request, and handed the receiver over to his assistant, Ensign Gloria Layworth, a German interpreter.

Sean and Alicia arrived in the CIC to the sound of Ensign Layworth conversing in German. This went on for several moments before she could stop to explain.

"I'm talking to a Colonel who doesn't seem to know who to transfer us to. He's getting conflicting orders. Hold on a second, there's another officer on the line. He speaks English, and wants to know who I am."

Alicia motioned for the Ensign to give the headset to her. "Who am I speaking to?"

The man answered in a heavy accent. "This is Colonel Weinmeister of the German Army General staff. Am I to assume you are responsible for the attacks today against Berlin?"

"You would be correct. I am Secretary of Defense Alicia Calhoun, the civilian authority of the United States naval task force that removed your leadership. It would be in the best interests of your country's wellbeing to get whoever is currently in charge to talk to me."

All they heard for the next five minutes was silence. With the thought the Colonel had broken off communications, Alicia was about to put the phone down when a different, heavily accented voice boomed over the radio. "This is Field Marshal Wilhelm von Leeb. Who am I speaking with?"

"As I told your Colonel Weinmeister, this is United States Secretary of Defense Alicia Calhoun, the civilian leader of the forces that attacked Berlin and your Führer at Wolfsschanze. I have a message for what's left of your government. Are you willing to listen to my conditions for a cease-fire, Field Marshal?"

Field Marshal von Leeb was formerly in command of Army Group North in the initial phase of Operation Barbarossa. He was the one responsible for the destruction of Soviet units in the Baltic Region all the way to the gates of Leningrad. When his offensive stalled and Hitler continued to meddle in his command, he asked to be relieved.

He was headed for retirement when Berlin was attacked, leaving him the highest-ranking official available for this conversation. Like most of the German High Command, he hated Hitler and his Nazi movement from the very beginning of their rise to power.

"Under whose authority do you demand a cease-fire if I was?"

"In case you haven't noticed Field Marshall, you are talking to one of the people responsible for toppling the Japanese government and now yours." Alicia then got real personal. "Keep in mind the simple fact that if I don't like what you say, there might be a bomb with your name on it already targeted on your location."

Now for the sugar. "Hitler is dead, along with both the leadership of the Luftwaffe and Kriegsmarine. This is a chance for you to take your country into a better future. Trust me when I tell you that if not for our timely arrival, over the next four years Germany would have been reduced to rubble.

"Instead I offer your government the same terms we gave the Japanese. Begin negotiations immediately with the governments of

England and the United States to end this conflict within the next week, or we will destroy your war machine piece by bloody piece until you do."

The lack of any mention of the Soviet Union in this strange woman's demands confused the general. "Does the omission of the Soviet Union infer they will not be included?"

"You can infer whatever you wish Field Marshal von Leeb, as long as our demands are met. My only concern is to end this insane conflict as soon as possible. Believe me when I tell you to continue will only result in unnecessary slaughter to the Fatherland.

"We expect to see the beginning of a phased withdrawal from the Soviet Union, and negotiations for a cease fire within two weeks. We will stay on station until we see the necessary steps taken in this direction. However, do understand that we will continue our annihilatory attack if Germany does not comply."

There was a long pause as von Leeb took the time to digest Alicia's comments. "It will be extremely difficult to disengage from this conflict without some assurances there will not be a repeat of the Versailles Treaty that destroyed Germany after WWI. What assurances do I have that this will not be the case?"

"I give you my personal assurance Field Marshal this will be a just peace. If that isn't good enough, remember it was your country that declared war on the United States and we would be completely justified in laying waste to Berlin right now – but as you can clearly see we are not. I sincerely hope for the sake of your citizens you come to your senses quickly." Alicia made a slashing motion to Osaka to end the conversation, which he did.

Even as Alicia was speaking to von Leeb, the struggle to take control of the German Government was playing out. In Berlin, General Franz Harder contacted Field Marshal Rundstedt in France and General Georg von Küchler in charge of Army Group North in the Soviet Union to get their support to assume temporary control of the German Government.

As far as von Leeb was concerned, the destruction of the Nazi leadership was a gift from God, as long as the Army acted swiftly to neutralize the symbol of the fascist regime, the Waffen SS. With Himmler and most of his staff killed, the odds were in the Army's favor by sheer weight of numbers.

After she finished the conversation with General von Leeb, Alicia turned to Sean. "Now it's your turn to convince Churchill to agree to a cease-fire."

Sean didn't hesitate. "Commander Osaka…"

"On it Sir." Osaka already had his fingers typing the encrypted communication.

Half an hour later, Churchill's response arrived with a simple greeting. "It's nice to hear from you again Admiral Phillips. I understand you've been busy over the skies of Germany."

"I'm sure your intelligence resources have already informed you of Hitler's death."

"I received the news earlier this afternoon. Congratulations on a job well done."

"So much for the good news," Sean thought. "Have your sources also informed you of our talks with Berlin since?"

This was news to Churchill. "Talks regarding what?"

"We offered von Leeb terms for a cease-fire."

Churchill exploded. "What makes you think you have any authority to offer terms to the Germans? Your arrogance is intolerable!"

"Be that as it may, the truth of the matter is it happened. You didn't question our motivations when you asked for our support to escort your convoy nor when you knew of our plans to attack Germany. What did we say that led you to believe we wouldn't involve ourselves in the peace? It's not like the world did such a bang-up job at Versailles in 1919. My advice to you would be to put your country's ego in a drawer for a moment and think about the opportunity we have laid at your feet."

This did nothing to placate Churchill. "Terms for a German surrender have already been laid out. Parliament will never abrogate their responsibility to a renegade military force to set terms outside the authority of any recognized government."

"Well you better convince them to try. Because if your government or the United States refuses to enter into immediate negotiations with the Germans, we will withdraw our support from the conflict and let it continue. At the same time, nothing will prevent us from taking our case to both the British and the American publics to explain who is responsible for the continued violence. Remember, you don't have the images of Togo and Hitler to demonize anymore."

"You've gone too far this time Admiral!"

"Remind me of that when you want our help to neutralize Stalin, Mr. Prime Minister. Since we will not be able to resolve this over the radio, I suggest you contact President Roosevelt after you read the message I am about to send to you. It applies to the American Government as well."

Sean had nothing left to add and motioned to Osaka to cut off communications. "Send it Commander."

Osaka sent the following message Sean and Alicia had written two nights ago, with the expectation their mission over Germany would succeed.

Mr. Prime Minister,

The German Government is in the process of reorganizing, and while this continues, they will disengage from the Soviet Union front. It could expedite matters if you would send your own communiqué through your contacts in Switzerland to reinforce the basics we have already laid out to German officials.

We are hopeful this will culminate with the complete withdrawal of German occupation from all conquered nations. I also need to advise you not to demand much in the way of reparations. History has shown that this war is a direct result of the burdens placed upon Germany under the Versailles Treaty, and it will become a major obstacle to peace if you insist on repeating the same mistake.

You must convince your government of the need for a speedy resolution. It will not be long before Stalin occupies Poland and the Balkans. If you hesitate, you will have to justify to the citizens of the British Commonwealth why they will need to expend their blood to stop him.

We are on station awaiting your next move and will be ready if the new German leadership needs another reminder that our patience is short.

Mr. Prime Minister, we are aware that it was you who convinced President Roosevelt to attack us while in the Canal, but we won't hold that against you if you are willing to engage in useful negotiations to end the hostilities with Germany. However, if you obstruct our efforts again, we will be forced to explore other alternatives, none of which will be to your or the British Empire's benefit.

Alicia Calhoun

United States Secretary of Defense

Civilian Authority aboard the USS Enterprise CVN-65

With this business concluded, Sean turned to what options remained for the warring nations. "Tony, you're the tactical genius. How do you think the next few days will play out?"

"So now I'm a genius?"

"Humor me."

Tony walked over to a vertical display with a map of Central Europe and pointed to the current German positions on the Soviet frontier. "If the Germans are serious about a cease-fire, we should begin to see German troop movements in the next few days as proof they are trying to disengage. Another indicator will be railroad traffic that carries their supplies to the front. The trains should be leaving Germany empty for the front if the German Army is trying to realign their forces on the ground.

"Commander Osaka, send a message to British Air Command and ask if they would be so kind as to keep us up to date on their reconnaissance missions over Germany."

"Aye Aye Captain."

Both Alicia and Sean were about to object to the idea of asking for support from the British Government before they responded to their cease-fire demands, but Tony stopped them. "I got it. You're worried about Churchill rejecting our terms. What choice does he have? He won't like it, but I'm sure after he gives it some thought he'll realize it's still in his best interest to comply."

"Makes sense." Alicia was quick to see the advantages. "If we continue to operate as if everyone is onboard, it will make it easier for all sides to gain some trust with each other. The Germans, Japanese, and Italians will think we are operating under Allied orders, and the Allies will be too worried we might turn on them if they refused a cease-fire. It's a great idea."

Sean was about to say something when he realized there was an important bit of business he had neglected.

"What is it?" Alicia asked.

"We lack a Captain on the Decatur, and I have the perfect fit."

Sean turned to the CIC Officer. "Get Captain Folger on the line."

When Folger answered, Sean ordered, "You need to relieve Barrish. You're also going to need to pick a new XO."

"Great. That will make the third one in three months I'm going to have to wet nurse," Charles complained.

Tony's eyes travelled over to Osaka.

Osaka thought he was about to be ripped again for his appearance, but instead Tony continued to stare at him. Then an evil smile appeared on the Chief of Staff's face.

"Osaka, you're with me."

"Yes Sir," the confused Commander responded as he policed his station.

When Barrish got on the phone, Sean ordered him to meet him on the flight deck without telling him why. After Sean put the phone down, he informed Alicia, "I'm headed over to the Decatur."

Ten minutes later on the flight deck, Commander Logan Barrish saluted Sean when he arrived.

"At ease, Commander. I am going over to the Decatur to inspect the battle damage and you're to accompany me. You are going to take command, and I expect you to put your ship in order as soon as possible."

It took a few moments for the surprised Barrish to react. "Thank you Sir." He hesitated before asking, "Do you believe we can save her?"

"Are you worried I'm putting you in command of a ship that might sink, Commander?"

This time Logan didn't hesitate. "If she sinks Sir, it will be because you ordered me to open the sea cocks."

Five minutes later, they were hovering over the severely damaged Decatur. Sean had the pilot circle the ship so they could get a good look at the mangled super structure. Sailors were busy cutting away the wreckage and throwing it overboard. Having seen enough, Sean ordered the pilot to land.

Chief Engineer Patrick Callahan, who appeared to be every bit the Irishman his name implied, was on the fantail when they set down. With his close-cropped red hair, the image was stereotypical down to the smart salute he snapped off.

"How's your crew holding up Chief?" Sean asked. "Is there anything we can send over?"

"We sure could use some more welding crews and gear to speed up resealing the hole in the deck the Harpoon made. We are shipping water with every wave that blows over the bow, and the sea isn't running high. If it does, we could have a serious problem."

"I am placing Commander Logan Barrish as Captain of the Decatur. If you need anything else, let him know. I'll have our staff send you over some welders and gear."

"Aye Admiral."

"Let's take a look at your new command, Logan."

They had trouble navigating around the blast damage as they inspected the ship. The missile struck at the base of the ship's forward superstructure and turned everything including the bridge into a tangled heap of wreckage. As amazed as he was that the ship survived the blast, the methodical manner in which the crew worked their way through the carnage reaffirmed Sean's admiration for the average sailor.

After an hour and a half of inspection, Sean left Commander Logan Barrish to familiarize himself with the ship and crew.

The next morning on the bridge, 18 February 1942, Tony placed the silver oak leaf insignia on Daniel's collar that increased his rank to Commander and saluted him.

Captain Charles Folger also saluted and addressed his new XO. "Commander Osaka, I think it is a good time to refuel and replenish the task force. See to it."

"Yes Sir!" Commander Daniel Osaka acknowledged before he informed Tony, "I have a recommendation for my replacement as Information Warfare Officer Captain Knox."

"Who do you have in mind?"

"Ensign Gloria Layworth, Sir. I know she is only an Ensign, but she has been soaking up everything she can about the communications technology of this era and is fluent in German. She stayed in the CIC most of the night monitoring radio intercepts. Further, her career in the Navy is helping pay for her Master of Science in Applied Mathematics at Yale, so you know she has already learned a lot about encryption codes. She is a quick study and an ideal choice for Information Warfare Officer."

"I will make it so Commander, and do you think she is ready for a promotion to go along with it?"

"Yes Sir, she has earned it and a bump to full Lieutenant will give her the altitude required to make sure her orders are carried out."

"Agreed. I will now leave you to your new duties, *Commander,*" Tony added with a grin.

As in the follow up to the strikes on Tokyo, a battle ensued in the power vacuum to determine who was going to lead Germany. The main contestants featured the Army and the SS. Field Marshall von Leeb didn't waste any time coordinating the Army's response. The Army senior officers quickly rallied under Field Marshall Von Rundstedt, who commanded German occupation forces in France. He immediately released two of his Panzer divisions to race back to Berlin while von Leeb surrounded the barracks of the SS. A stalemate quickly ensued.

Field Marshal Von Rundstedt's Panzer units reinforced von Leeb thirty-eight hours later and forced the trapped SS forces to surrender without bloodshed. Because they had not fired on the Army and after signing an oath declaring their repudiation of the Nazi Party, they were disarmed, put into civilian clothing, and allowed to return to their homes.

After seven years of brutalizing Europe, the most feared element of the German military ended with the burning uniforms on the parade ground. The German Army completed the disarmament of the remainder of the SS still on the battlefront with a minimum of violence and distributed their personnel throughout the regular army.

Field Marshall von Leeb went to France to take command of the German occupation forces so Field Marshal von Rundstedt could return to Berlin to take over the government. He assumed the title of Chancellor with the promise he would reconstitute the Bundestag.

Von Rundstedt's first order was to General von Küchler to disengage from the fight for Leningrad. Because of his superior tactical abilities, General Heinz Guderian replaced Field Marshal Günther von Kluge as Commander of the Second Panzer Army. Rundstedt ordered Guderian to come up from Moscow to protect the German southern flank as they withdrew from Stalingrad.

When Lt. Layworth relayed the news to Sean and Alicia, they worried about what Stalin's reaction would be to a vulnerable German Government. This was one of the reasons Alicia didn't want Stalin included in the negotiations. They wanted to put pressure on the Governments of England and America to reach a cease-fire with Germany. That way if Stalin insisted on continuing the war, a new alliance between the Allies and Germany could slam the door before his Army followed the German retreat into Poland, the Balkans, and Czechoslovakia.

On the second day after the attack on Germany, reconnaissance photos from the RAF revealed the German Army had stopped offensive actions all along the Eastern front.

Not long afterward, Lt. Gloria Layworth received a call in the CIC that she relayed. "Admiral, General von Rundstedt wishes to speak to Secretary Calhoun."

In the Admirals Quarters Sean replied, "Thank you Lieutenant. We are on our way."

He then turned to Alicia. "It's show time, Madam Secretary."

Seated in the CIC, with Lt. Gloria Layworth interpreting, Alicia began the conversation. "It's good to hear from you General Rundstedt. We have noticed a general redeployment of your forces on the Eastern front over the last two days. Does this mean you have good news for me?"

Through the interpreter, his response was swift. "The German Government will send emissaries to the proposed peace conference if you can give us assurances England will cease all offensive operations. However, while these talks take place, our forces on the Eastern Front will continue to hold their ground. We reserve the option to strike back if the Soviets interpret our cease-fire as a sign of weakness.

"I look forward to meeting you soon, Madam Secretary. Will your role be to act as the intermediary between Germany and the Allies?"

"This is how we have seen our role all along, General."

General Rundstedt had one final warning. "I wish to reiterate that as a nation we will continue the defense of our country if there is any sign of betrayal during this process."

"We will stay on station to ensure this will not happen. Thank you for your time General."

The end of this conversation began a whirlwind of activity over the next two days as the dynamics of world politics tacked away from all-out war. Envoys arrived in Paris from America, England, the Free French led by General Charles de Gaulle, Germany, and Japan. The discussions included talks on the timetables for the withdrawal of Japanese troops from Manchuria, China, and Singapore, in return for the resumption of oil supplies delivered to the Japanese home islands. The American and British Navies had moved major portions of their Pacific fleets into Subic Bay in the Philippines in case negotiations stalled and the need for further military intervention was called for against Japan.

The Soviet Union sent a strongly worded protest from Stalin, when he discovered preliminary discussions proposed the return of national sovereignty to the Balkans, Poland, Rumania, and Czechoslovakia. Stalin's rambling missive to continue the war against Germany played into Sean and Alicia's plans.

Alicia now spent most of her time in the CIC keeping track of the peace talks taking place. After an update from the British Foreign

Office, Alicia returned to Sean's quarters and wasn't very happy. Seated at the conference table with charts of the Atlantic in front of them, Sean and Tony were plotting the course to take the group back to Norfolk. Quick to notice her mood, Sean asked, "Problem with the Soviets?"

"Considering he doesn't want anything to do with these talks, Stalin is doing everything in his power to disrupt the meetings. Commissar Maxim Litvinov is sending out letter after letter with ridiculous demands that would all but ensure Soviet control over all of Central and Eastern Europe. He's threatening military action against the Allies if agreement is reached without consideration of these demands."

She took a moment to pour a glass of wine. "You want one?"

"No thank you," Sean replied.

Tony picked up a glass and handed it to her. "I will if you're pouring.

"So, big surprise," Tony continued. "Stalin is being the pain in the ass you expected. Has it pushed Britain and Germany closer together like you hoped it would?"

"I think so," Alicia answered. "The German Government sent their new Vice-Chancellor, Grand Admiral Erich Raeder, aided by Field Marshall von Leeb to represent their interests. The head of the British team, Lord Halifax, has maneuvered brilliantly to keep the Soviet demands from having any influence on the agenda.

"A treaty with Japan appears to be a given, though fortunately for us this won't happen quickly. All of the intrigue is taking place in the preliminary discussions for the implementation of a formal ceasefire in Europe. The Polish, Danish, and Norwegian Governments in exile are to return to their respective capitals immediately. Commissioners from the United States and England will oversee investigations into German atrocities.

"Churchill and Roosevelt sent a letter to the Soviet mission in Washington, warning Stalin they would consider it an act of war if the Soviets tried to enter the Balkans or Poland. Stalin responded to this with the recall of his Ambassadors from both England and the United States. Hold on a second; I need more wine. This goes on for a while."

After she poured herself another glass, Alicia continued her narrative. "Another point of contention slowing negotiations was determining who represented the interests of France. Marshal Petain of the Vichy French was in opposition to General Charles de Gaulle and it looks like there could be French civilian casualties if an agreement isn't brokered fast."

Twenty minutes later after Alicia finished, Tony summarized in his usual way. "It appears we got what you wanted, a reason to go after Stalin. So remind me again, where exactly is all of this is supposed to take us?"

Even Tony's witty cynicism couldn't darken Alicia's mood. "Hopefully to a place where we won't be involved at all, that's where. You mean to tell me you don't find anything fascinating about being a central figure in the most incredible adventure in human history?"

Tony wasn't convinced. "I'm sorry, but the longer we are here, the more I see everything works the same as it did in 2014. The only difference is they didn't have the means to kill so many at once."

Sean was concerned about his friend. There was something else going on and he had an idea what it was. "I've been thinking. With the ceasefire in place with Germany, we should have a peaceful voyage back to Norfolk. I think it would be a good idea to inspect the Missouri."

"You going to take Alicia?"

Alicia and Sean looked at each other as if to ask, "Is he a complete idiot or what?"

Finally, a tiny light bulb went off in Tony's head. "Oh, you want *me* to go. I somehow remember a conversation that put the kabob on senior staff fraternizing. Besides, who's going to be around to make sure you two don't go Napoleon and Josephine on us?"

Sean had to laugh. "I can't think of anything either Alicia or I have done to cause you to worry."

Alicia walked over to Tony and grabbed his hand, pulling him from the chair. "Now why don't you be a good boy and let Renée know you're coming."

Tony grabbed his hat. "Make sure you don't ground the task force on a shoal." He was out the door before they could say another word.

Alicia threw Sean an evil look. "Don't worry. If I see anything resembling a Napoleon complex in you, I'll start my own revolution."

Sean walked over and despite her protests, picked her up and headed to the bedroom. "Viva La Revolution."

It took Tony only twenty minutes to pack a bag, board a Seahawk, and arrive on the Missouri. Renée was there when he stepped off the chopper. "So, you want your cabin back?"

After Brewster's death, Renée had moved into the Captains Cabin, purged of all of the shrines, of course.

"Why are you really here? If anyone was going to inspect the Missouri, I'd think it would be the Admiral."

"So many questions, so little time. Why don't we head to *your* cabin so we can talk?"

Renée led the way through the ship. "Seriously Tony, why are you here?"

"Well, I don't know, it all happened so quickly. One minute I'm bitching to Sean and Alicia about how the assholes from this era don't seem to be any different from the assholes we left behind, and boom, they kick me off the ship. Go figure."

"Maybe it was the only way they could spend some time alone without you hovering all the time."

Taken aback by the comment, Tony protested. "I don't hover." He then made the same monumental mistake most men make when they get defensive. "Unless you feel my presence here means you're worried I will be hovering around you and Commander Eddington."

Renée was quick to make him pay. "You've got to be kidding me! You're jealous of Commander Eddington? God, are all men stupid, or is it just you?"

Never one to pass up an opportunity to stick his foot further down his throat, Tony added fuel to the fire. "Look, it's none of my business if you and the Commander got together. After all, he is quite a bit younger, and his ass is almost as nice as mine is. You could do worse."

Renée shook her head in disbelief that Tony was so oblivious to her signals. "Do I keep torturing him or spell it out?" she thought. "Idiot!" She grabbed his arm, pulled him close, and kissed him hard on his lips.

Renée didn't want anyone to see, so she quickly broke away. "Look at this; we're at the door to *your* cabin." Renée turned with her back to the door and looked Tony straight in the eye. "I'm not looking for a weekend on the beach Captain Knox, because if that's all you're after, I'm not interested."

For the first time since he arrived on the Missouri, Tony made the right move. He kept his mouth shut, opened the door, lifted her off her feet, entered *her* cabin, and slammed the door behind them.

On the 24th, two days after the task force left the North Sea, they held a memorial service on the Enterprise to bury the Decatur casualties. A general malaise hung in the air as the sober service brought home that it could have been any one of them sliding into the water. After the service was over, the senior staff met in the Admirals Ready Room for an update on their next step. The mood was sober, with little of the normal banter that would occur prior to most meetings.

Alicia was off by herself looking over her notes as reference points to make her case to President Roosevelt. It was imperative that he get behind the idea for world leaders to meet for a conference about what the postwar world should look like. Sean had acted as a sounding board while she put it together, but Alicia felt she hadn't hit the mark.

She accepted the cup of coffee Sean offered and set it on the table before she handed him the letter. "If you don't mind, will you read it to me? Maybe it will help give me a different perspective."

"I'd be happy to."

Tony reached over and grabbed the papers from Sean could react. "Don't you all think *I* would be better suited to get the most out of what the Secretary wrote?"

Sean could see Tony was trying to loosen up the mood in the room, so he sat back with a smile.

Captain Mark Daily of the Seawolf couldn't resist. "If by better you mean overly dramatic, yeah, I'd say you are better suited, like a drama queen that is."

"He's certainly more disposed to it than his better half," Commander Regis Goddard of the John Paul Jones said while laughing. By now, everyone in the room was aware of Tony and Renée's relationship. Unfortunately, without knowing it, the junior officer had crossed the line, which brought all conversation to a halt.

Fortunately for the young Commander, Renée came to his rescue. "That's okay Commander Goddard; you're still young and allowed a little latitude when you stick your foot in your mouth." She looked over to Tony, who this time wisely remained silent. "Though it is true Captain Knox and I share common interests outside of our command duties, it would be in *your* best interests to refrain from comment."

Alicia finished for Renée. "I think what Captain Aslan means Regis, is the Chief of Staff will make you his bitch if you don't."

That did it. Everyone but the chagrined destroyer Commander

broke up, followed by a round of further abuse. When the laughter died down, Sean took the papers back from Tony and began to read.

Mr. President,

Our unique knowledge of the future compels in us a moral obligation to attempt to make a difference for the good of all humanity. Every generation spends the majority of their lives trying to clean up the mess their ancestors left behind, all the while continuing the conflicts left over from animosities passed on from father to son and mother to daughter. Each new conflict compounding those that came before as history records only the version determined by the victors. Versions that demonize their enemies and perpetuate animosities between cultures and religions that are never resolved.

During the early years of human tribal communities, leaders did not need to do much to unify their group in a world where every day was a struggle to survive. With strength in numbers, you could defeat those who tried to steal your crops or livestock. In this early history, if you lived to the ripe old age of thirty you were an elder wise man. As violent as this world was, it was still much bigger than the body of humanity that populated it. Therefore, genocide here, genocide there, made little difference to whether the species of Homo sapiens itself survived.

The rise of the great human urban centers changed this equation over four thousand years ago. As the killing machines utilized by these expanding societies grew more lethal, the amount of treasure needed to support them increased accordingly. Narratives passed down over the centuries describe the brutal battles of conquest fought by King Xerxes of Persia against the Spartans and Athenians in 486 BC. Stories of the great sea battles between the Phoenicians and the Romans were the prelude to 500 years of Roman dominance over most of the known world. The one constant being the ever increasing costs to feed the killing machines.

With the introduction of gunpowder came the epic sea battles fought between the French, Spanish, and British who battled for control of the New World colonies for over two hundred and fifty years. Following this were the French and American Civil Wars, preludes of the massacres to come as weapons reached maturity to mow down hundreds of lives in seconds. These weapons improved until the world was able to decimate an entire generation of Europeans in the trenches of France in WWI. It is hard to imagine over one hundred thousand deaths in a day and the stench of the rotting corpses strewn across miles of cratered landscapes. At the end of this bloodbath, who could have realized how much worse it would become a mere twenty years later.

The one constant in everything I've described is an unbroken time line of greed, terror, and violence humanity has given up trying to alter. This brings me to why we are attempting the impossible. We possess technologies that every nation on this planet would die to get their hands on. Only we will be very careful about whom we share them with. To find out how we plan to share this knowledge, you will need to invite representatives from every nation to meet in Paris.

If you question our motives, you only need to know they lie in the truth of what we have witnessed in your future. Our loyalty will be with those who help us change the world to where genocide is no more than a historical reference in the dictionary.

Alicia Calhoun

United States Secretary of Defense

Civilian Authority aboard the USS Enterprise CVN-65

Sean finished reading the letter and sat down. "Okay, let's hear what you think."

Tony didn't hesitate. "I know you've put a lot of thought into this Alicia, and I hate to rain on your parade, but even if you convince this generation to lay down their weapons, how long will it be before the next generation blindly follows another monster to start the cycle all over again?

"You already know that I have as much contempt for the citizen who can't name their own Senator as I do for the greedy Captains of Industry who drive the economy off a cliff every fifty years. Hell, only ten percent of the population when we came from was well informed, disciplined in their abilities, and willing to sacrifice for the greater good. And this is the reason why the next Fascist monster most likely will come from the United States, when all we have left to claim in leadership will be from the guns of our cloaked ships."

Captain Gordon Lincoln shook his head. "So you'd rather some country other than the United States have this technology?"

"No, I'd rather the United States be world leaders in something other than its military industrial complex."

"I'm sure we all wish the same thing," Gordon agreed. "However I do disagree with your contempt for big business. How can you begrudge anyone who creates his or her own wealth under a system designed for such outcomes?"

Alicia tried to intercede, but Tony quickly responded. "Good point, though personally I don't have a problem with their wealth. It's the lengths these greedy bastards go to destroy anyone who challenges their dominance once it's established that bothers me. In the first decade of the 20th Century, it bothered the government enough to break up the trusts of the day. In a perfect world, governments wouldn't need to penalize businesses that become so successful they dominate a market."

Captain Lincoln countered. "The antitrust laws are a form of governmental terrorism. Congress wrote antitrust law with such ambiguity that every guilty verdict automatically becomes a case for the Supreme Court to review. Sounds like socialism to me."

Tony smiled for a moment, satisfied Gordon was off balance, and in his most humble voice countered, "That isn't fair. You do know I read more than the sports page and Iron Man comic books, don't you? Though seriously, I think you are blind to what these egomaniacs do to the loyal customers who paid to build their businesses once the threat of competition ends. Instead of servicing the community, the community becomes a slave to their products. It seems to me these sociopaths spend most of their lives trying to return the world to the good old days of Feudalism. Start with the day a child is born and get him or her in debt to the Lord of the Manor for life."

Sean had heard enough. "So *Alicia*, remind me again what exactly is it we're trying to accomplish?"

Happy to get back on point she jumped at the chance. "With our ability to control the game, we can force the most militarily aggressive nations to allow the weaker ones to compete. We can't change human nature, but maybe we can level the playing field for a brief moment in time."

Tony still wasn't satisfied. "Seems to me one of two things can happen. Some will proclaim us as prophets and follow us around, think Life of Brian, until they see we bleed like everyone else and, in their disillusionment, nail us to the nearest cross. Or, they can skip the first part and go straight to the cross. Either way, I'll be glad to be around to see the fireworks, because if a greater power put us in this situation as humanity's last chance, the responsible deity must be pretty desperate."

Sean realized there was a microcosm of society sitting right here in this room. He could tell by the conversation that nothing would satisfy those as fundamentally grounded as Captain Lincoln. "I understand both Tony and Gordon's concerns, but we have to show a united front if we hope to succeed at anything. Thank you."

Most stuck around and socialized for the next hour, except for Tony and Renée who took the time to escape to *his* cabin.

The next day, the 25th, Rebecca was asleep in the Missouri's infirmary when Tony arrived and asked the Corpsman how she was doing.

"She will be in a sling for four weeks, but will make a full recovery."

Rebecca sensed Tony's presence and opened her eyes.

Tony winked at her. "How's the little warrior doing today? I'm told Dr. Strangelove won't be siring any little maniacs after the hurt you put on his little buddy."

"I heard about all those sailors who died when I lost control of Specter. I'm sorry I failed to stop the missile launch Tony. I should have gone over to the Princeton and repeated the same diagnostics programs I ran on the Missouri."

"First off, you didn't put the laptop in his hands. The person who did is now fish food, so let it go. Second, you were a little busy fending off a mad scientist who mistook you for some kind of evil monkey. What do you think? Was he trying to steal your ruby slippers?"

Tony saw her face light up at the image he had painted, but he knew it would take some time for her to accept there was little she could have done to save the sailors who died. After getting to know her over the last month and a half, he had an idea of what would speed up her recovery.

"So you ready to get back to work? We still have a lot to do over the next, oh I don't know, maybe the rest of our working lives. You know it's never easy when you're tasked with saving the world."

Rebecca seemed to ignore what he said, her mind already on what she needed to do. "Dr. Phelps called me an hour ago and told me how Dr. Strangelove manipulated the Princeton's computer when he first hardwired Specter into its mainframe. I'd like to see if he repeated it in any of the Missouri's programs, though he was pretty vague on how he did it."

She tried to get up from the bed, but winced from the sharp pain and fell back. "Can I get a little help here Captain?" With Tony and the Corpsman's help, she staggered out of bed and walked around the room to regain her equilibrium.

Tony conferred with her doctor and they agreed there wasn't any reason to keep her in Sickbay as long as she returned to her cabin for a few days to rest.

Tony took her hand and while he helped her get ready to leave thought, "Yeah, like I'm going to let her do that."

After Alicia polished and then sent her message to President Roosevelt, she headed to the hangar deck where she met Sean for an informal meeting with the assembled sailors. To her surprise, the questions dealt more with the future disposition of the crew into the mainstream of society than with the war they were fighting. As of yet, neither Sean nor Alicia had figured out all the angles of this recurring problem.

Sean spoke to their concerns as honestly as the facts allowed. "To give you assurances we'll find a way for a smooth transition into society would probably be a lie. Put yourselves in the shoes of the average person, who is used to the daily reality that comes at him or her at a steady rate, digesting events incrementally. Some make sense, some are scary, and others beyond understanding. New car models, your kids are another day older, and church on Sunday means a new dress. In other words, despite the highs and lows of living in 1942, their reality is as predictable as the steak, potatoes, and peas they had for dinner.

"Then we appear, throwing everything into question. From their basic beliefs taught in Bible school, to the incredible pressure the public will put on the government and the scientists of the day to explain the meaning of our existence. What cannot be explained, will be feared. Look at your own beliefs and ask yourself one simple question. How have your beliefs been impacted since you were ripped out of your time and place? How would you relate to people who already know your future?

"Let's say you meet up with Charles Manson as a child. Do you kill him or let his life play out and hope for the best? How do you live with yourself if history repeated and Sharon Tate dies all over again?

"We have already experienced these fears, borne out by President Roosevelt and Prime Minister Churchill's attempt to seize our ships in the Panama Canal. I can't find any fault with their actions. They acted to protect the public from what they saw was a threat greater than those posed by Germany and Japan.

"Look at it from another perspective. How secure would you feel if you were back in 2014 and a starship appeared in the skies above Washington DC and every other major city around the world? After landing, little green men teleported straight into the White House and every other major seat of power around the world. Don't you think fear would be the immediate effect of losing control to a force that could move at will through your defenses, while at the same time they are telling you it's for your own good?"

Sean recognized a sailor from the back of the room who had stood up. "Sir, so what is our future if we're such a threat to this world? You don't expect us to remain aboard ship for the rest of our lives do you?"

Alicia answered the sailor. "No I don't, which is why it's so important to bring the world's leaders together to discuss the future direction humanity takes and then get off the stage. Afterward we can utilize the technology at our disposal to buy all of us the freedom to settle as a community in a yet to be determined location. I hope over the course of a few years our assimilation into society will begin. There is still the possibility that our scientists can figure out how to return us to where we belong, so we wouldn't want to spread throughout the world too quickly.

"Dr. Cutler from Comstock Technologies has already discovered some of the physics involved, and this will continue to be the focus of her efforts. Meanwhile, I want you to know Admiral Phillips and I are doing everything in our power to give you the best chance for as normal a life as this situation will allow."

Sean decided to close the meeting before the discussion went into the absurd, which based on earlier experiences was assured. "And we'll continue to stay honest with you as we negotiate our way through this maze. Thank you and carry on." The officers and crew stood to attention as they left the hanger deck.

Sean gave her a quick kiss when they were out of sight. "I've got to go to the bridge to check on Commander Osaka and make sure he's not steering us into the Missouri. Charles has been making Osaka's life hell to find out as soon as possible if he is up to the task. I'll see you a little later." The instability of their situation left little room for a commander who could not react with the right instincts in an emergency.

That afternoon, Sean learned from the British Admiralty that negotiations with the German Government appeared headed for a successful conclusion. The only sticking point for the German delegation was the lack of a formal agreement from Britain and America to commit their armed forces against Stalin's offensive. In a move that signaled his complete disregard of the current political reality, Stalin cut off communications with the British Government. This made it easy for Roosevelt to send the little known General Dwight Eisenhower to England to prepare the ground for the deployment of American troops.

"Looks like Uncle Joe can't help himself," Tony joked when Sean relayed the news.

Stalin's actions were not a surprise to Sean. "The man thinks he's Attila the Hun reincarnated. However, he underestimated Hitler's brutality when he accepted the 1939 Molotov-Ribbentrop Pact that divided Poland between Germany and the Soviet Union, which began WWII. Despite repeated warnings from the English Government, the Germany Army was two days into Operation Barbarossa before Stalin mobilized his Army. A military genius he's not."

Tony chuckled. "You and Alicia counted on it. Neither Churchill nor Roosevelt will be happy to learn you want to use Europe as a bargaining chip."

"Be that as it may, Alicia is looking forward to the challenge. She can give them a more palatable option, and that is where it will get interesting. By the time she's finished with them, everyone will leave believing they won something."

Tony took a moment to think about this before he responded. "How can someone as sane as Alicia enjoy the insanity of geopolitical politics? I never could understand why she jumped ship to work with the State Department, considering she was the highest ranking female at sea at the time."

Sean immediately shot back. "They would never have let her captain an aircraft carrier, let alone hang a flag on a task force, that's why. Why do you think Renée left her command to join her?"

Tony hadn't considered the glass ceiling, and how it limited women he knew were more qualified than some of the male commanders he had served under. Then a light bulb went off in his sometimes-dim head. "So, as Captain of the Mighty Mo, Renée is living the dream right now?"

"You think?" Sean loved his friend dearly, but knew he needed further evolution before he overcame his own chauvinistic traits. "Hopefully this is one of the societal issues we can speed up by a few decades."

At the White House, President Roosevelt was having lunch with Harry Hopkins. Harry was reading Churchill's latest correspondence to the President and the look on his face betrayed his feelings about its content. He jumped out of his chair and stormed around the room. "I don't know how we are going to do it, but you're going to have to bring these guys under the rule of law. The very fact they recognize your constitutional right to command, yet refuse to submit to it is treasonous.

"It's difficult enough to deny to the media what they've accomplished against the Japanese. Now we have to explain their attack on Germany, which included descriptions of alien aircraft, and all we can tell the public is nothing. I can't wait to see what's next in their bag of goodies. They can dictate whatever they want, whenever they want, and however they want. Add to that, the defection of the Southern Democrats when you hit them over the head with civil rights legislation and I don't see us able to pass any meaningful legislation. Everything we've worked for will turn to dust and the voters will throw us out on our asses."

He walked back to his chair and plopped down in surrender. "Oh well. I'm too old for this shit anyway."

Roosevelt thought for a moment and hit on an idea he knew would lower his friend's blood pressure. His smile said it all. "We make their plan our own. What would be the downside if we expose who they are to the public? If we make the public aware they are a United States Naval Task Force under my authority, their success becomes our own. Add to this their need to resupply, and we will have the leverage we need to dictate terms which will neutralize them. This strategy also gets us off the hook about this civil rights disaster. I'll explain to the country that because of the turmoil reported from the Southern States against the Negroes it's for their safety."

His interest stoked, Harry leaned forward. "It's perfect, and we have eleven days before the summit to arrange everything." He stopped and smiled, then added somewhat deviously, "I have a suggestion. Let's see if we can get Churchill here as soon as possible to stand alongside you when you deliver the news."

Now both men were smiling.

On 27 January 1942, while the Enterprise Task Force was still three days out from Norfolk, the two leaders rocked the world to its foundations when they stood before Congress and exposed the truth about how Japan and Germany were defeated. After their address, they stood on the steps of the Capitol as the Ambassadors from Japan and Germany announced they had agreed to a peace settlement. While the uproar associated with this fantastic news raced from Wall Street to Main Street, behind the scenes the attempt at civil reforms died quietly. Following this charade and with Roosevelt more popular than ever, the Southern Democrats returned to the Democratic Party.

In the Enterprise CIC, Lt. Gloria Layworth picked up the phone and called Sean. "Admiral, you're not going to like what I've just picked up."

Chapter Three

Congress

Once again, the senior staff sat in the Admirals Ready Room with only Tony and Alicia aware of the depth of Sean's anger. He sat quietly doodling on a piece of paper. When he looked up, the green in his hazel eyes stood out like an oncoming storm. Those eyes now bored like a laser through those in the room. Then with a slow cold voice, he announced to the stunned gathering, "The President has betrayed us again."

Sean went on to explain what the intercepts they picked up out of Washington meant. "Without any other viable options, Secretary Calhoun and I have come to the conclusion we must wage war against our own government."

This statement elicited a breakdown in the usual military protocol as the room burst into a cacophony of disagreement.

"Settle down people," Sean shouted. "I don't mean we're going to launch missiles on Washington. The war the Secretary and I want to wage is in the political arena. I ordered this meeting because we intend to broadcast in the clear an invitation to every journalist in New York City, the nation's number one media center, to come aboard the Enterprise. We will show them transcripts of our talks with the American, British, Japanese, and German leaders." It was abundantly clear from the tone of Sean's voice that the President shouldn't have pissed him off a second time.

Alicia felt it necessary to add some context. "It is obvious negotiating secretly within the government has allowed the President to use his political skills to back us into a corner. What he fails to understand is with the country no longer at war, we don't need to tread so carefully."

Sean and Alicia spent the next hour convincing those on the fence what they planned to do. By the time the meeting ended, everyone agreed that their plan was their only option.

Later that afternoon, they sent an open invitation to every credentialed news service they could dig up to come aboard the USS Enterprise at 1000 hours the morning of 30 January 1942. There wasn't any mention of the agenda for this gathering in the release, which was designed to add to the President's discomfort. Further adding insult to injury, there wasn't any attempt made to contact him. In fact, Sean gave orders not to respond to calls from *any* government official.

President Roosevelt was at dinner with Eleanor and Churchill when his porter handed him a note. After reading it, the President excused himself and wheeled himself from the room to find Harry Hopkins waiting.

"What happened?"

"It appears our friends have some skills of their own. Secretary's Hull and Stimson are waiting for us in your office."

"Send for Winston to meet us there."

When Roosevelt entered his office, he immediately phoned his Attorney General, Francis Biddle to see if he had any legal recourse to ban the reporters from going out to the Enterprise.

Hopkins pushed his finger down on the phones hook. "We already told the world what heroes they are. You would look like an idiot if you barred the press from meeting with them. Besides, without the ability to know where they are, they could bombard the airwaves wherever they wanted with whatever they wanted anyway."

Roosevelt put the phone down as Churchill arrived. For the next twenty minutes, Roosevelt and his staff ran through their options, all of which led to the likelihood of political embarrassment, or worse.

Churchill quietly listened until there was a break in the discussion. "It would be difficult, but not impossible for them to turn you away if you decided to show up with the media." He then flashed his famous smile. "However, if you care to take a minute to hear me out, I can guarantee you a way to get invited aboard."

The morning of 30 January 1942 at 0900, the task force was ten miles outside of New York harbor as Sean, Alicia, and Tony prepared for the deluge of reporters who were set to descend on the Enterprise. The crew, including Alicia, would wear their dress whites to drive home the point that this was a powerful United States Navy task force. When they met on the flight deck, Sean noted this also made Alicia more attractive than he thought possible. The cut of her uniform accented her shapely body and presented her as someone born to power. "I think you couldn't look sexier if you were wearing your forest green teddy," he whispered.

She smiled and whispered, "Thank you for the compliment. Now behave yourself or you won't be seeing that particular piece of clothing for a long time."

Sean feigned the look of a lecherous land shark. "Maybe we should forget all of this nonsense and hop a steamer headed for the Bahamas."

When Alicia laughed, it caught Commander Osaka's attention, which prompted Alicia to break away from Sean. "I told you to behave yourself."

As the Enterprise slowly worked her way toward the harbor, the wind was gusting at fifteen miles an hour, which added a bite to the 20-degree winter weather. Five miles from the entrance, the number of pleasure boats heading out of the harbor gave them little seaway to avoid the crush closing fast on their cloaked course. Tony ordered full stop for every ship except the Enterprise. "Slow to five knots. Steady on course. Bring the crew to attention Commander Osaka."

Osaka keyed the order and announced on the ships intercom. "Man your stations on the flight deck." Immediately hundreds of white clad sailors rushed out to line the flight deck.

The pleasure craft nearest to the cloaked Enterprise began to troll back and forth across the aircraft carrier's projected course in an attempt to get the best vantage point when the mystery ships arrived. Like most of the boats in the harbor, she was loaded to capacity. One of the women onboard scanned the horizon through a set of binoculars, when all of a sudden the massive bow of the Enterprise filled her lenses. While screaming, she fell over backwards. As the rest of the massive shape slowly materialized out of thin air, the white-clad sailors lining her decks added to the grandeur of the moment.

"Stop all engines."

The sailors snapped to attention and saluted as she glided to a halt, her massive anchors sliding into the sea. On the silent Enterprise, they could hear a wall of sound, which after a few moments they recognized as a cheer from the approaching mass of pleasure boats.

As they viewed the choked harbor through binoculars, Sean and Tony picked out a yacht that stood out from the rest. It was painted white, with two smoke stacks and was over one hundred fifty feet long from bow to stern. Tony was first to recognize the historic vessel. "It's the USS Potomac, the Presidential Yacht, and there's the old goat himself seated on the fantail."

"And there's Eleanor Roosevelt sitting next to him," Sean observed.

Churchill knew Sean and Alicia would find it impossible to be rude to the First Lady in front of the entire country. They would know how bad it would look to the American public to insult their *Queen*.

President Roosevelt was not used to being in such a vulnerable position. When Winston proposed the idea of bringing his suffragist wife Eleanor along to gain access, he was intensely opposed at first. He conceded to the idea only after Hopkins convinced him it was his only chance to head off a political disaster. However, everyone had agreed Churchill should stay away so as not to complicate matters further.

Because Eleanor Roosevelt already disagreed with her husband on issues she felt strongly about, this tactic was the proverbial double-edged sword. She spoke publicly against the country's racist policies after she failed to convince the President to continue to fight for the bill Alicia had demanded. She would find allies in Sean and Alicia.

Alicia grabbed the binoculars from Sean's hands to see for herself. "He's using his wife as cover. Who do you suppose came up with that idea?"

"You might as well flip a coin," Tony answered.

"I bet it was Churchill," Alicia surmised. "He knew we wouldn't refuse to let the First Lady come aboard. Has the man no shame?"

"Fine, we let her aboard, and deny him," Tony sniped.

"Let it go Tony. We lost this round. We still have plenty to work with, and remember we have the home turf advantage." As the Potomac maneuvered through all the pleasure crafts to come alongside the Enterprise, Alicia's mind raced through the implications the First Lady's appearance represented and realized this gave them a unique opportunity.

"Sean, I think it would be a good idea to change our strategy and let me do the talking. Let the press wait until we have a chance to see if I can have some influence over the First Lady."

Reluctantly Sean gave the order. "Prepare to greet the President and his wife Commander Osaka.

Commander Osaka scrambled to make the necessary calls to get the honor guard set up for when the President and the First Lady boarded the Enterprise.

Bowing to protocol, and against Tony's protest, Alicia had convinced Sean the President should board ahead of the reporters. "I say we should have let them board right after the last of the ice cream venders."

"Yeah that would have looked good splashed across the New York Times front page." Even while standing right off the boarding ramp waiting for the President's hoist to be rigged, Alicia and Tony kept at it.

"At least you two are not dressed like the little brats you're acting like." Sean imagined what a cross-country car trip would be like traveling with these two in the back seat. "Let it go."

Alicia took a moment to admire her men. "Tom Cruise had nothing on you two in Top Gun. Too bad I can't get you in those dress whites more often."

Tony wasn't about to let her get in the last word and was about to respond when the sight of Roosevelt's chair cleared the ships side railing. "Attention!" At once over five hundred sailors snapped to attention as the President was set on the flight deck.

With the long cigarette holder clenched in his teeth as depicted in a hundred pictures, Roosevelt was all smiles. "Good morning to you all. What an incredible ship you command."

The President's son wheeled him over to the receiving line, where Captain Folger smartly stepped forward. "It is an honor for you to come aboard Mr. President."

"The honor is mine." Roosevelt glanced back to see Eleanor reach the deck. "And let me introduce the First Lady."

Eleanor reached out to shake Folgers hand. "I must say I am at a loss for words."

Alicia gave a nod to Folger and stepped forward. "It is my pleasure to introduce Rear Admiral, Retired and Secretary of Defense Alicia Calhoun," Captain Folger announced and stepped back.

"Oh Yes. A pleasure to meet you Madam Secretary," Eleanor Roosevelt acknowledged.

Alicia went on to introduce the rest of the Senior Staff to the First Lady, leaving Sean for last. "Rear Admiral Sean Phillips."

After shaking both their hands, Sean motioned for them to follow. "Shall we get to it?"

The First Lady showed off her gracious nature right from the start. "When Franklin informed me of his meeting in December with Admiral Phillips and Prime Minister Churchill, I didn't believe the truth of your existence, but frankly the size of your ship goes beyond his description. Where are the rest of the ships the President told me would be present?"

Alicia answered the First Lady with a smile. "Well frankly Mrs. Roosevelt, because your husband has now twice managed to avoid living up to agreements he made with us, we don't trust him. We decided to expose only this ship to any new surprises while we take our case to the public."

The First Lady shot her husband a look of confusion that he quickly addressed. "The issue in question alludes to a set of political points which under current realities are impossible to put to the American public without causing major social unrest."

Alicia quickly countered. "The issue the President refers to would be the one you have placed closest to your heart, civil rights for all."

"As I stated, let's take this conversation somewhere more private." Sean led them to the elevator that would take them to the hangar deck.

For the next half-hour, a hundred members of the media boarded the Enterprise. Sailors lined the route to a curtained off area of the hangar deck to keep the press from wandering into restricted areas. When they reached the hangar deck, other sailors funneled them to rows of chairs set up to face a large screen. During this process and regardless of the incessant questions thrown at them, silence was the only response.

Tony ushered the President and First Lady to the front row of seats, while the press in animated discussion about the Enterprise filled in the rest of the chairs. After everyone sat down, Sean and Alicia approached a podium set up to the left of the large movie screen.

"Good morning. I am Admiral Sean Phillips, Commander of the United States Navy task force this ship is a part of." He then turned to Alicia. "And this is United States Secretary of Defense Alicia Calhoun.

"President Roosevelt met with us in December in the waters off Oahu, but even he is unaware of some of what you are about to see. You will have many questions afterward that I am sorry to inform you, no one under my command will answer. We've invited you aboard as a courtesy, so please refrain from any activities that will force me to have you thrown off my ship."

After this warning, black out curtains were drawn, and images appeared on the screen. To get everyone focused, Sean and Alicia wanted to shock the reporters to the worst of humanities evolution first thing. Hydrogen bombs detonated in the Nevada desert, on remote Pacific Islands, and dropped over the cities of Hiroshima and Nagasaki drew a gasp from the visitors as scenes of nuclear mushroom clouds filled the screen. Scenes of the devastation of those cities and their people followed. This visual representation of the abject failure of humanity to reign in its self-destructive nature took all of twenty minutes. When it ended, Sean returned to the podium to witness shocked silence as he looked out at the faces in the audience.

"This is the reality your children and grandchildren will live and die under if we cannot convince you and the public at large that change must come. That's all I have to say for now, so if you please follow the direction of the sailors and return to the flight deck, I would appreciate your cooperation." The President's surprise appearance forced him to interrupt the program until after they found out Roosevelt's motive for doing so.

Sean left the podium and motioned to Tony to escort the President and First Lady to the Admirals Ready Room. This also signaled the sailors who surrounded the guests to escort the press up to the flight deck to wait. It took a moment for the press to recover their senses, but when they did, they all jumped to their feet and shouted out questions that as promised went unanswered.

Sean and Alicia made their way to the Admirals Ready Room, where the President and First Lady waited. Alicia's first words sounded like the little girl who just met her idol. "Before I begin, once again I want to tell you what an honor it is to meet you Mrs. Roosevelt, and how much I respect your efforts to bring about equal rights for both minorities and women."

The tone in Alicia's voice turned serious as she walked behind where the President sat. "However, I must be blunt about how the President's attempts to break several agreements he reached with us has made it impossible for us to negotiate any future agreements. As we showed you in our presentation, there will be millions of premature deaths from now to well into the next century if you persist in using us for your own political gain. It is essential for this nation and its leaders to rid itself of its moral hypocrisy if we are to be taken seriously by the rest of the world."

Mrs. Roosevelt began to put some of the pieces together, which prompted her to ask. "One of his agreements wouldn't by any chance be the civil rights bill he introduced to Congress and then pulled back three days ago?"

The President realized he needed to get ahead of the coming storm. "As a matter of fact it is Eleanor. I pulled it because the Southern Democrats promised violence and to exit the party if I refused. This is just a continuation of the same argument I have had with you for years. The country is not ready for it yet." Though he gave it a brave effort, the President knew there would be no winning this one.

Alicia moved away from the President and took her seat. "The problem with your thinking Mr. President, is you are the one ultimately responsible for every injustice suffered if you turn a blind eye while you sit in the Oval Office. The nation wasn't ready for it in 1964 either when another President, apparently braver than you, rammed the same Civil Rights Act through Congress. And yes, Federal troops spent years in the Southern States to quell the violence it spawned.

"Nevertheless, I digress from the main point of my argument. Because of this and other just as glaringly political hypocrisies, the United States lost the moral ground it needed to lead the world. If you act now, instead of the loss of this moral authority, we can truly create the country that is a beacon of light for the world to follow."

The First Lady was confused. "It seems to me with the technology you possess, you could fabricate any reality you choose to convince us of almost anything."

Alicia answered. "Unfortunately, everything we shared with you is real, including the consequences of the social reforms the President championed.

"What did you think would happen Mr. President, after you gave absolute control over the largest amount of money ever collected by the Federal Government to a group of the most egocentric members of our society?"

Roosevelt was accustomed to defending his program. "It doesn't matter. We built enough safeguards into the program that corruption would be limited."

As soon as the President said this, Tony burst out laughing. "Yeah like handing out pork wasn't enough for Congress, you had to hand them blank checks that decades later they were still cashing whether or not they had the funds to cover them.

"Mr. President, I don't mean to show disrespect, but your so-called protections led to Congress using Social Security as a slush fund to explode the size of the Federal Government to the tune of four trillion dollars by the time we left."

Alicia shot Tony, a *that's enough* look before she took over. "This one entitlement program began a slew of legislation that led to a complete takeover of personal responsibility by the Federal Government. Deductions by Local, State, and Federal Governments removed thirty-five percent of the wages from every one of the average American workers' paychecks.

"This paled in comparison to the burden governments placed on small businesses that by law paid out another forty percent above the employee checks for the honor to employ these workers. It became impossible for anyone except those with multiple college degrees to succeed. And if this wasn't bad enough, by the year we left the dollar was worth only three percent of what it is right now. Now throw in a population that doubled in size, with over sixty percent untrained and uneducated, and you can see why we might seem a little aggressive in our pursuit to alter the equation."

Alicia's arguments did not persuade Roosevelt. "So if I were to believe your dire warnings, how would you address the inequities which left over half of this country's population destitute? Is your solution to abandon them?"

Eleanor Roosevelt had her own concern. "When you say the social programs Franklin put into place were a failure, do you mean there were still millions of children going to bed starving, or do you believe they should be abandoned?"

"Certainly not Mrs. Roosevelt. In any crisis, it is the government's responsibility to aid its citizens. Only this support should have been temporary, as your husband's predecessor, Herbert Hoover, intended. Instead of an enlightened society, you created a nation of crybabies who grew dependent on the government.

"When we left our time, the country, as well as the world, was in a depression every bit as great as the one that began in 1929. In fact, the root causes of the 1929 Depression were never resolved, so every time the country slid into recession, the Federal Government would print more money and push the problem further down the road."

The President was getting agitated with the conversation and his wife's willingness to engage in it. "I'm not a dictator who can force Congress to pass laws it doesn't want to pass."

Eleanor snapped at her husband. "Maybe this wouldn't be the case if you stopped letting Mr. Hopkins *dictate* to you what is politically possible." It was obvious the First Lady and the President had danced to this tune before.

Sean figured this would be a good time to move things along. He got Alicia's attention by pointing to his watch.

Alicia nodded and quickened her pace. "Getting back to the here and now, if we hadn't interceded against Japan and Germany, you were looking at the loss of twenty million lives in Europe and Asia by the end of 1945. Two-hundred and fifty thousand of these would have been American. What you did in the way of thanks was to ignore our only demand. Therefore, we will tell the truth to the reporters who are waiting for us on the flight deck and the only question is, do we tell them or do you Mr. President? If you'd like, we prepared a few words for you." Alicia handed the President a few pages of print.

After he browsed the pages, the President took off his glasses and rubbed his eyes. "If I read this to the press and then tried to get it into law, I'd never get the votes to see it pass. In fact, it would make governing this nation impossible with the violence it would create."

"You're right about one thing Mr. President, legislation that will guarantee equality for all will lead to civil strife and will divide the country. However, if you make the attempt, we will neutralize the threat Stalin poses."

"And there it is," Franklin thought.

The First Lady pushed her husband. "You've never backed away from a conflict you thought was worth fighting before. You have this prophetic view of the future staring back at you from everything this ship and its crew represent, so why would you shrink from trying?"

Sean decided the conversation had gone as far as it could in this direction. "I think I have a solution that can shelter you from the political storm you're worried about. Why don't you let Secretary Calhoun address Congress after you announce your call to reintroduce the civil rights bill? Within the context of our accomplishments against the Axis, this should give you enough leverage to convince the American public to finish the work Abraham Lincoln began."

Then in a show of determination, Sean threatened the President. "If this doesn't work, we will take our technology to countries who will listen. Like maybe England or France, both of whom have centuries of national perspective to help them see the possibilities of the future that we have experienced." Sean saw a slight smile on the First Lady's face.

Defeated, the President only slumped deeper into his chair. "Considering the excitement you have already stirred up in the press with this stunt of yours, it appears this fox has gone to ground."

Alicia did not want to let Roosevelt off the hook so easily. "No offense Mr. President, but your incessant need to manipulate us politically made us release the hounds in the first place."

Without any other choices, a smile returned to the President's face. "I'll agree to Miss Calhoun speaking before Congress, but I don't see how this will change the political reality. I will not be able to get a bill out of committee for a full vote, unless she gives a speech for the ages. But if you insist, I'll call for a special session day after tomorrow, if this isn't too early for you to prepare."

Alicia shook her head in agreement before Sean could object. "That will be fine Mr. President. I assure you I have years of experience dealing with bigger sharks than those who sit in Congress today."

With another agreement in place, Roosevelt turned his attention to the other urgent matter he needed to discuss. "By the way, I think I should make you aware of events taking place in Eastern Europe. Units of the Soviet Army have swung south and are trying to take control of the Balkans. Negotiations with the German Government have allowed us to reach an agreement for their withdrawal from France by the end of April, with elections for a new French Government scheduled for the following month. Prime Minister Churchill requested the United States Army begin to ship the troops we have already mobilized to Europe as soon as possible; with the expectation we'll be fighting the Soviets instead of Germans."

As far as Sean was concerned, this strengthened their position. "If we can receive assurances from Congress that our ideas will be heard, those soldiers won't need to fight in Europe. I hope for all our sakes you choose not to deceive us again or we will carry out our threat to take our business elsewhere."

With this warning, the conversation ended, and they left to deal with the reporters. When President Roosevelt informed them of his intention to reintroduce the civil rights bill to Congress, a storm of obscenities came from those in the audience whose opinion sided with the racists of the era. With a nod from Sean, the President let him take the podium.

"What those of you who mock the President's remarks fail to appreciate is that decades of violence to rectify the lack of liberty and equality you now deny to a few will with certainty be your legacy.

"The nuclear explosions we showed are a direct result of the kind of blind ignorance we are trying to end. Humanity does not have the luxury of such shortsighted thinking when a single misplaced reaction will have the capability of killing millions. If you want your grandchildren to have any chance of a future, you will have to learn to lose the bigotry and hypocrisy you cling to so desperately.

"As you witnessed when you scanned the lines of sailors who escorted you here, the men and women who serve aboard our ships come from every walk of life and ethnicity. They know the quality of their service to their country is the measure of the person, not the color of their skin. If we can't as a society resolve what should be the most obvious of injustices, then no other advancement is possible."

From one of the front rows, a reporter stood up and questioned Sean. "Do you carry the weapons you showed us aboard this ship? And as a follow up, what would keep you from dictating what you want if you do?"

Contrary to his earlier statement, Sean felt answering this question wouldn't hurt. "That's a question I will answer in two parts. First, we don't want anything to do with forcing our will on the United States Government or its citizens. We are sworn servants of the United States of America who defended our country against the aggressions of Japan and Germany to save millions of innocent lives. We will return under government authority as soon as the threats to *our* future end. Second, this ship, as well as the others outside your view, can bring great technological advancements that if used properly have the capacity to create a world where every nation benefits.

"Imagine everybody in this room transported back to the Civil War era, and how they would perceive you. Would you have tried to keep the slaughters of Gettysburg or Vicksburg from happening? More recently, would you try to stop the First World War, or would you sit back and let it unfold?

"Then there is this. Is the country my crew and I have sworn to serve worthy of our loyalty? Because I can tell you right now, this ship is crewed by one of the most ethnically integrated groups the world has ever seen. I can guarantee you that they will not fight for a country that allows innocent American citizens to be lynched from a tree because his racist neighbor doesn't like the way he looked at his daughter."

Sean had enough and walked away from the podium to a cacophony of follow up questions. After an acknowledgement from the President that he had nothing further to say, Sean gave the nod to Commander Osaka to escort the reporters off the Enterprise. Then with Tony and Alicia, Sean took the President and the First Lady to review the sailors who lined the decks. He wanted the couple to see up close and personal the diversity of the crew to drive home to the President who he should be fighting for in Congress. After the President and his wife left, Tony ordered the Enterprise back out to sea.

It didn't take long for the extraordinary press conference to work its way through the fabric of the American public, whose first reaction was another round of disbelief. It was one thing for the President to have talked about their existence, quite another to actually see and hear from them. This reaction was comparable to the Orson Wells radio broadcast of *The War of the Worlds* on Halloween 1938 and the hysteria that followed.

Church leaders from around the country split between the beliefs their appearance was God's will and the work of Satan. Some of the more fanatical fundamentalists went so far as to suggest Sean was the Antichrist.

Roosevelt restored order with one of his famous radio fireside chats, where he assured the public they operated under his authority. This helped to balance out the reporters exaggerated descriptions, if you could believe it was possible to exaggerate the nuclear devastation they had witnessed.

The violent backlash to the reintroduction of the Civil Rights Act instigated unprovoked attacks on Black populations in the Southern States. It wasn't out of any sense of altruism the President sent units of the United States Army into the South to quell the violence. He knew if he ignored the groundswell of positive expectations now set loose throughout the rest of the country, he wouldn't have a base left to govern from. Once he made the decision to send in the Army, he realized the potential benefits about how historians would remember his presidency if his name were tied to finishing Lincoln's work.

After two years of bloody conflict, and its sudden conclusion, the rest of the world was too busy celebrating to care much about how it happened. In Japan and Germany, the work to build new governments obscured the means of their defeat.

The exception to this rule was the Soviet Union, where Stalin turned up the pressure on his generals to push their soldiers ruthlessly. When the American press confirmed how Germany and Japan lost to a naval force from the future, he recalled his spies from America to face firing squads for their lack of initiative to discover their existence earlier.

Unfortunately, he didn't change his goal to occupy Eastern Europe. In fact, he saw it as an opportunity to maximize the millions of troops he had under arms. Stalin demanded his Commanders push the attacks along the extended battlefronts against the German forces. He also ordered every available division held in reserve to deploy to the battles raging around the cities of Minsk and Kiev.

As these additional forces arrived, they put Stalin in the position to move on the German's northern flank and to continue the drive west to threaten Czechoslovakia and southern Poland. It did not matter to the butcher that millions of Soviet citizens were starving to death to support his offensive. All he saw was the opportunity to expand his territory and bring the millions of people in these lands under his despotic rule.

Winston Churchill arrived in Paris for the peace conference on 31 January 1942. His first order of business was to add his signature to the treaty that ended the war with Germany. Later Churchill met alone with Chancellor Rundstedt and they talked well into the evening about the threat Stalin represented to the newfound peace. This led to a proposal from Churchill to blockade the Soviet ports in the Baltic. If this didn't back Stalin down, England and her Commonwealth nations would send armed forces to the continent and join the German Army to stop the Soviet advance. Churchill was aware there were opponents to this course of action in Parliament who argued against military action against the Soviet Union. He also knew the political capital he gained from Germany's sudden surrender would vanish if they didn't quickly bring Stalin to heel.

On the morning of 1 February 1942, the Enterprise Task Force was seventy-five miles off the mouth of the Potomac River as Alicia finished getting ready for her trip to the Capital. Sean, Captain Mark Daily, Captain Renée Aslan, and a SEAL squad were to accompany Alicia to the Capital, while Tony stayed aboard the Enterprise to command the fleet.

"I'm beginning to feel like the third wheel on a date. While you two get to trip through Washington society, I'm left to rot both figuratively and literally at home again to watch the kids," Tony whined.

Alicia never missing an opportunity to bust his chops couldn't help herself. "As if you've ever looked forward to putting on a tux and socializing with political wonks. Cheer up, Tony. I'm sure if everything goes according to plan, in a few days we'll be back in the North Sea and you'll have plenty of time to enjoy life on the Missouri to, you know, keep an eye on things."

Tony struck back. "Based on what I read of your speech to Congress, I wouldn't get too excited about your chances. After all, you plan to tell them everything they already know is wrong. Make sure you stick close to your SEAL squad. I wouldn't want to see some boozed up redneck Senator whack you with his cane. And, as far as a return to the Missouri goes, someone has to keep you two honest."

At 1000, they boarded the Seahawk to transport them to the Capitol Building where Alicia would deliver her speech to Congress at 1100. For this important appearance, she dressed as the Secretary of Defense in a dark brown pantsuit with a plain white blouse, more suited for diplomacy. Sean was in his dress whites, accompanied by Renée and Captain Daily of the Seawolf, who performed the duty of Sean's adjunct. Commander Thornton led a six-member SEAL squad from the Enterprise to ensure their safety. Thirty minutes later, their Seahawk approached the mouth of the Potomac. As the nation's Capital came into view, they could see an ocean of humanity on the national mall waiting for them.

"My God, it looks like there are a couple of million people down there." Alicia thought back to the President's inauguration in 2008 and remembered a crowd similar in size for that revolutionary day.

The effect on the mass of people as they cleared the Washington Monument gave Sean a sense of the enormity of the moment. "Imagine what they're thinking, watching our Seahawks approach. Most of these people don't have the slightest concept of what a helicopter is."

As they neared the Capitol Building, a space in the parking lot opened up below for the Seahawks to land. The Seahawk with five SEALs landed first so they could establish security, then it immediately took off and orbited south of the Capital.

When the group with Commander Thornton disembarked from the second Seahawk, Roosevelt's Secretary of State Cordell Hull waited to escort them up the Capitol steps. Off to the side and cordoned off, they noticed a large group of white men violently protesting. Some of them carried crude signs that explicitly expressed their opinion about race relations.

As they entered the Rotunda, a part of Alicia felt at home, having spent four years roaming these halls. Another part brought out her memory of the first time and how she felt the presence of all the moments great and tragic that oozed from the marble edifice. When they entered the House of Representatives chamber, she could feel the conflicted emotions of the members of Congress, from curiosity to the hatred from the block of Southern leaders.

Halfway down the aisle, a single Senator leapt up and began to clap with enthusiasm. This brought a majority in the chamber to join him. Mayhem threatened to break out, as the racists from the Southern block then rose as one and began to scream obscenities.

Thorny recognized things could turn violent at any moment and motioned for the surrounding SEAL squad to quick time the group the rest of the way to the podium. Sean stepped up to the Speaker of the House Sam Rayburn who furiously pounded his gavel to gain control of the chamber. "Let Secretary Calhoun handle it."

Rayburn shrugged his shoulders and sat down.

Alicia made her way to the podium and stood there with a blank look on her face. At first, this added fuel to the fire, but after three minutes without any attempt to quell the petulant crowd, a strange thing happened. Like children allowed to cry themselves to sleep, the chamber slowly became quiet as even the rabid dissenters took their seats.

Alicia took a deep breath and dove right in. "I will come straight to the point. You must pass a comprehensive Civil Rights Act that guarantees equal rights for all Americans."

This brought another round of jeers from the Southern block, which forced Alicia to pause again until they died down. "This is not debatable," Alicia sternly rebuked. "This country cannot stand as moral arbiters to the world while terrorizing its own citizens because of the color of their skin."

She paused for a moment to stifle a quick chuckle while directing her attention to the Southern Senators. "I am sure you would be horrified to know that your brethren helped to elect a Black President a few years from now. He took the oath of office in front of this building, so you had better get used to the idea that racial equality *will* come to America.

"Once the Civil Rights Act is passed and signed into law, the leadership of this government can then take the moral high ground to address the three main issues that will destroy civilization as you know it. They are overpopulation, religious radicalism, and the oppressively large Federal and State Governments of the future.

"By the second decade of the 21st Century, the world's human population will explode past seven billion human beings who went about obliviously depleting the resources of the planet faster than a hoard of hungry locusts. This over population destroyed native habitats, led to the extinction of hundreds of animal species, and wiped out indigenous plants worldwide. The seemingly endless supply of food from the seas vanished, as fleets of massive floating processing factories captured entire schools of fish.

"With the additional energy needed to support this population boom, concentrated levels of carbon dioxide in the atmosphere created a greenhouse effect that helped to melt fifty percent of the world's polar ice caps. Because of this, scientists estimated rising sea levels would threaten thirty percent of the world's population, creating the potential for the largest mass migration in human history. Seven billion people, on six continents, all competing for the same finite resources. Seven billion people all scrambling to get whatever they can for themselves, in a world where talent is cheap and dissent is punishable by death."

Alicia paused, took a drink of water, and looked out on the faces of the political leaders to see she had everyone's attention. "The Constitution you swore an oath to uphold became nothing more than a propaganda tool when the wall separating church and state was breached and Fundamentalist Christians took control of the Republican Party. If all of that wasn't bad enough, the world became captive to a wave of religious fundamentalism that spawned terrorists, who demanded that you subjugate your life to their vision of their God or die. Martyrs with bombs strapped to their bodies blew up hundreds of innocents at a time. Terrorists hijacked passenger planes and flew them into the highest skyscrapers in New York City, killing thousands.

"I am not here to argue against faith or one's personal beliefs. I will argue however, the same logic our founding fathers did. Religion does not belong in the governance of this nation. The very nature of religion deals with absolutes, driven by leaders who are sure of a place in the afterlife for their followers. This does not allow for compromise in the here and now, and compromise is the basis of politics in a civilized society. Religion is antithetical to freedom and must stay out of politics.

"This brings me to the last issue. You in this hall are responsible for laying the groundwork that led to corruption on a monumental scale. The Federal, State, and Local Governments of this country choked its citizens with a steady flood of taxes and regulations, most of which didn't do anything other than render both the economy and more importantly the individual impotent.

"The Executive Branch and Congress created regulations at the point of a gun held by megalithic corporations that threatened the collapse of the economy if ignored. Unlike their predecessors, who Theodore Roosevelt wrested control from at the turn of the 20th

Century, this time society had no white knight to ride to the rescue." You could hear a pin drop as Alicia paused to drive the point home.

"This all began innocently enough with Social Security. An entitlement program designed to ensure our elders who spent their lives working received the necessary resources to live out a fruitful retirement. In its original form, the rest of the Federal budget could not use the taxes collected under Social Security to fund other government activities. Nevertheless, your future brethren managed to *borrow* all of these funds to finance an ever-expanding and oppressive Federal Government. It became more politically profitable to blame their political rivals for the lack of action at election time than to make the adjustments required to track with the demographic changes.

"By the early 21st Century, the budget of the Federal Government was over three trillion dollars, and the country was sixteen trillion in debt. A debt mostly owed to foreign nations whose interests rarely coincided with those of the United States. Yes, you heard me right, sixteen trillion dollars of debt that allowed hostile governments to hold our foreign policy decisions hostage.

"What the American taxpayer got for their four trillion dollar budget and a national debt of sixteen trillion dollars was an economy stuck in never-ending stagnation, thousands of dead American soldiers fighting ill-defined wars, and the well-earned hatred from almost every citizen in the world.

"Another byproduct of this massive intrusion into the capitalist model was the burden it placed on the small businesses that would under normal conditions power half of the American economy. Buried under mountains of regulations and taxes, these American businesses could not economically compete with the rest of the world. Entire industries shriveled up and died, which left large tracks of rusting industrial ghost towns across the country.

"That it was so easy for the government to enslave the population to this reality, also said much about how compliant the population had become in the belief their needs, now provided by the government, was their birthright. The public's ignorance was also responsible for allowing the government to throw billions of dollars into nationalizing education. This led to a society with millions of poorly educated young adults with meaningless lives on the fringes of society.

"Compounding this failure, Federal Government policies promoted a binge of debt spending by the public to keep the economy spinning and then bailed out the financial institutions that financed that debt when the economic bubble burst. The government printed trillions of dollars of new currency, claiming these companies were *too big to fail*. I believe the audaciousness of these plunderers would have made the Rockefellers and Carnegies shake their heads at the sheer greed of it all. No one went to jail as crime in American boardrooms stole billions of dollars to support lifestyles that would have made Nero envious.

"I don't profess to have all the answers, only a mountain of evidence exposing what doesn't work. To ignore this evidence is to lose the sense of individuality that is so uniquely American.

"To sum it up, the United States became the largest debtor nation in the history of governance with poorly educated and civically ignorant citizens. That is your legacy.

"If you decide to continue business as usual, we will use the technology we possess to spend our lives in blissful wealth, selling it off piece by piece to the highest bidders. We also have the means to protect ourselves from any attempts to take these technologies from us, if you were foolish enough to try. Thank you for your time, gentlemen, and now I have to get back to my ship."

As Alicia left the podium, Commander Thornton nodded to his SEAL squad Communicator to contact the Seahawks and motioned for his squad to take up their positions. From his front row seat, Sean joined Alicia. Renée and Captain Daily followed behind as they walked up the aisle and out of the chamber. Unlike the chaos that announced their arrival, this time there was an eerie silence.

Sean whispered in Alicia's ear. "From their body language it looks like someone kicked sand in their face."

Under normal protection detail, two of the squad members would have shouldered an M14A1 carbine, but Sean was concerned about the image this would present to the public and ordered side arms only. With Commander Thornton and the squad Point Man, Lt. Franklin Morris, leading the way, two SEALs took positions on their flanks and two in the rear. As they cleared the bottom of the Capitol steps and away from the Army soldiers, the crowd outside moved toward the small group. Commander Thornton gave the sign for the SEALs to quicken the pace to get their charges to the Seahawk before the crowd completely collapsed in on them.

On the right, three men separated from chaos of the surging the crowd intent upon cutting them off. One of them pulled a shotgun from under his overcoat and shouted, "It's time for you nigger-loving assholes to die."

The Point Man caught sight at the same time and called out as he brought his weapon to bear. "Shooters at ten o'clock!" Before the man with the shotgun could raise it to aim, Lt. Morris fired three well-directed shots into his chest from his M11 Sig pistol. Immediately Commander Thornton and the SEALs on their right flank drew their side arms and fired at the other two assailants who had pulled out pistols.

The explosion of gunfire panicked the crowd into running over one another in their haste to escape. The ones who ran ahead of the group discovered to their dismay that they had to contend with the massive spinning rotors of the Seahawk and veered off. With the path now clear, the SEALs pushed Sean and the others forward as the barrage of fire continued. Sean heard a scream from behind, but his momentum kept him from seeing who uttered it. They quickly covered the distance to the Seahawk, where two of the SEALs threw them onto the floor and landed on top of them to shield against any further gunfire.

"Get this thing off the ground, now!" Commander Thornton screamed, as he remained on the ground with his men.

Before anyone could untangle their limbs, the Seahawk lurched into the air and tilted violently forward. When the Seahawk finally leveled off, the man who had covered Sean with his body writhed in pain. Sean gently rolled the man off him and asked, "Where are you hit?"

Between gasps, he pointed to his side.

Sean turned and yelled out over the noise of the Seahawk's engine, "I need help here. This man has been hit!" Then to Sean's relief he saw Alicia sit up with the help of the other SEAL. They made eye contact, assuring each other they were okay. However, their relief was short-lived. This time the yell for help came from Captain Daily, as he ripped open Renée's jacket.

"Oh my God," Alicia screamed and kneeled at her side.

Sean wanted to follow her, but he had to stay at the wounded man's side. He wasn't alone for long, as the other SEAL squad slid to his side with a first aid kit.

"Could you help me Sir, so I can get back to Captain Aslan?"

"Of course."

During the short trip back to the Enterprise, the inside of the Seahawk resembled a battlefield MASH unit. Sean held a compress against the wounded man to stop the bleeding while the other SEAL connected an IV to Captain Aslan. Renée was breathing in shallow fits and starts with her eyes open, but unfocused. All the way back to the Enterprise Alicia pleaded with her not to give up.

The copilot radioed ahead to the Enterprise to have medical teams ready to receive casualties. Tony was on the flight deck with the Corpsmen when the Seahawk set down. As the door opened, the sight of blood all over Sean's bright white dress uniform brought Tony running to his aid.

"I'm not hit."

Corpsmen lifted the wounded SEAL onto a gurney as Tony anxiously waited for Renée. When he saw Alicia exit the door, also covered in blood and her face streaked with tears, his anxiety turned into desperation. He attempted to board the Seahawk, but Sean blocked his effort. "She's hurt bad."

The crew lowered the stretcher carrying the now unconscious Renée out of the Seahawk. Without a word, Tony rushed to her side and held her hand all the way to Sickbay, as Sean and Alicia followed.

When they arrived, Alicia, with a nod from Sean, followed Renée into the ER. Tony tried to accompany her, but once again, Sean blocked him. "We can't get in their way. You have to let them do their job. Alicia will stay with her."

Sean flinched, when his friend raised his fist to punch him. Instead, Tony wheeled around and slammed his fist hard against the bulkhead.

Tony paced back and forth. "What the hell happened? Did Roosevelt screw us again? Was he responsible?"

"The government had nothing to do with it. It was a race-related assassination attempt. Our bodyguard reacted quickly, but it all happened fast."

"What all happened fast? You're telling me rednecks were able to shoot their way past six of the best-trained warriors in the Navy? How the hell were they able to do that?"

Though Sean knew it wouldn't do any good to console his friend, he tried. "We were in the middle of a crowd that only left short sight lines to see where a threat might come from. Thornton's squad reacted heroically considering the gunmen were only ten yards from us. I'll know more after I get their reports."

Unsatisfied, Tony continued to pace the corridor until his anger got the better of him. He stopped just short of Sean, and with his teeth clenched, he announced in a cold measured voice, "We're going to find out who was responsible for this, and when we do, don't get in my way."

An Ensign approached Sean and saluted.

"At ease. What is it?"

"CIC reports there's a call from the White House for you Admiral."

Sean reached for his radio and contacted the CIC. "Inform the President I'm not available. Also call the task force to General Quarters."

Sean put down his radio. "Thank you Ensign. That will be all."

"Yes Sir."

Sean would not have taken the call if it had been George Washington back from the grave. Though he wanted to stay with Tony until Renée's condition could be determined, he needed to find out who was trying to kill them.

Sean walked up to Alicia who had come out of the ER, and in a whisper asked, "Is she going to make it?"

"She's lost a lot of blood, and one of her lungs collapsed. It doesn't look good." She threw her arms around Sean and began to sob. "She's so pale and hasn't moved once. I'm so scared we're going to lose her."

Sean held her tight and kissed her ear. "We got her here in the golden hour. If anyone can come through, it would be her." Survival rates dramatically improved when a wounded soldier received medical attention in the first hour.

Impatient to know what was happening, Tony interrupted. "Is she going to make it?"

Alicia wiped her tears away. "She's hanging on."

Sean decided he needed to act and said to Alicia, "I've got to go find out what happened. Call me as soon as you know anything about her condition."

Sean then gave her a quick kiss and whispered in her ear, "Keep a close eye on Tony."

She gave him a gentle kiss on the lips, and as she pulled away loudly echoed Tony's sentiment. "Get the bastards who did this."

Commander Thornton and the SEAL squad, minus the one in Sickbay, rose as one in a sharp salute when Sean entered the Admirals Ready Room.

"At ease gentlemen. Have a seat. Lt. Morris, tell me what happened."

With little emotion, Lt. Franklin Morris replayed the event. "As the Point Man, it is my responsibility to see forward threats Sir. I'm sorry to say I caught sight of the assailants too late. It's my fault Captain Aslan and Petty Officer Granger were wounded."

"Nonsense Lieutenant," Sean contradicted. "No one could have reacted as rapidly as you and your squad did under those conditions. Let's deal with what you observed before the shooting started."

"Yes Sir. Three men separated from the crowd on our right about ten feet in front of us. The first warning I had was when I could tell that the angle they were taking would cut us off from the Seahawk. As soon as the first shooter saw that he had caught my attention, he pulled out the shotgun.

"I immediately called out the warning as I drew my weapon and fired three rounds hitting the man in the chest before he could bring his shotgun to bear. Commander Thornton and Petty Officer Kendrick on our right flank exchanged fire with the other two assailants. The three remaining members of my squad rushed the four of you to the Seahawk."

At this point Commander Thornton took over. "My target got off two rounds before I put a bullet in his head. Petty Officer Kendrick took down the last shooter with two shots to the chest. At the time, we were unaware Captain Aslan was a casualty. Petty Officers Johnson and Granger boarded the Seahawk with you while Lt. Morris, Petty Officers Kendrick and Jackson, and I covered the rear until you were aboard the Seahawk and took off. The four of us then formed a defensive stance with our weapons trained on the crowd as the second Seahawk landed to pick us up."

Sean took a moment to absorb the report before he stated his own opinion. "Commander Thornton, I'm sure you would agree with me your squad responded in the finest traditions of the United States Navy."

Thorny wasn't so easily impressed. "They did their jobs Sir. Nothing more, nothing less."

After the SEAL squad left, Sean was about to call Sickbay for an update on Renée's condition when the phone rang. The first words he heard made his heart drop.

"She didn't make it Sean. Tony is taking it hard and I need you here."

Sean slammed the phone down, his head spinning from the emotion of her loss. He went over and sat on the couch to get his emotions under control. "As much as Renée's loss hurts me, Alicia and Tony's grief must be tenfold," he thought. "Damn it, why is it fate comes along and kicks him every time Tony seems about to get his feet on the ground. Renée was the only woman in the twenty years I've known him, who not only shared his passions, but could also stand up to him as an equal."

When Sean returned to Sickbay to console Tony, Alicia started toward him, but he motioned for her to stay away.

"I'm sorry Tony. Her loss is a tragedy for all of us." Sean realized how hollow these words were even as he said them.

"What did you find out?" Tony asked. "Did they hear the assailants say anything about who ordered the attack?"

"No, they didn't. Look, we're going to find out who is responsible, but in the meantime it's been a long day, so let's go back to the ready room."

This angered Tony. "I don't want to go sit on my ass and feel sorry for myself. I want to find out who killed Renée. I have an idea.

Why don't you call up your buddy at the White House and demand that if he doesn't help us, we'll withdraw from the agreements we made."

"Because if I call him and he refuses to help, I'll be forced into a no win situation. Are you ready to go to war against your own government? Do you really believe we could convince our sailors to launch weapons against Americans? I will take his call when I am ready."

"That's not good enough!" Tony shouted.

From across the room Alicia weighed in. "I know you're not listening very well right now, but try to listen to him Tony. As much as I hate to say it, Renée was an officer of the United States Navy who died serving her country. She is the latest that includes the crew of the Orion and the forty-two on the Decatur. If we let our love for her influence the decisions we make, then we don't deserve our jobs. Do you need Sean to find someone to replace you until you can separate your grief from your responsibilities?"

That did it. Tony leaned up against the wall, lowered his head, and began to cry.

Alicia walked over and hugged him until she felt his body relax. She pulled away and wiped the tears from his face. "Let's do as Sean asks and take a little time to gain perspective."

A relieved Sean placed his hand on Tony's shoulder. "You two go ahead. I'm going to arrange for Renée's body to go over to the Missouri. It would be best if we had the service on her ship."

Tony didn't say a word as he followed Alicia to the Admirals Ready Room.

After Sean finished with the arrangements, he went to the bridge to inform Captain Folger and Commander Osaka. Sean ordered the task force to stand down from General Quarters, and updated his senior officers about what happened. Afterward, he delivered a short speech broadcast throughout the Enterprise Task Force.

Something was gnawing at Sean's gut. It wasn't until he finished with the broadcast that he reacted to what it was telling him and called the CIC to set a southern course.

Finished, he headed back to the Admirals Ready Room where he found Alicia and Tony already well on their way to finishing off a bottle of Tony's best Tequila. Though overwhelmed by her own grief, Alicia had pushed her emotions down for the sake of being there for Tony. Sean made a mental note to make sure he was able to spend the next morning returning the favor to her. When Tony finally passed out on the couch at 0100, Alicia threw a blanket over him and they headed into the bedroom.

After a restless night mostly spent with Alicia wrapped tightly in his arms, Sean got up to see Tony had left. He poured coffee and placed a call to his steward to order breakfast. When he returned to the bedroom, she was sitting up, her eyes puffy and pink from hours of intermittent crying. Sean sat down next to her, gave her a quick kiss, and handed her a cup of coffee. "Tony is gone. I hope he went back to his cabin and sleeps until noon. How are you doing?"

"To tell you the truth, I wish I didn't have this damn hangover right now."

"I'm sorry I had to leave you alone with Tony last night. Thank you for putting aside your own emotions to help him."

"What are friends for? You have any Tylenol around here?"

"I've already requested the steward bring you some with breakfast."

Alicia grimaced. "I don't think food is a good idea just yet."

"Toast and poached eggs, with a glass of Alka-Seltzer on the side should be okay. I have to get dressed and after we eat, make an appearance in the CIC. Are you going to be all right?"

"Go ahead. I'll try to eat with you, take a long shower, and then hopefully be coherent enough to talk to the President." She took a sip of coffee and noticed he didn't respond. "You do want me to talk to him, right?"

"I think we've let him sweat long enough," Sean answered. "I'll bet he's been trying to reach us all night. Think you'll be up to it by 1100?"

Alicia sat on the edge of the bed with her head in her hands. "I'll be fine. Meet you in the CIC?"

"It's a date," Sean replied, as he got up to take a quick shower.

During breakfast, neither of them made mention of Renée, which was an unsaid recognition they had important business to see to.

When Sean arrived in the CIC, he was shocked to find Tony there. The atmosphere was sullen, as Tony's mood emanated a dark aura that squelched all incidental conversation.

Without moving or acknowledging Sean's presence, he said in a matter of fact voice, "The President's people called again."

Sean ignored the comment. "Anything happen that I should be made aware of?"

"Renée was transferred over to the Missouri an hour ago."

"What do you think about following her over? I think Commander Eddington could use some support, considering he's never commanded a destroyer before, let alone a battleship."

Tony finally turned and faced Sean. "I don't think that would be wise. We have the Missouri right off our starboard quarter, so if there is a problem, we're right here."

"Okay, we'll see how he holds up for now. At 1100, Alicia will contact the President. Based on what he tells her, we'll plan our next course of action."

"And if he hasn't anything enlightening to share? What then?"

Sean didn't want to answer that question just yet. "One step at a time Tony."

An hour later, Alicia arrived in the CIC. President Roosevelt was on the phone within 15 minutes and had enough sense to begin the conversation with what he had discovered about the attack. "I've received the initial FBI report on the attack you suffered, but before

I go any further, was anyone from your group hit?"

Before Alicia answered the President, Sean put the call on the overhead speakers so they all could hear the conversation. "Mr. President, we lost one of my senior staff, Captain Renée Aslan, to a bullet fired by the very racists your policies have legitimized."

"First off, let me offer my condolences for your loss, and second, the Director of the FBI J. Edgar Hoover informed me they were all from Alabama. The FBI found a letter in the pocket of one of the dead men that directed the citizens of Alabama to take action against you. The contents of this letter came from a speech by Governor Frank M. Dixon excoriating your attempts to – and I quote from his speech, *'tell the great citizens of the State of Alabama how we should treat our niggers.'*"

The very mention of that word in conjunction with Renée's death sent Sean into an internal rage. He looked over to Tony and saw he was clenching and unclenching his hands, struggling to remain silent. Alicia choked down her own emotions and asked, "So what's your response going to be to his provocation Mr. President?"

"There's nothing I can do to the Governor. Nothing in the letter expressly orders them to kill anyone."

Sean noticed Tony was about to explode and motioned for him to keep quiet. "Then I guess for the moment we have nothing further to discuss," Sean interjected. "We'll be in touch."

"What do you mean we have nothing to discuss? Your lady friend stood up in Congress and savaged my Presidency. We have much to discuss if your plans involve destroying the people's trust in their government."

Alicia answered. "Since when does destroying trust equate with historical truth? What you are trying to do is admirable in concept. Unfortunately, it comes into conflict with another experiment begun long before any of us were ever born. Maybe you are familiar with the date July 4th, 1776."

With this, Sean made the motion to break off contact and turned to face Tony. "It's a good thing I've already plotted our course south. You up for kidnapping the Governor of Alabama?"

"Kidnapping no, beating to death, yes."

"And we're going south to do exactly what?" Alicia asked. "Invade the Old South all by ourselves?"

Without skipping a beat, Sean answered. "As a matter of fact, yes we are, and I need you to find any information you can on our target, Governor Frank M. Dixon of Alabama."

The political implications concerned Alicia. "I wouldn't mind at all if you can tell me what you hope to gain by mounting a military operation against civilian authority. I think it will validate every fear we've been trying to avoid."

"This isn't about political risk," Sean argued. "If we don't strike back immediately against those who attacked us, it will be open season on us everywhere we go. We are doing this to send a message that we can get to anyone, anytime, anywhere. What happens to Governor Dixon after we get him will be determined by how Roosevelt reacts."

Alicia wasn't completely convinced. "And if it turns out the most logical conclusion to this little adventure is to set Dixon free, you and Tony will be all right with that?"

Tony didn't immediately respond. Then without emotion he answered, "It would have to be a damn good reason."

"Great," Sean concluded. "The sooner you can get what we need on the Governor, the sooner Tony can plan the tactical operation, agreed?"

Alicia dropped her concerns, but remained skeptical. "Talk to the senior officers to make sure they are onboard."

"Good idea. Thank you."

Throughout the rest of the day, Alicia tracked down a brief history of Alabama politics in the 1940s, while Sean communicated his intentions to the senior officers. With the same argument he used with Alicia, he convinced the Southern born Captain Frederick Johnson of the righteousness of the mission. The other Captains didn't need too much convincing before they too agreed.

Early the same evening, Alicia arrived at Tony's wardroom to share what she found out about the Governor. The work had kept her emotionally grounded, but she lost control as she reached the door to his cabin. She took a moment to bring her emotions under control before she knocked.

"Come in Alicia."

Tony was standing over his conference table covered with maps of the Atlantic and Gulf of Mexico when she entered the room. "Montgomery, Alabama is too far for Seahawks to reach from the east coast of Georgia. We will have to enter the Gulf of Mexico, which will add another two days. You said you know where we can find Dixon?"

The coldness Tony had shown earlier in the day held firm. This was a side of him Alicia hadn't seen before, and it annoyed her. She could also tell if she tried to talk about it, he would probably make her the object of his anger and decided to leave it alone for now. "Yes, I did. You're welcome." She handed him pictures of the Governor's mansion, titled the Moses Sabel House.

Without a word, Tony briefly looked up, took the photos, and fed them into the copier.

Alicia decided she had nothing positive to gain by sticking around, so she dropped the rest of her notes on the table and left without a word.

Later that night in the Admirals Quarters, Alicia was in the bathroom brushing her hair. "I'm worried about Tony."

"I'd be more worried if he was acting normal. It's only been two days since we lost Renée." Sean came up from behind and wrapped his arms around her waist. "How are *you* doing?"

"I'm fine until it hits me we'll never see her again." Alicia turned around and kissed Sean hard, then pulled away and gave him a hurt expression. "Maybe you can do *something* to help me get some sleep tonight."

As strange as her request was, Sean was never one to shirk his responsibilities, so he eagerly rose to her request. As it turned out, after a very intense hour of relieving her grief, Alicia finally fell asleep. Unfortunately, Sean spent the next two hours wide-awake, circling back to the thought, "Why us?" Renée's death took all of the fun out of his belief God had a strange sense of humor. Clearly, in this situation, It did not.

On 4 February in the Gulf of Mexico, Sean, Tony, Commander Thornton, and the squad leaders who would be on the raid, sat around the Admirals Ready Room conference table. Because the mission only required resources from the Enterprise, the other members of the senior staff weren't involved.

The meeting began with a jolt from Tony. "I hope you don't have a problem with it Sean, but I'm going with them."

Commander Thornton looked to Sean, who only shrugged and stated, "I won't if you remember that if you kill Dixon, every member of this task force will pay a price for your vengeance. So convince me."

"What, do you want me to give you my word? Okay, here it is. I, Captain Anthony Knox, will make sure Governor KKK makes it back alive if you see your way clear to allow me to accompany Commander Thornton and his men."

The sarcasm emanating from Tony toward the *Admiral* froze everyone in the room. Thorny reacted quickly to defuse the situation. "I'll put you on one of my birds Captain. But if you try to go back on your word or put any of my squad in danger, I'll shoot you myself." By the look of menace he projected, everyone knew he meant it.

That evening a light rain fell and intermittent fog banks added to the somber mood. The three Seahawks took off at 0230 the next morning for the hour and a half flight through the Alabama countryside. Sean made sure Thorny formed the SEAL squads around an ethnic and gender blend guaranteed to unbalance the Governor.

Commander Thornton agreed with the sentiment and went a step further. Tony's sense of humor briefly returned when he climbed aboard the Seahawk and looked at his companions. "Any of you got some extra face grease? I'm feeling awfully pale back here."

Not one to miss an opportunity, Thorny fired back. "Wouldn't do you no good no how, white is as white does, and you're one of the whitest dudes I've ever known."

Tony was quick with his retort. "That's not what your sister Rachael said after we dropped you off in Atlanta."

This elicited a few catcalls among the other SEALs, which Thorny quickly silenced with a scowl.

"It's the truth, you know."

"Shut up Tony."

While the Seahawks were in the air, Sean and Alicia went to the Admirals Quarters to take a quick shower and change. Alicia reiterated her concerns. "I'm worried about how easy the whole thing could blow up in our face. You know if I let my emotions have their way, I'm right there with Tony. Let's burn the bastard. Nevertheless, we have to make sure the perception of this course of action doesn't come across as vigilante retribution. If anything happens to the Governor, it will destroy everything we're trying to accomplish, and that wouldn't be much of a memorial for Renée."

"That's a fair argument," Sean agreed. "And if I told you it wasn't the first thing on my mind when I came up with the idea, I'd be lying. After mulling over the pros and cons of making an example of the governor of a state that sanctions terrorism, I concluded that it might not be a bad idea if we used our abilities on our home turf. It might go a long way to move our agenda forward. Besides, I think it's time our own government received the message that we don't have another cheek to turn, especially when their actions lead to the murder of a member of this task force. This will also signal to the crew that their safety is our first priority. If everybody does their job, everything will be fine. You ready to go?"

As the Seahawks approached their target, the spotters with night vision goggles reported the perimeter around the house and outlying areas were clear, and gave the go to land. The first Seahawk landed at the rear of the building, the second to the front, while the third Seahawk, after unloading its passengers, took up a position five hundred feet above looking for any threats stirred up by the noise. The house was located in a sparsely populated area and the few people the commotion brought out, quickly retreated at the sight of the three alien craft.

Inside the house, the Governor woke to the sounds and ordered his wife to stay put. He grabbed the loaded pistol off his nightstand, and headed toward the stairs. He made his way slowly down the stairs and headed to the kitchen, where everything looked in order. He lowered his gun and started to head back to bed when a round metallic object crashed through one of the living room windows. The Governor froze and his eyes went wide as it rolled across the floor. Before his brain could order his feet to move, the flash bang went off, knocking him to the floor senseless. His addled brain barely registered the two imposing individuals who scooped him up like a rag doll and raced out the front door. Within a minute, they were all aboard the Seahawks for the return flight.

Tony wrapped his right hand around the terrified man's neck and all he could think about was how easy it would be to snap it. Instead, he took an old picture out of his uniform and stuck it in the terrified racist's face. "Because of you, this beautiful woman is dead. Well now you're going to wish you were too." The look on Tony's face made the racist wet his pajamas.

A SEAL applied a strip of duct tape over the Governor's mouth while another zip tied his hands and feet, and put a hood over his head. Everyone then sat back and relaxed, pleased with the rhythm and timing of their operation.

Tony couldn't resist. "Black enough for you Thorny?"

A smile was Thorny's only response.

When the choppers were within ten miles of the Enterprise, Sean left the CIC to meet their guest. He stood on the flight deck when the first Seahawk touched down. The first to get off was Commander Thornton with a fat unlit cigar in his mouth, followed by the two SEALs with the hooded captor between them and Tony bringing up the rear.

Tony stoically removed the hood from the disheveled Governor's head. "The little weasel wet himself." The look on Governor Dixon's face was a mixture of shock and hatred as he tried to regain his composure by staring down the men in front of him. This was too much for Tony. "You are clearly *still* not aware how pissed off I am." He followed this up by landing a quick punch to the Governor's solar plexus dropping the gasping man to his knees in convulsions as he struggled to regain his breath.

"I suppose I should have seen that coming," was Sean's only reaction.

Commander Thornton watched as his two SEALs dragged the still gasping Governor Dixon away to the brig. By prearrangement, they would keep Governor Dixon in solitary confinement.

Tony shook his hand to try to reduce the pain the delivered punch caused. "Okay, we have him. Make the call to the President."

Sean thought for a moment before he rejected the idea. "I think it would be a better idea to wait until we return to Norfolk."

This isn't what Tony wanted to hear. "I think it would be a *better* idea to find out if he's going to indict Dixon for murder now. That way if the President declines, we stay here and give the Southern people something else to worry about."

Sean shook his head no. "When he hears about what we did, and we don't respond for the next day and a half, he'll think the worst has happened to Governor Dixon. Don't worry Tony, this whole exercise is to prove our patience has its limits and we will take action against anyone who threatens us." Sean hoped this was enough to placate Tony for now, because if it didn't, he would have to force his authority on his friend.

"Will that be all, *Admiral*?"

"So this is how it's going to be?" Sean thought. "Yes, *Captain*. You can return to your duties." He wanted to add, "Until you get your head out of your ass," but there were others present.

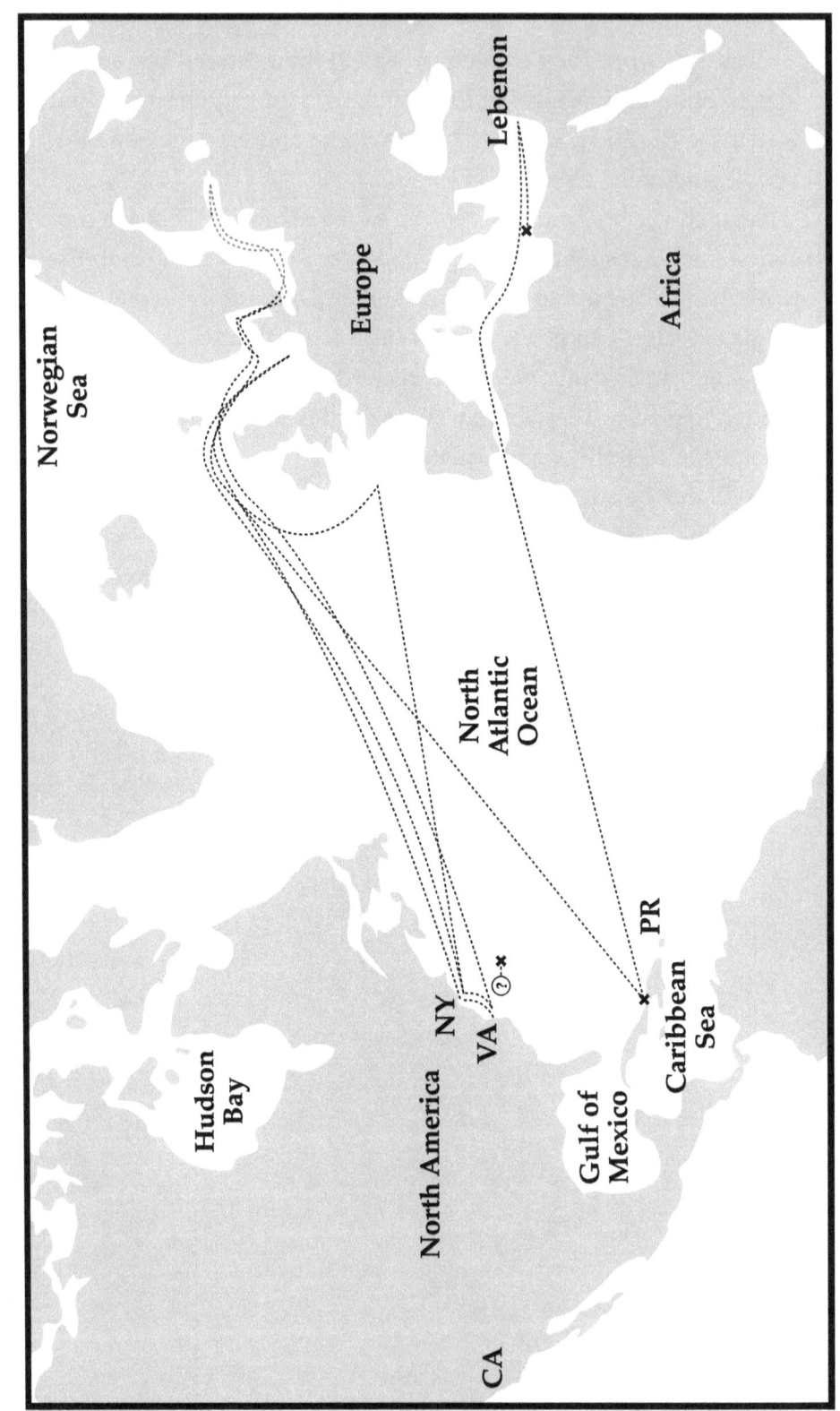

Chapter Four

Stalin

After a couple of hours in the darkness of the brig, Governor Dixon, in a moment of rare illumination, realized these people were going to kill him. As these thoughts swirled around his one-dimensional brain, he finally noticed the makeup of his guards when they entered the lit interior of the brig. He was horrified to see they were all black, and each one of them looked strong enough to break him over their knee.

Commander Thornton quietly said something to the two Marines on duty.

"Yes Sir." They then left the room.

This left Thorny alone with Governor Dixon. He turned on the cell lights, entered, put his face within an inch of the frightened Governor, and in his best Uncle Tom voice told him, "We ahl want to welcome y'all to the Enterprise, massa Dixon."

Then in a deadly serious voice, with eyes that bore through the terrified Governor, he further menaced, "You managed to get a very special person killed with your hatred. The Admiral gave me orders to keep you alive, but I got the impression if both of your legs got broken, he wouldn't lose any sleep over it. So my advice to you, piss ant, is don't give me an excuse."

With a smile, he stepped out of the cell, shut off the lights, and left Dixon once again in the dark alone with his thoughts.

Two hours later, it was Sean's turn. It amused him when the Marine opened the outer door and the lights were out. "Turn the lights on," he ordered. When the lights came on, Dixon winced. "You don't look very happy Governor."

Dixon stood up in his cell and noticed Sean's rank. His bravado was quick to return. "What do you want with me, *Admiral*, and what makes you think you have the right to kidnap the duly elected Governor of Alabama?"

"Quite simple, you and people who think like you were responsible for the death of one of my crew, who unlike you was irreplaceable. So, we're going to make an example out of you."

"You come out of nowhere with your nigger loving ideas thinking you can ram them down our throats and we'd swallow it without fighting back. You don't know anything about Southern pride."

"I'm assuming it's the same pride you rely on to assemble a mob all boozed up to hang a man simply for *sassin' his massa*. For way too long people like you terrorize those who cannot defend themselves, all in an effort to make your own miserable lives more important. However, I am not here to argue against what you represent. I'm here to say you will pay for the death of one single white woman."

"You don't have the legal authority to do shit, unless you plan to kill me, which would only prove to the country how dangerous you are to our great democracy. You are still part of the United States Navy, and sworn to obey the President's authority, even if you are from a different place in time. Yet you mock that very authority by operating outside of it. Your plan seems to be to enlighten all of us to the wisdom of your prophecies as if you were the second coming of Jesus. Well I'm not buying your horseshit and neither will any of my Southern brethren."

Sean had to give the man credit. He was smart, which made it unfathomable how one so obviously well-educated could be immune to the suffering of an entire ethnic group. "Regardless of what we are doing or why, at the end of the day, hate filled people like you will be exposed and become as extinct as the dinosaurs. Hell, your own kin helped elect a black man as President of the United States. Chew on that while you sit alone in this cell for the next couple of days." With Dixon yelling out obscenities, Sean left the brig to go take a shower. He suddenly felt dirty.

The next morning, still two days out of Washington, the sailors of the task force assembled for the services that would culminate with the interment of Renée's body to the sea. The weather was unseasonably warm and clear, as first Sean, followed by Alicia, and then Tony gave the eulogy for their friend, confidante, and lover. The service ended with her flag-draped body sliding into the water as rifles blasted out their salute.

Afterward, Sean and Alicia met with the senior staff. Their faces reflected the two months of stress they had all been under since they first deployed out of San Diego, in what now seemed a lifetime ago.

Tony was lost in his own thoughts. Within the gloom of the moment, he remembered the dissatisfaction he felt serving twenty years in the Navy without a single action against equal forces. He compared this to the three previous months, and in his mind's eye, there was little difference between then and now. As far as he was concerned, an Ensign right out of Annapolis could have been as successful beating up the Japanese and Germans. The frustrated romantic warrior in Tony now also carried the added burden of the missed opportunities of a love forever lost. As he mourned, one more piece of the child in him slipped away.

Sean was in the CIC with Alicia two days later, the Enterprise Task Force now twenty miles east of Norfolk. They both agreed it was best Tony not be there when Sean talked to the President. He nodded to the Communications Officer to make the call.

"Good morning Mr. President. I'm sorry for the delay getting back to you but we had some urgent business to attend to."

A clearly agitated Roosevelt wasn't in the mood for trivialities. Sean had cut off communications six days ago, the last three in which the President had to deal with the political firestorm the kidnapping set off. "What have you done with Governor Dixon Admiral?"

"Since you made it clear there wasn't anything you could do to him, we arrested him, and he is sitting in our brig awaiting a military trial."

"I have military Commanders from the South including General Marshall trying to convince me to take military action against you. Congressional representatives from four Southern states, in both the House and the Senate walked out in protest over your actions."

The President paused, unhappy to validate the positive results of Sean's reckless adventure. "Ironically, this paved the way to achieve what you wanted in the first place. Without their opposition, I was able to pass the Civil Rights Act, which I signed into law yesterday. Now that you've got everything you wished for, release the Governor."

Sean smiled, and under his breath asked Alicia, "Still a bad idea?"

She whispered back. "So how are you going to justify giving him back?"

"Watch and learn grasshopper."

Sean responded to the President. "If we turn Governor Dixon over to you, what will you charge him with?"

This wasn't what Roosevelt wanted to hear. "Didn't you listen to what I just told you? You won! Throughout the rest of the nation, public support over the loss of your Captain allowed for the passage of the bill. So please make it easier on all of us, and release the Governor. If I did anything but send Governor Dixon back to Alabama, there is a good chance a full-blown rebellion will break out in the rest of the South. Your actions have already set off horrific repercussions. All across the South, whites are burning the churches, homes, and schools of the very Negroes you are trying to protect."

"I appreciate public support is behind us, but Governor Dixon incited the attackers that murdered a member of my senior staff, and he needs to answer for it. Further, it would be a disservice to the sailors aboard my ships to allow her death to go unpunished." Sean needed to push the issue to ensure the President understood he would deal with anyone who preached violence against his command, regardless of the political fallout. "I won't hand him over to see him come home to a hero's welcome."

During the days following the kidnapping, Roosevelt had consulted with his advisors to discuss this possibility, and he had a suggestion prepared. "If the Governor stood with me, in front of the national media, and humbly apologized for unwittingly encouraging the attack, would you be satisfied?"

"It would be a good start."

Alicia motioned for Sean to hold on a minute.

"Excuse me Mr. President; I'm going to put you on hold."

"Tell him the Governor needs to come out in support of the bill he just signed."

Sean took the President off hold. "Secretary Calhoun requested we give the Governor a choice between supporting the bill and standing trial for murder."

The President didn't see how. "He'd never do it. He would be signing his own death warrant."

Sean knew how to convince Dixon. "Don't worry, Mr. President, I'm sure he will be happy to comply."

Although Roosevelt wasn't convinced, he needed to move on to the other issue keeping him awake at night. "Your Miss Calhoun excoriated my policies in front of Congress without any regard to the disruptions this caused to the markets. Is it your aim by saving the country from a horrible war, to now drive its economy off the same cliff we've spent eight years in this government trying to steer clear of?"

"First off Mr. President, I appreciate the political capital it took to see the bill through. You will find there will be a need to keep troops in the South for a while if the history I grew up in is any sign. Second, we will not dictate public policy from here on out. This doesn't mean we won't point out to the public the fallacy of your socialist policies. We will continue to argue the Federal Government does not belong in the business of running entitlement programs. It is just not good at it. The place for government is exactly where our Founding Fathers described it should be in the Constitution."

"I don't need you working against me Admiral Phillips. Therefore, if you release the Governor, I will set up a meeting for tomorrow to hear out all of your suggestions. Let's see if we can reach agreement on how we can get you and your ships back under civilian control. Then if you think you could do a better job, you can run for my office."

Alicia shook her head in agreement.

Sean and the President worked out where they would deliver Dixon into the hands of federal agents.

Alicia stated the obvious as Sean ended the call. "Tony isn't going to like it."

"Leave Tony to me." Sean turned to the CIC Officer. "Have Captain Knox report to the Admirals Ready Room."

Sean was waiting alone when Tony arrived. "Where's Alicia?"

"I wanted to talk to you alone." Sean handed Tony a shot of Jack Daniels Single Barrel.

Tony glared at Sean while shaking his head. "Roosevelt convinced you to let Dixon go, and the Secretary of Defense was too chicken to stick around to tell me. So what did it take?" Tony downed the shot and nervously paced the room.

"We've got to look at the big picture. The longer it takes us to return him, the more likely he will be seen as a victim."

"I don't care. We let him go, and it will be open season on us from every moron with a gun. Besides, do you think I will sit on my ass while he struts around bragging about how he got away with killing Renée?"

"That's not going to happen." Sean then explained the details of the agreement he had worked out with Roosevelt and finished with a warning. "To tell you the truth, Alicia isn't here because I didn't want her feeling sorry for you. You know I love you like a brother, but you have to get it together."

"And exactly how do you propose I do that? We have the person responsible for Renée's death in our hands and you let him get off scot-free."

"Are you kidding me, scot-free? How long do you think Dixon can survive in Alabama after he endorses the Civil Rights Act?"

This got Tony to calm down a little. "So what makes you think Dixon will commit political suicide?"

"I don't know. But, I figured you should be the person to convince him it's in his best interest." Sean coyly stated this with his back to Tony while he refilled his shot glass. When he turned around to hand it to him, he saw Tony smile for the first time since Renée died.

The next morning the 9th, Tony went down to the brig and walked up to the Marine on duty. "Why don't you go get a cup of coffee?"

"Yes Sir."

"And leave the key with me."

The Marine smiled, dropped the key into Tony's outstretched hand, stepped back, saluted, and left.

Tony picked up a chair, walked over to the Governor's cell,

placed the chair, and sat down. He took his pocketknife out and began to clean his nails.

Lying on his bunk, Dixon chose to ignore his presence.

"I thought I'd come down here and share with you the debate we're having with the President about your disposition."

Dixon remained silent.

"My preference would be to strap you into one of our planes and eject you at fifteen thousand feet in the middle of the Atlantic without a parachute. Unfortunately I'm having a difficult time convincing the Admiral, who is leaning toward letting you rot right here."

Dixon swung his legs out and sat up. "If you could get away with any of your threats, you would have already carried them out. My read on the situation is you can't do anything but release me."

Tony smiled as he continued to clean his nails. "If this was the case, then why am I here, and not the Admiral?" Tony leapt to his feet and in one swift motion threw the knife, which flew right by the Governor's head and bounced off the metal bulkhead. This sent Dixon sprawling to the floor, as Tony unlocked the door and entered the cell. He picked Dixon off the floor and with one hand around his neck pinned him against the bulkhead. "You really don't understand I don't care what the President, or even for that matter, what my own Commander wants, shit head. The woman you killed was a very close friend of mine."

To drive his point home he squeezed his fingers tight enough to cut off the struggling man's ability to breathe, until he almost passed out. When he released his grip, Dixon slumped to the floor. Tony picked up his knife and sat down on the bed.

"Here's how it's going to go. When we release you, you will stand alongside President Roosevelt and give him your complete support for the Civil Rights Act Congress passed and the President signed earlier this week. Afterward, you will then become a voice in the South to ensure your brethren implement it – Capish?"

Violently coughing, Dixon slowly got up off the floor. Between coughs he spit out, "Or what?"

Tony slowly stood up, and before Dixon could react, punched him in the stomach, sending him once again to the floor. "Or I spend the next twenty minutes beating you to death."

Dixon began to panic. "You wouldn't dare! You kill me and you'll have the entire South rise up against you."

Tony picked Dixon up by his collar and slapped him hard in the face. "Your fellow bigots are a little busy with the troops the President sent to worry much about what happens to *you*." Tony slapped him once again. "You're mine." Tony dropped him to the floor and returned to the bunk.

Dixon didn't make any attempt to rise, as he looked at his assailant, who he could see was more than willing to carry out his threat. When Tony stood up again to continue, the Governor raised his hands in surrender.

Tony leaned down until his face was inches from Dixon's. "If I hear the word nigger come out of your mouth or of you bragging even once about Captain Aslan's death, I promise you nothing will stop me from finding and killing you – very, very slowly. Do you understand me?"

Governor Dixon had no doubt the man was serious, so he capitulated and shook his head in agreement.

Tony left the cell, locked it, and walked out of the brig to return the key.

After they turned Governor Dixon over, Sean and Alicia arrived at the White House and sat across from Roosevelt in the Oval Office. In a chair to the right of the President sat Harry Hopkins and to his left, Secretary of the Treasury Henry Morgenthau Jr. and Secretary of the Navy Frank Knox.

After the introductions, Roosevelt turned his attention to Morgenthau. "Seems to me Admiral Phillips agrees with your economic instincts, Henry."

Sean interrupted. "Actually, Mr. President, everything I learned about economics came from Miss Calhoun after she got tired of hearing me complain about how the system is manipulated. When one of my senior officers, Captain Mark Daily, learned of my interest, he supplied me with books written by the leading economists of the day. Personally speaking, I think terms like Perfect Competition, Micro and Macroeconomics, Marginalism, and Utilitarianism are as alien as the bills Congress passes. But I digress; the conversation here today should be directed to Miss Calhoun."

The President was eager to hear why they were so adamant his policies led to ruin. "Fair enough, then let's get started. Miss Calhoun, you said in your speech, and I quote, 'The verdict is in on the New Deal, and the verdict is failure.' Even if everything you stated came to pass, and it all began under my administration, am I to assume over thirty percent of America still lived in poverty?"

Alicia straightened in her chair before she answered. "The issues of our time were more than if you got enough to eat or had shelter over your head. The population of the United States had risen beyond the ability of industry to supply employment opportunity. As a result, the Federal Government, following your lead, mounted stimulus program after stimulus program to prop up an economy that no longer had the means to absorb the new numbers."

This got Secretary of the Treasury Morgenthau's attention. "I've had arguments with the President about the destructive nature of an overreaching government and the negative long-term affects this intervention would have on the markets."

Alicia was already aware of this. "I read about your disagreements with the President, Secretary Morgenthau, and you should have held your ground. The economy would have begun to grow by now, instead of the stagnation you are still experiencing eight years into the New Deal.

"The only thing that kept the illusion going for the next seventy years was the constant state of war the world was in much of the time. The growth of the Military-Industrial Complex, which became the largest employer in the nation, fed this illusion of a thriving economy. The trillions of dollars of debt spending to develop this arsenal led to a technology explosion beyond our ability to control.

"As an Admiral attached to the diplomatic corps, I witnessed how the world depended on the United States Navy to protect the world's sea lanes. Yet the cost in national treasure to run a Navy this size for decades is insane. The federal budget for the military-industrial establishment in the year we left was one and a half trillion dollars; the balance of the national budget for the year came to two and a half trillion dollars. So in effect, the economy is still rolling down the same slope you put it on. To pay off the government's national debt, every citizen would have to write a three hundred thousand dollar check."

This led to two hours of an aggressive exchange of ideas, with the outcome helped along with a suggestion by Sean. "You're looking to stimulate growth in the economy to get the twenty percent of Americans now currently unemployed back to work. We have the stimulus engineered into our ships. We will license our technology in exchange for the use of the Naval Base at Guantanamo Bay, Cuba. The license fees will provide for the ships and sailors. The fees will continue uninterrupted for fifty years, paid annually, tax-free, and without constraint. To prove businesses can fund their own development, none of these payments will be collected from the national budget or from taxation. You get economic stimulation and we get safety and financial security. Everybody wins."

Secretary of the Navy Frank Knox was growing impatient with the lack of discussion on the issue most important to him. "Nothing you've said resolves the issue of who upholds authority over your ships, Admiral Phillips. My understanding was you would return to civilian authority."

Alicia was quick with an answer. "You must agree with our

concerns that once we give control of our destiny over to this government, we lose the ability to protect the interest of our sailors. We have borne witness to the abuses this country has shown those who served in uniform in the past.

"Regardless of our sworn duty under the constitution, we've concluded it would not be in our best interest to give up our autonomy at this time. We will be at our country's disposal to protect from any foreign threat, but this will only happen if the threat is real. If we don't agree with the use of force in a given situation, we will not interfere with US military operations, nor will we aid them."

Secretary Knox rose up in violent disagreement with this idea, mainly because it kept the task force out of his control. "This sets a bad precedent to have an advanced naval unit funded with private funds outside of the control of Congress and answering to nobody. Do you really believe the people of this nation will tolerate a military force outside of civilian control?"

Sean used to believe this was true. Now he knew better. "They will be too busy enjoying the rewards from the jobs created to care much at first. Over time it will become obvious to the American public the last thing we want to do is run this government. Considering this is a one of a kind situation, what you gain far exceeds your worries about command and control authority.

"Besides, the President wants to send this fleet back into European waters and force the Soviet Union to end its current offensive. Do any of your senior officers have the knowledge to operate our systems and therefore be able to plan the strategy to carry out their use?"

The President interjected. "Let's not get too far ahead of ourselves trying to resolve every issue your assimilation into society will entail and stick with the immediate turmoil you've created. First off, Churchill has been on my back every day to see that you return before he commits British troops to battle Stalin. The Germans want a timetable on when this will happen and are using this as leverage in the peace talks.

"You will also be interested to know Stalin has gone underground. British intelligence believes he's moving around to avoid the same fate as the Japanese and Germans. He isn't having any trouble communicating with his theater Commanders though. This has been confirmed by radio intercepts."

Alicia reached into her briefcase and handed some folders to the President. "In these folders you will find a series of innovations we know will help jumpstart the economy. This should help you calm the markets as some of these breakthroughs create new economic opportunities around their use. Have your scientists pay special attention to the development of solar cells and more efficient batteries that become integral to weaning the world off of the oil-based energy you now depend on."

After she gave the President time to glance at the documents, Alicia handed him papers that outlined the agreement for maintaining the base in Cuba. It also included guarantees to the fleet personnel and what their status would be when they left the Navy to return to private lives.

With little changes made to the overall scope of the agreement, they ended the meeting with one last warning from Sean. "Humanity is on the clock toward collapse if you can't get the world to agree on some formula to reduce the world's population."

Roosevelt, realizing there was little he could say to combat their arguments, decided there would be more to gain if he gave his agreement to remain open to their suggestions. "Why don't I agree to accept your proposal for a one-year period and revisit it after we see if it's still acceptable to both parties?"

Sean looked over at Alicia. She agreed and thirty minutes later, they were back on the deck of the Enterprise.

While they were gone, Dr. Rebecca Cutler didn't find it difficult to convince Captain Eddington to have a Seahawk fly her to the Enterprise under the premise she discovered something important about their trip through time. In a state of excitement and pacing the floor like a caged lioness, she waited for Sean in the Admirals Ready Room.

Sean and Alicia had barely entered the room, when Rebecca rushed over and exploded. "The most far out thing has happened. I've been able to repeat the conditions on the computer, simulating the environment from when we got zapped into this history book gone wrong world. There is a chance I can get us back to where we belong. However, if we think the unthinkable and forces beyond our knowledge are pulling the strings, all bets are off." She had their attention.

"I think I know why Senator Boyle split when we jumped into the past. He was the only person aboard any of the ships who was alive in 1941. I think he didn't transfer into this era because his spiritual mass already existed in this continuum. Everything else, including our ships existed in undeveloped form."

"So if I read you correctly," Sean surmised, "you can return us to 2014 unless an alien entity is responsible? If this is the case, why would this entity allow us to return to any other time and place if it already wanted us to serve a purpose by putting us here in the first place?"

Rebecca demurred. "Personally speaking, I would never question the motives of a deity or some bad ass who could just snap their fingers. I don't know if they would have fingers, but if they did have fingers, to snap them and, poof, we're in hell. Because I have to tell you Admiral, I will not survive well in this world."

Sean decided it was time to cut to the chase. "When you say you can mirror the event, does that mean you think there is a strictly scientific means to return us where we belong?"

The phone interrupted before Rebecca could answer. "Excuse me Rebecca."

Alicia didn't wait for Sean. "So, what have you got?"

"I don't see why we can't replicate the event. We still have the same technology, and I'm sure if you could run your ships into the same type of storm as before and in the same place off San Francisco, it's possible."

Sean had one ear to their conversation. "We will be leaving for European waters after we resupply. Do you think you can keep Specter operational for another three weeks without blowing another hole in one of my ships?" He immediately regretted his choice of words when he saw the look on her face. "I'm sorry. I didn't mean it to come out that way. We all know it wasn't your fault."

"Don't worry about it Admiral. Specter's complex programming makes it impossible for anyone, including me, to find every trap Dr. Safire laid. If I was the one who created the programming and was crazy as a loon, I could have destroyed every one of your ships by now and nobody could have stopped me. However, forget all of that. As I've already stated, there's a better chance than I thought about getting us back home, barring the possible existence of superior entities."

Rebecca grabbed Sean's arm and led him over to look at a copy of Specter's schematics she brought with her. She explained to him the steps she needed to take to create the necessary overload. "As I said before, Specter's programming could do it automatically under the same conditions. Believe it or not, we've actually been lucky there haven't been other preprogrammed commands Specter could have triggered without Strangelove's input."

"You're just a fountain of good news." Sean thought about the options this represented. "We'll keep Specter offline until we reach the North Sea. It's likely the weather would make it impossible for the reconnaissance planes of this era to locate us anyway."

"That works for me. There isn't enough time in the day as it is to ferret out the other issues that I know are still buried in the coding."

"Thank you for your efforts Doctor. Let me know if there is anything you need."

Along the Eastern Front, ten divisions of the German Army retreated from Minsk and took up positions east of Warsaw, Poland. Another eight divisions had moved south to counter the Soviet attempt to occupy Czechoslovakia. The German field officers were enraged when they received orders not to engage in offensive operations to drive the Soviet Army off their flanks. Their mood didn't improve with the knowledge they were taking heavy casualties while retreating from territory they had shed so much blood to conquer.

Though Chancellor Rundstedt tried desperately to convince Churchill to let the Germans continue the defense of Minsk, he refused and insisted they needed to be out of the Soviet Union before the British could commit troops to the defense of Poland.

When the German Army abandoned Minsk, Stalin ordered Field Marshall Georgy Zhukov to continue the offensive against the retreating Germans. He also sent orders to Field Marshal Ivan Kulik to swing south with five divisions to secure Ukraine. The door was wide open for Stalin to sweep through Ukraine, with nothing to stop his Army from occupying the Balkans.

Churchill knew he could not get the Allies mobilized fast enough to keep the Soviets out of the Balkans, but he was desperate to save Czechoslovakia. This elicited the repeated telegrams Roosevelt referred to in the meeting.

It was one thing to plan the tactics of the mission to the Soviet Union without knowing Stalin's location, and quite another to find him within their reach. The truth about most sociopaths is they are also in the upper ranges of the intellectual scale and Joseph Stalin was no exception. After he decided to continue the war with Germany, Stalin moved his quarters into the sprawling metro systems, specifically designed as bunkers below the streets of Moscow. The brutal dictator was over five hundred miles from the Baltic Sea, the nearest deep water to Moscow. Still, he wasn't going to make himself an easy target after his intelligence sources reported the precision with which the American naval force decapitated Japanese and German governments.

On 20 February 1942, as Soviet forces arrived along the Czech border, the Enterprise once again was off the Northwestern coast of Ireland with Specter engaged before they entered the North Sea. Tony was having trouble with his plan to take out Stalin. "We have to find a way to draw him out of hiding. Even if the history of this guy is only half-right, I don't see him coming up for air anytime soon. Not unless he's convinced we're nowhere around."

Sean calmly laid out a solution. "Why don't I go to him instead?"

Alicia looked at him as if he had lost his mind. "You can't be serious. What viable reason could you possibly have to meet with Stalin that won't get you killed?"

"Think about it. Can you think of a better way to draw Stalin out of hiding than to have the opportunity to sit down with the person who is responsible for putting him there?"

"I'll repeat again, *that won't get you killed*," Alicia said forcefully. "Tony, talk some sense into him."

Instead, Tony was thinking of something shiny enough that would draw a man like Stalin's attention. "Why don't we set up a little demonstration for him to see we can be a hell of a lot more brutal than he is?"

Tony said this in such a matter-of-fact manner it took Alicia a moment to catch his meaning. "When you say brutal and demonstration in the same breath, it could only mean one thing. You want to threaten him with one of our tactical nuclear weapons. I think that is a very bad idea."

It wasn't what Sean had in mind, but he realized Tony's idea could fit into the one he had. "It shouldn't be too difficult to find an unpopulated area in the vastness of the Soviet Union. It wouldn't be any different from the nuclear tests we did in the Nevada desert. Besides, it could act as a great diversion for the idea I have. We could use the variable yield B83 set to 3 kilotons, which should make a big enough show. I don't want the blast to be so small he mistakes its true potential." Sean knew the atomic bomb that leveled Hiroshima carried a 10-kiloton yield, less than one percent of the B83's devastating 1200-kiloton potential power.

Tony grew excited about the idea. "When I spent six months attached to the American embassy in Moscow, I spent time touring around and there's plenty of empty space south of Leningrad near Novgorod. If we did launch a low yield bomb in this wilderness, there should be only minor casualties and its close enough to Moscow to scare the shit out of him."

"You're not helping Tony," Alicia cried before she turned her wrath on Sean. "What makes you think he won't kill you on the spot after your *demonstration*? I'm not willing to let you take that risk."

Sean tried to assure her. "Don't worry. I know it will be dangerous, but the only way to get at Stalin is to give him something he wants, and that would be a chance to get ahold of our technology. Tony will plan the operation, and there's nobody better at what I have in mind."

Alicia wasn't convinced, but from what she knew about Sean, he was going. "We'll need interpreters to get through the Soviet military channels to set up the meeting. I'll contact Lt. Layworth. Oh, and you can be sure he'll demand the meeting be held in Moscow where he can control the environment."

Through the rest of the night they ironed out the details of the plan, with the assumption Stalin couldn't resist the bait. At the end of the day, there wasn't any way to avoid the simple truth that Stalin might kill Sean the minute he appeared. When dealing with crazy, you sometimes get crazy.

By the next morning they were back in the North Sea. Throughout the rest of the 21st, they cruised under Specter's cloak east-southeast toward Denmark. The task force continued through the Skagerrak Strait, the Kattegat Sea, into the Baltic Sea, and then finally their destination, the Gulf of Finland.

Lt. Layworth had recruited Lt. Anatoly Ginsberg to interpret what the Russians had to say. With a little help from their XO, Commander Osaka, regarding the encryption code used by the Soviets, they broadcast a repeating message. They waited impatiently throughout the day for a reply, but the airwaves remained silent.

Sean worried he had read the man wrong; Stalin's sense for survival might be overruling his curiosity. Nevertheless, this didn't feel right for a man whose sole goal in life was to bring as much of the world under his despotic rule as one lifetime would allow. However Stalin's mind worked, he had survived for so long without someone putting a bullet in his head it made Sean believe the odds of getting to him might be in his favor. Not many depots as brutal as Stalin managed to live long enough to die in their sleep.

Finally, on the 23rd, the message from the Soviet High Command in Moscow they were waiting for came in. Lt. Ginsberg transcribed the message and Lt. Layworth forwarded it to Sean and Tony on the bridge. The message was from the Southwestern Front Commander, Chief of Staff Aleksei Antonov, headquartered in Moscow. It read simply, "We have received your request for a meeting with General Secretary Stalin, and it would please him to meet with you at your earliest convenience."

Information Warfare Officer Lt. Gloria Layworth was talking to Lt. Anatoly Ginsberg when Sean entered the CIC with Alicia and handed Layworth his response accepting Stalin's invitation. It also included a request to allow a single Seahawk to transit from the Gulf of Finland, at an altitude of two thousand feet and airspeed of one hundred and thirty knots. If shot down, Sean wanted to make sure it wasn't from a lack of communication.

Sean turned to Lt. Ginsberg, "You have any problem acting as my interpreter, Lieutenant?"

"No Sir, it would be my honor to serve my country however you see fit."

Sean wanted to make sure. "Considering your Russian background, is there any reason to believe you would have a problem being in Stalin's presence? I guess what I'm asking is, do you have any ancestors he was particularly brutal with?"

"Sir, half of my ancestors on my father's side were either executed, or as in my great-aunt Yevgenia Ginsberg's case, spent years suffering in one of his gulags. When I was old enough to understand, my parents made me read a book she wrote that described her experiences under Stalin. I grew up with stories about her pain and the suffering Stalin brought to my family. So yes, I have a problem with Stalin. And if by my interpreting for you we are able to cut his nuts off, so much the better."

"Good answer," Sean replied.

The Soviet response came through ten minutes later. Sean laughed after he read it. "At least he's consistent."

He handed it to Alicia who read aloud. "'The General Secretary would welcome discussions with Admiral Phillips at his earliest convenience.' Isn't that what he said last time?"

"Like I said, he is consistent," Sean agreed.

He then turned to Lt. Layworth. "Let them know I will depart in an hour, and have the Soviet's relay the coordinates where they want us to land."

This time it only took five minutes for the Soviets to reply, which included the coordinates and instructions for landing at the Khodynka Field airport northeast of Moscow.

With a nod from Sean, Alicia followed him down to the armory to enter the codes necessary to gain access to the B83. The munitions officer in charge, with well-armed sentries at his side, verified the

Admiral's authorization codes and added his own. Twenty minutes later, as they looked on, a special plane crew attached it to the centerline hard point of an F/A-18F.

He then walked over to Air Wing Commander, Captain *Dash* Nelson, who saluted as he approached. "At ease Captain. Are you clear about the parameters of your mission?"

"Yes Sir. Pretty straight ahead, outside of the ordinance I'll be carrying. As you ordered, there will be eleven F/A-18s flying escort, but we'll be in and out before they can react."

"Just make sure of your coordinates before you launch Captain."

With everything prepared, Sean and Alicia, with Anatoly in tow, headed to the flight deck where the Seahawk sat with its rotors turning.

Tony came down from the bridge to send them off. Over the noise, he assured Sean, "Your escort of 3 cloaked F-35s will arrive over Khodynka Field the same time you do. Make sure your pilot keeps to the hundred thirty-knot profile, so if the situation turns ugly, they are on station to cover your ass. Good luck, and I'll see you this evening."

Alicia stopped Sean before he could board the Seahawk, and in a voice that left no doubt she was serious, threatened him. "If something goes wrong and you don't make it back, I'll never forgive you."

"I guess I better make sure nothing goes wrong then." He gave her a quick kiss and started to board, but turned back, shrugged his shoulders, and gave her a, *what, me worry* smile.

That wasn't the assurance Alicia had in mind. "He better come back," she thought. After what happened to Renée, it would not go well for Stalin if anything happened to Sean. Though diplomacy was her chosen road, plans for retribution were already taking shape in the former Admiral's mind as she watched Sean disappear into the helicopter.

Moments later the Seahawk cleared the deck and tilted its nose south to Moscow. Tony returned to the bridge, and Alicia headed to the CIC.

After they were in the air for 30 minutes, the copilot notified Sean and the Enterprise that multiple radar contacts were converging on their heading. Sean expected the Soviets would send up fighters to track them. With visibility out to ten miles, the pilot identified the approaching fighters as American built Bell-P39 Airacobras and British Hawker Hurricanes. Ten minutes later, the copilot reported another large formation was on a course north toward the task force. That could only mean bombers. Sean remembered, for all of the Soviet skill in the development of bombers, because of Stalin's many bloody purges they had to rely on imports from England and America to fill their fighter ranks.

The Soviet fighters took up positions on all four axis of the Seahawk, and came close enough for Sean to see their animated conversations, he was sure were about the strange appearance of the Seahawk. Sean felt the irony that it was a Russian, Igor Sikorsky, who pioneered the early development of the helicopter and Soviet bomber designs after the revolution in 1917. Fearing for his safety under Stalin, he immigrated to America in 1919. The company Sikorsky formed still supplied the armed forces of America, as well as the civilian market with state of the art helicopters in 2014.

On the Enterprise bridge along with Captain Folger and Commander Osaka, Tony could see on radar the formation of Soviet bombers closing from the south. He ordered the bridge Communications Officer, "Take the task force to General Quarters."

"Aye Aye Captain!"

Minutes later hidden under Specter's cloak, everyone topside on the ships of the task force could see them, twenty miles out passing to starboard. The Soviet bombers headed fifty miles out to sea, and then made a ninety-degree turn to the west. The bombers conducted a grid search that took them away from the task force.

In the CIC, Alicia contacted Tony on the bridge. "Should we let Sean know about this?"

"Sean already knows, and the Soviet fighter escort is with the Seahawk, so any deviation from the flight plan will mean trouble."

Alicia knew better than to belabor the point.

When the Seahawk reached the outskirts of Moscow, Sean reported to the Enterprise Task Force by way of the E2D Advanced Hawkeye stationed thirty thousand feet above them. Alpha Whiskey confirmed his covering force was on schedule and flying at twenty thousand feet.

They continued flying over the streets of Moscow where to the west of their position Sean could make out the shape of the Kremlin. Below them, he identified scores of antiaircraft batteries with their guns trained on the Seahawk as they passed overhead. He silently prayed they had orders not to fire. After five minutes of white-knuckle tension, they approached Khodynka Field.

Sean contacted Alpha Whiskey one more time to confirm his covering force was overhead and ordered the pilot in.

Armored vehicles and enough soldiers to fill a division clogged the area around the landing field. According to plan, the Seahawk swooped in and found a location isolated from the Soviets. It set down and was back in the air seconds after Sean and Anatoly jumped to the ground.

The mass of soldiers rushed toward the helicopter in an attempt to keep it from lifting off. As they raised their weapons to fire on it, out of nowhere three F-35s roared across the field straddling the Seahawk, now fifty feet in the air. The attack aircraft sent rounds of gunfire pounding into the ground in front of the approaching soldiers forcing them to the ground. Before they could recover, the Seahawk disappeared to the north along with the F-35s.

"Put your hands in the air Lieutenant. I don't want to give them an excuse to shoot us considering they're probably pissed off they couldn't get at the Seahawk."

Sean was well aware of Stalin's penchant for stealing Western technology whenever possible. During WWII, he inherited two B-29s with battle damage suffered in a bombing raid on Japan and kept them to reverse engineer his *allies'* planes. There wasn't any way Sean would let him get his hands on the Seahawk.

The troops quickly recovered and led them to a nearby hangar. Trying to act calmer than they felt, Sean and Anatoly walked at a deliberate pace. When they entered a cramped office, they met a slight man with a glimpse of a smile on his face who appeared to be in his mid-sixties.

"Good afternoon Admiral Phillips. That was quite a demonstration you put on. My name is Maxim Litvinov, the Soviet Ambassador to the United States. I'm here to take you to the General Secretary, unless you have some more surprises for me."

Sean recognized the name and put his hand out to shake Litvinov's extended hand. "You helped negotiate the Mutual Aid Pact with Secretary of State Cordell, and if I'm not mistaken, you also voiced concerns of Hitler's duplicity before Molotov took your job in 1940. It's a pleasure to meet you, Ambassador Litvinov. This is my interpreter, Lt. Anatoly Ginsburg.

"In regard to any more surprises, it depends on what the General Secretary's intentions are. If he has aggressive designs, I can assure you my officers have orders to deal with them, even if I'm still here on the ground."

"Why don't we talk to him and find out?" Ambassador Litvinov led them out to a car, which became a part of a convoy headed back toward Moscow. Twenty minutes later, they stopped at a nondescript farmhouse in a secluded wooded area.

"I apologize Admiral, but I insist you allow us to search you before we enter the house."

"I understand perfectly Ambassador."

With a nod from Litvinov, two serious looking men in civilian clothes brusquely patted them down. Satisfied, the men escorted the small group through the front door. As Sean's eyes adjusted to the darkness, he made out the pockmarked face of Joseph Stalin sitting in a chair facing the door. Even in the darkness, Sean could see his eyes were dark as coal, making it impossible to see through to the dark soul hiding behind them.

He stood up to greet Sean and extended his right hand to him while saying in a cold voice that Ambassador Litvinov interpreted. "General Secretary Stalin wants to know why he shouldn't arrest you for attacking his soldiers at the airfield."

Sean could tell this greeting unnerved Lt. Ginsberg. "Calm down, and tell Secretary Stalin that if his soldiers hadn't threatened our aircraft it wouldn't have been necessary." After Anatoly interpreted, Sean continued to address the tyrant. "I am not here today to listen to empty threats."

Stalin showed no reaction at all. "It would seem to me it is you who is here to threaten the interests of my country," Stalin snapped back with, "It is you, who has the unfair advantage. What chance do I or any of my countrymen have in stopping what we can't see?"

Sean figured Stalin's frustration stemmed from his military's inability to figure out the location of the Enterprise Task Force. "I am sure you are fully aware of the results from the last time we acted in our country's defense. It doesn't help my level of trust when you had a division of soldiers greet us. I can only surmise you wanted to capture my transport." Sean watched Stalin's reaction while Anatoly translated, and found Stalin's body language revealed little of what he was thinking or the slightest betrayal of an emotion.

"So, Admiral Phillips, have you come to the heart of the Soviet Union to assassinate me?"

"The only reason I'm here today is to convince you to practice a little pragmatism. Do you seriously think Great Britain or the United States will let you occupy the countries they went to war to save in the first place? All you will accomplish is the slaughter of thousands of soldiers and civilians for an unavoidable defeat. I've come here to change your mind."

It didn't take long for Stalin's response, which Litvinov translated with little emotion. "Let's say I decide to continue the rightful defense of my country, and throw both you and your attaché into one of my Gulags as criminals of the state as well. What do you have to offer that would make me not want to give this order?"

Sean smiled as he returned the volley effortlessly. "Because you would be dead before the end of the day if you did. What you fail to understand is I am here to keep you from making the same mistakes that led to your country's demise. In the history I came from, the war with Germany lasted another three years with millions of additional casualties, but with the same outcome, Germany and Japan destroyed and defeated. After the carnage was over, you did manage to control the countries you seek to occupy in the vacuum of the German retreat. The problem is General Secretary, in doing so the world remained in a constant state of war." Then Sean returned the same cold emotional detachment right back on Stalin. "I have both the means and the will at my disposal to see this isn't repeated."

They had arrived at the breaking point. Did Stalin believe Sean would sacrifice his own life? The thought Tony would have been better suited for the role of a crazed sociopath crossed Sean's mind.

"You do not have the authority to dictate terms to me for what is in the best interests of the citizens of the Soviet Union. The only talks I will pursue are those that put Poland, Romania, Czechoslovakia, and the Balkans under the protection of the Soviet Army so they can be assured Germany will not rise to threaten them ever again."

There it was. Stalin stated the same terms that led to the fifty-year stalemate of the Cold War. "Before I respond to your justification for sacrificing millions of lives at the altar of your own ego, let me offer you the same opportunities I've negotiated with England and my own country. You see, I'm more concerned with the welfare of the world community than any single nation, including ones ruled by despots. We will give your scientists and industries the same technologies to develop certain beneficial technologies that can ensure your place of power in the Soviet Union. That is, if you are willing to stand down your armed forces."

Stalin figured that as long as he controlled Sean, he might as well see what else was on the table. "What proof do you have that what you offer to my scientists is equal to those you release to the people of your own government, Admiral Phillips? But if I hold on to you, I'd be in a much better position to dictate terms I know will benefit my people."

Sean ignored Stalin's ploy. "If you keep pushing your Army into formally occupied nations, we will intervene to stop you. Knowing you need proof of our seriousness, a demonstration has been arranged for your benefit." Sean took an exaggerated look down at his watch. "In two minutes you'll know exactly what I mean."

***

Tony had cleared the twelve F/A-18Fs for launch after the armada of Soviet bombers passed a hundred miles further to the west of the carrier's undetected position. The nuclear-armed F/A-18F was the last to slingshot off the Enterprise flight deck.

Captain *Dash* Nelson did not relish the idea that he would become the first pilot to drop a nuclear weapon outside of a test range, even if the target was in a desolate region. As he neared the target, *Dash* became increasingly uncomfortable as the minutes passed without orders to abort. He chuckled and imagined changing his name to Paul Tibbets.

Now 20,000 feet over the Novgorodskaya Oblast region, between Leningrad and Moscow, Captain Nelson armed the B-83 as he passed over the eastern shores of Lake Ilmen and entered the target area. When satisfied that he covered every procedure required in ensuring the proper delivery, he firmly toggled the release on the bomb and quickly executed a sharp turn back to the north.

The B-83 was set to explode five hundred feet over a heavily forested area to reduce the size of the blast area. Nevertheless, in Novgorod they could see and feel the effect as the city shook and the signature mushroom cloud rose into the sky seconds after the detonation. The small yield limited the destruction to a one-mile radius, but unfortunately, it still managed to incinerate seven people and all wildlife unlucky enough to be within the blast radius.

After the explosion, the telephone lines to the Kremlin overloaded with thousands of calls. It wasn't long before the military leadership in Moscow relayed the news to the Commander in charge of Stalin's protection, who entered the house and relayed the news.

Before Stalin could express his rage, the sound of explosions and F-35 cannon fire rocked the perimeter of the house, followed by more explosions, small arms fire, and men yelling. Stalin glared at Sean, and opened his mouth to order him shot when the rear wall of the building exploded, knocking everybody in the room to the floor.

Four SEALs charged into the breach and systematically took out the Commander and the two serious looking men in civilian clothes. Sean rolled over Ambassador Litvinov to protect him from the onslaught. The gunmen grabbed Sean, Anatoly, and a struggling Stalin, leaving Litvinov as the only living witness.

The SEALs rushed them through the breach to a Seahawk that had just touched down. Reminiscent of the experience in Washington, the assault squad threw their charges unmercifully through the door as small weapons fire exploded behind them. No more than a couple of seconds separated the time between when the rescue Seahawk took off and the two support Seahawks fully loaded with the rest of the SEAL squads egressed from the assault zone. The second they cleared the area all Hell rained down upon the pursuers, delivered once again with precision from the orbiting F-35s.

While his heart rate slowly returned to normal, Sean looked on as the two SEALs zip tied Stalin's wrists and applied duct tape to his mouth. With a big smile on his face, Sean leaned over the restrained dictator. "I told you that you didn't have a clue about our capabilities. Now you can spend the rest of your life in solitary confinement letting your demons drive you stark raving mad, you sick bastard. These negotiations are now over." After Anatoly translated, Sean took great pleasure in watching Stalin's eyes finally show emotion, even if that emotion was pure hatred.

Sean removed the earpiece tucked deep in his ear that allowed him to track the mission as it played out. Sean's Seahawk had been equipped with the tracking equipment, which directed the other Seahawks with the SEAL assault squads to the farmhouse location. A second flight of the other three Specter equipped F-35s had arrived so the original three cloaked F-35s that had stayed in range of the airport after the Seahawk dropped Sean off could return to the Enterprise and refuel. Captain *Dash* Nelson and his flight of twelve F/A-18Fs that flew over Novgorod now flew cover over the returning Seahawks.

The force of F-35s and F/A-18s spread out to intercept the approaching Soviet fighters sent after news of the attack and abduction reached the Kremlin. They decimated what turned out to be fewer Soviet aircraft than expected. Because Stalin had ordered so many of his air assets out to search for the task force, there weren't enough in reserve to give much of a fight.

Within minutes, they were west-southwest of Novgorod where they could see the distinctive shape of the B-83 mushroom cloud. The area of devastation was in stark contrast to the heavily wooded landscape that surrounded the square mile blast zone. Sean had convinced Alicia to explode the bomb whether the abduction was successful or not as a warning to Stalin, or the men who would replace him.

Tony and Alicia were on the flight deck when they returned to the Enterprise. After the SEALs removed Stalin from the Seahawk and took him to the brig, Tony walked up to Sean to report as a still weak-kneed Lt. Anatoly Ginsberg stood by. "The task force is on course to the North Sea and most of the escort fighters are back aboard. We lost three SEALs and another six injured during the raid on the farmhouse. Considering the scope of the fire fight during your extraction, our casualties were light."

"Were we able to recover the dead?" Sean asked.

"We didn't leave anyone behind. They're in the other Seahawks. Captain Nelson wasn't too pleased you didn't abort his mission."

"He'll get over it."

Sean watched the survivors exit while Corpsmen rushed to care for the wounded and remove the dead.

"Tony, I want closed-circuit cameras in the brig to monitor Stalin. If anything happens to him while in our custody, I want a record of it. Alicia and I are heading down to the CIC to see how the Soviets react and who they put in charge.

"Lt. Ginsberg, you're with me."

"Yes Sir."

Sean noticed Alicia was unusually quiet as they made their way through the ship and stopped walking. "Lt. Ginsberg, continue on to the CIC. We'll be right behind you."

Taking this as a *get lost* command, Anatoly quickly obeyed. "Aye Admiral, Madam Secretary."

As soon as the Lieutenant was gone, Sean opened up. "Okay, let me have it."

Alicia's expression turned deadly serious. "If you ever decide you want to play Rambo again...," was all she could get out before she needed a deep breath to hold back an emotional surge.

Sean wrapped his arms around her and gave her a kiss on the forehead. "I'm sorry to have put you through it, but I was the only bait Stalin would accept. Believe me, I wouldn't have taken the risk if it wasn't our only option."

Alicia wasn't consoled. "We lose Renée in a supposedly nonthreatening environment, which was tragic enough, and then you put yourself in the hands of one of the most ruthless, psychotic individuals in human history. To be honest, I don't know how I could stand losing you so soon after… well you know."

Caught off guard by Alicia's sudden display of vulnerability, Sean's own emotions backed up in his throat. He had to clear it before responding. "I can't promise you there will not be other circumstances that demand I lead from the front, but I will always return to you."

"If this was true, Renée would still be with us," Alicia countered.

Sean was quick with his retort. "Who knows, maybe she is back in 2014 sipping martinis while trying to explain what happened to a roomful of panicking politicians."

In spite of herself, Alicia laughed at the image of a defiant Renée scolding the President and his advisers for questioning her sanity. "I'm sorry for getting so morose on you."

Sean smiled. "Don't be silly. If this is you being morose, I've got you beat by a mile. Wait until you see how bad I can get."

With another piece of their relationship in place, they continued to the CIC. When they arrived, Sean approached Lt. Layworth. "Try to reach someone in the Kremlin."

After a few minutes, an angry Georgy Zhukov, Chief of the General Staff of the Red Army came on the line. Anatoly rapidly translated. "Your unprovoked attack on the Soviet Union is an act of war. I demand you return the General Secretary at once."

Sean calmly responded to the general's histrionics. "Tell him we don't have any intention of returning General Secretary Stalin, and neither he nor anybody else in the Kremlin is in a position to order anything.

"Further, if you declare war against the United States, I guarantee you it will be a quick one, and whomever you put in the Secretary's place will not live to see it concluded. If you do not stop your offensive, you will force me to detonate another bomb like the one near Novgorod, but this time right over the Kremlin." After Anatoly translated, Sean made the motion to cut off communication. "It should take a day or two for them to sort things out."

Alicia looked up from some papers she was reading. "My money's riding on Lavrentiy Beria, head of the NKVD [forerunner of the KGB, the Soviet secret police], who will come out on top with the support of Molotov. I think the next communication we receive will come from Beria, because he knows where all of the bodies are buried. Considering he was the one who buried them, most of his rivals will be too worried they might be next. Be prepared for announcements of public show trials, with Khrushchev, Malenkov, and the man I talked to, General Zhukov, on the docket."

Alicia was thinking about whom she would have to negotiate with in the future. "Though it is true he is Stalin's hatchet man, he lacks the guile to run the apparatus, so he'll need a puppet as his public face, as Putin did with Medvedev. They'll trot out Molotov because of his political abilities and connections."

Lt. Layworth interrupted. "Admiral, I have a call from Foreign Minister Molotov for you."

The call surprised Sean. "That was much quicker than we thought. You're on Alicia."

"This is United States Secretary of Defense Alicia Calhoun, the civilian authority aboard the USS Enterprise. What can I do for you, Vyacheslav Mikhailovich Molotov?"

"I wish to talk to Admiral Phillips, not his secretary."

"How surprising," Alicia thought, another egomaniacal male who couldn't conceive of the idea a woman had risen to a position of political authority.

"I'll repeat Mr. Molotov, I am the person in charge, and it will be me you speak to. Now, what do you want?"

Molotov took a moment to consider his options before he

responded. "Very well." Molotov then spent the next ten minutes reading off a list of crimes they had committed against the Soviet Union. Alicia could tell a committee had written the message, which told her the Politburo was still in upheaval. "…and we demand you return General Secretary Stalin, or give us proof he still is alive."

"Finally, to the point," Alicia thought. "The only thing the Kremlin wants to know is if Stalin is still alive. This makes sense. They're worried he could return to purge those who didn't attempt to retrieve him."

"Foreign Minister Molotov, it doesn't matter now whether Stalin is dead or alive. He refused to negotiate an end to your country's aggressions, so he no longer has a say in the matter. Are you as stubborn in your objectives?"

"Am I to understand that I too will be forcefully removed or assassinated for opposing your suggestion to order the Army to stop defending my country against the fascists who invaded it? I hope you understand that any leader who replaces Stalin and gives such an order will be dead before tomorrow's sunrise."

"Suppose instead that Stalin is still alive, but could never return to power. Suppose also for a moment that instead of ordering the Red Army to retreat from their current areas of operations in Romania and the Ukraine, their orders are to hold their ground and wait for resupply. Would a person who gave those orders feel threatened?

"Suppose then, after a few weeks that person would then request to be included in the disarmament talks in Paris. That way any valid claims the Soviet Union have against Germany could be addressed."

Alicia's deft maneuvering impressed Sean. She had supplied Molotov the cover he needed.

"Even if the situation you describe is possible, what assurances do I have you will not launch attacks on Soviet soil or its armies outside of the country?"

It was clear from the direction Molotov was leading the conversation that the Politburo would turn inward until the battle to succeed Stalin was resolved. However, after two decades of Stalin's reign of terror, they also needed assurances Stalin would not be coming back.

"Mr. Ambassador, the Soviet government's actions will dictate if there is a need for any intervention in Soviet politics." Alicia then made sure to assuage his fears. "I will tell you we are not in the business of carrying out actions contrary to those we have already expressed. However, I will take this time to inform you that we will not stand by while the neighborhood bully decides to roll their tanks through a weaker neighbor."

Molotov wasn't through posturing. "It is hard to believe in your altruistic ideology while you use weapons of war to enforce these views. I will not offer any agreements to your wild attempts at demanding what is in the best interests of the Soviet Union, and further I demand you return our leader or admit you murdered him. Until then we will continue with our efforts to defend our sovereign rights." With this final warning, Foreign Minister Molotov cut off communications.

Tony's reaction was unexpectedly hostile. "Let's see if I've got this straight. We now have the Japanese Navy in control in Japan, the Army in Germany, and now the NKVD is in control in the Soviet Union. And we have them right where we want them?"

Surprised by his reaction, Alicia felt it necessary to defend their actions. "I think history validates this as the only way to move forward, and with our help Japan and Germany will follow a similar path to align their economies with those of the United States and Europe. In addition, although brutal thugs will still control the Soviet Union, we will have prevented fifty years of the Cold War."

"That remains to be seen," Tony countered. "As far as I can tell, things couldn't possibly be any more screwed up. I'm going to the bridge." Without another word, he left the CIC.

His attitude finally brought Sean to anger, but Alicia grabbed his arm before he could react. "Let it go." Alicia could see the discomfort in the CIC personnel and lowered her voice. "Let's finish this discussion somewhere more private."

On the way back to the Admirals Ready Room Sean couldn't let it go. "The plan all along has been to get in and get out. Well, outside of setting some boundaries, we're done, finished, kaput. So regardless of what he thinks we *might* be able to influence, it can't be by intimidation. Which reminds me Alicia, have you given any more thought about your idea to address the international community?"

"I don't know. There is so much to think through before I will feel confident enough to deliver a Marshall style plan. It's one thing to see everything from our own historical perspective, but the longer we're here, the more obvious it becomes it's still the same people who inhabit the planet."

Sean stopped. "Okay, you've lost me."

"I don't have the words to express what I mean yet. The bottom line is I don't know if anything we have to offer from here on out will make any difference. I wake up every morning asking how any plan can survive the human element. I'm going to need more time."

"Not a problem," Sean counseled. "At most, you have a couple of weeks to come up with a plan equitable to every nation on the planet. No pressure at all."

Later that evening Sean couldn't fall asleep. Alicia's earlier comments made him think about what they had accomplished so far with so little loss of life. When he imagined, in what now seemed a lifetime ago, that they could reshape the world of the 1940s, he didn't imagine how quickly it would happen. He hadn't given much thought about how their actions would affect future political realities, because this was Alicia's realm and she was the one who excelled at it. Sean always hoped he could fade into the background once they completed the military mission. Unfortunately, he now recognized he wouldn't have this luxury.

A sense of loneliness he hadn't felt since a small child suddenly overcame him. Sean had known for years his commitment to the Navy wasn't the only reason he remained single. His mother was not the touchy feely type portrayed in the 1960s suburbanite sitcoms. One of the unfortunate side effects of taking care of yourself at the age of four was you spent more time observing the imperfections in the relationships around you than the joys.

As he lay in bed, Alicia asleep by his side, Sean reflected on the hundreds of relationships he had witnessed in his life. It seemed all relationships lived or died in a single moment. If it was the right moment, it could lead to a lifetime of commitment and new branches on a family tree, or more likely, based on what he had witnessed, to suffering through the hate and pain of yet another lost opportunity. Sean realized he was in one of these moments, and worried this would be his last chance to share a love that finally matched up in time and space. Even if that time and space happened to be complete insanity.

By the 26th, they were cruising through the North Sea again. Alicia convinced Sean it was time for the secrecy that had surrounded the task force to peel back and show more of their humanity and less militancy. She wanted to disengage Specter and steam into the French port of La Havre.

Later in the Admirals Ready Room, when Sean asked Tony what he thought of her idea, he was livid. "What makes either one of you think after all of the deceit we've been shown this won't be seen as an open invitation to strike at us again?"

Alicia defended her plan. "Because with all of the positive press we've received, it would be political suicide if Churchill or Roosevelt did."

This didn't satisfy Tony. "There's no way in hell we can defend our ships if you anchor the task force in the harbor. Besides, do you want to expose to the world that the Decatur is severely damaged?"

That argument got Sean's attention. "That's a good point."

Tony continued. "Personally, I don't understand why it would be a problem to fly in. But if you and Alicia feel a need to anchor in the French harbor, why don't you use the Amelia Earhart?"

With a smile, Sean deflected the insult. "Somehow I don't think showing up in a cargo ship would do much to project the image Alicia had in mind."

Tony was quick to continue his beratement. "If all you want to do is put on a show, arrive with an escort of two Seahawks, while a flight of F-35s and F/A-18s put on an air show as you land."

Sean smiled. "What about it, Alicia?"

"Okay I concede. Specter stays on and we stay in the middle of the North Sea."

Leaving out the specifics of the raid, Alicia filled Churchill in that afternoon about their Soviet adventure and their new guest in the brig. Churchill could hardly contain his enthusiasm at the despot's downfall, and wanted to fly out to the Enterprise as soon as possible.

Alicia disagreed. "I don't think it would wise Mr. Prime Minister, if the English Government became implicated in our actions against the Soviet Union. Until you can achieve dialogue with the Soviets, it would be best if your involvement didn't become public knowledge.

"At this point, we intend to stand down from any further military operations."

With Churchill in such a good mood, Alicia felt this was the perfect time to announce her intentions. "This leads me to the last demand we are going to make of the international community. Two weeks from today on March 12, I would like to address the world leaders at Versailles, after which our role as arbiters will end as well."

This made Churchill suspicious. Nobody with this much power ever willingly stepped away from trying to dominate everything their weapons would allow. "I can't see you or any other members of your team ever being satisfied on the sidelines. With the threat the Soviet Union still poses to the security of Europe, the pressure you provide will be necessary to keep Europe safe."

Alicia grew tired of the conversation. "To be honest with you Mr. Prime Minister, based on the history I have already lived, let's see if you still feel the same way after you hear our suggestions about how the people of the world can take a break from killing each other."

Churchill wasn't buying it. "You'd have better luck teaching a monkey how to steer one of your ships than change the basic need man has to covet what his neighbor possesses. Based on what you have revealed about yourselves, I doubt this truth has changed much sixty years from now. The citizens of Great Britain and her Commonwealth owe you a debt which is incalculable in lives saved and national treasure. However, you're doomed to failure if you think in a mere three months you can solve the problems of the world, even with the knowledge you possess."

"You can't blame a girl for trying, can you?" Alicia cheekily replied.

"Before I go, my radio operator is going to send you a list of the nations I want represented. Your government, among others, will be unhappy to see England currently rules many of them as colonies. I want them to have opposition leaders present and not the usual provisional puppets who mirror their imperialist masters. If you cooperate, this will be the last set of conditions I make. If Great Britain, France, or the United States refuses to cooperate, our technology will stay out of reach to all of you."

Churchill didn't have long to wait for the list. When he considered the implications to current British economic health and foreign policy, he realized these demands would be an impossible sell to Parliament.

The Enterprise Task Force spent the days cruising in the North Sea, giving the world's governments the time needed to send their representatives to Paris. France was going through major civil unrest because of the political vacuum the German withdrawal created. Factions from the Communist, Socialist, and Radical Parties were trying to form a coalition, while the Vichy government officials under Philippe Petain were busy trying to keep angry partisans from stringing them up in the streets.

The Americans and the British had installed De Gaulle as head of the provisional government, so the soldiers of the Free French and the Resistance were still under his wartime command. This did not stop a series of assassinations of political collaborators, including Pertain, whom the partisans gunned down in the town of Vichy. In Paris, the violence against Nazi collaborators had already passed its peak and the city was settling down.

President Roosevelt returned his friend William Bullitt, the Ambassador to France before the war, back to this posting. The problem with this appointment was he was enamored with the Socialists and far too engaged in the social intrigues of French society. Simply put, Ambassador Bullitt was a gossip. Not surprisingly, he leaked the news that President Roosevelt was aboard the new battleship USS North Carolina BB-55, crossing the Atlantic to join in the talks.

Further news came in that a Soviet delegation headed by Molotov would arrive in Paris. An uneasy stalemate had ensued when the Red Army stopped its advance on German forces in Poland, indicating the Soviets decided not to test Alicia's warning. Churchill had arrived ahead of time to prepare for the Soviet delegation's arrival and sent a message they were making every effort to assure the representatives Alicia requested would be there for the conference.

The aggressive pressure from the gathering diplomats to have Sean and Alicia come ashore finally reached the point that Alicia convinced Sean they should make an attempt at diplomacy. "I can see how it would be taken as an insult if we don't recognize the representatives of the French Government, considering we're the ones who demanded this conference. Let me contact Ambassador Bullitt and ask him to set up a little soirée with De Gaulle. To tell you the truth, I should have done it earlier, but I understand the need to appear neutral."

Sean agreed. "Go ahead and set it up."

At 1800 that evening, Sean in his dress whites, and Alicia in a black skirt with matching jacket, boarded a C-2 Greyhound cargo plane with the same SEAL squad that accompanied them in Washington. The C-2 had the added benefit of the extra space for fifteen Marines to supplement the SEAL squad. Tony was the one who demanded they bring the extra protection.

They first flew to Beauvais airport, where they could see remnants of the Luftwaffe still in the process of turning it over to French authority. After a fifty-mile drive to Paris, their convoy arrived at the American Embassy, which sat on the northwest corner of Place de la Concorde. Ambassador Bullitt greeted them and escorted them into the salon where he introduced the rigid medal-bedecked General De Gaulle to Sean and Alicia. He in turn gave them the customary French greeting of kissing them on both cheeks.

Ambassador Bullitt interpreted for the General. "President De Gaulle wishes to express his country's gratitude for your efforts to drive the German's out of France, but he also wishes to express his displeasure over your rebuffs of his earlier requests to meet with you."

Sean and Alicia couldn't tell how much of the displeasure was De Gaulle's or the Ambassador's for the lack of access. It was also difficult to ignore the self-proclaimed title of President.

Bullitt continued to press. "President De Gaulle and I want to know if it would be possible to see Mr. Stalin. The Soviet government forwarded this request to confirm whether he's still alive or dead."

"Nothing like getting right to the point," Sean thought to himself.

Alicia swatted down the request. "I'm afraid we will not allow anyone to see the former General Secretary. We are monitoring him twenty-four hours a day, and until the conference ends this order will stay in effect."

Through the Ambassador, the next question invoked the stereotypical arrogance known of the French. "The President has concerns about the affect your presence might have on our ability to stabilize the French Government."

De Gaulle's question offended Alicia. "What you meant to ask, *General*, is do we have any intention of interfering in France's struggle to form a new government. We would rather drink a glass of cyanide than get involved with French politics. If the new Soviet leadership cooperates, we don't have any intention to remain in European waters once I address the conference. We will not influence who leads your nation no matter what strife your nation suffers, even if you choose to murder every Nazi collaborator, and every opposition leader. Your internal affairs are none of our business, though they would have an impact on any future agreements you might want to make with us."

With the expectation a diplomatic nightmare was in the making, Ambassador Bullitt looked like he wanted to crawl under his seat. Instead, De Gaulle smiled after the Ambassador relayed Alicia's words. They spent the rest of the evening trying to avoid anything remotely political. Three hours later, they boarded the C-2 for the flight back to the Enterprise.

After Sean strapped in, he vigorously rubbed his temples. "Just put a bullet in my head if this is what we have to look forward to."

"You pussy," Alicia teased. "This is how I've spent the last four years of my life. You think domestic politics is bad; it's the minor leagues compared to international politics. However, I have to admit De Gaulle reminds me of Bush II in his self-righteous manner."

"Whatever. All I know is Cuba is looking mighty nice right about now."

Chapter Five

New World

The days leading up to the conference went without incidence. Not wanting any chance for a repeat of their tragic experience in Washington, Tony convinced Sean to bring the Enterprise Task Force into the English Channel 50 miles northwest of La Havre, France to transport them by Seahawk to Paris. The cloaked task force would remain there until the Seahawks returned from Paris. He planned it so the two Seahawks with Sean, Alicia, Commander Thornton, and a 7-member SEAL Squad would land in an area of the Versailles expansive garden after the authorities cleared it of all personnel.

Sean enjoyed the irony of this peace conference held at the Palace of Versailles, considering the royal blood that gave it life. Especially since the treasure gained from the French Imperialistic past paid to build it. Everything this palace of decadence represented was what they hoped to end.

The flight was uneventful, and 35 minutes after they left the Enterprise the Seahawks touched down on the formal grounds of the Palace of Versailles.

When they entered the Hall of Mirrors, Alicia noticed a podium set up in the middle of the hall, with representatives seated in chairs lined up facing it from both sides. She liked the arrangement because it gave the illusion of parity to the invited guests.

The buzz of conversation abruptly ended as everyone's attention turned to Alicia. She gazed first to her left, and then to the right, and thought how much the situation reminded her of a Broadway play. Armani and minks in the front rows, polyester in the balcony, and every seat in the hall occupied.

President Roosevelt sat near the podium next to Winston Churchill, who wore a dour expression having already gotten a glimpse of what she was here to propose.

She took a deep breath and began. "As I stand before you now in this elegant palace, I'm awed by the talent that went into its design and construction. I also understand Louis the XIII built it in 1624 with wealth plundered from the New World. Every great civilization throughout history built their foundations on the ruins of those who came before." Alicia stared directly at an unhappy Churchill. "From Mesopotamia in 3100 BC to Britannia today, there is only one common thread connecting each one of these great societies – they collapsed."

Now looking out on the audience, she continued. "Whether they collapsed because of years of decadence or superior weapons technology, the fact remains archeologists have documented the violence humanity can never seem to get enough of.

"Though it is obvious we can't change this basic flaw in human nature, all we wish to convey to you today is that you better begin to try. In case no one here has noticed, modern war technology is getting very good at shredding human bodies. What you don't know is sooner than anyone here in this great hall can imagine is it will threaten to wipe out humanity as the dominant species on this planet.

"This isn't to say our planet couldn't use a few less human beings stripping its natural resources. Right now, there are over three billion human beings populating the earth. By the turn of the next century, there will be close to seven billion.

"This explosion of humanity stretched natural resources to the breaking point, while the waste humanity spewed into the environment threatened the..." Alicia stopped short. "This is all wrong," she thought. "Who do we think we are to believe we have the intellect or the incredible wisdom it would take to lead the world to some great epiphany?"

Alicia looked out once again on the audience, picked up her notes, and without emotion, let them flutter to the floor. "Blah, blah, and more blah. I don't need to give anyone in this room a history lesson on how horrible human beings act when manipulated into believing their way of life is threatened. To tell you the truth, I've given a lot of thought lately about what you would need to do to keep this from happening."

Alicia stepped away from the podium, walked down the aisle, and stopped in front of a thoroughly surprised Sean. She bent over, gave him a quick kiss, and winked as she stood back up.

"Now I was going to offer what I thought were sufficient bribes to this august body that would keep you all so busy trying to get filthy rich off of, you wouldn't have a reason to develop the weapons that will end humanity.

"Instead of trying to appeal to your basic greed, I will only say if you do not get your houses in order, we will do it for you. You will come to an agreement to keep your populations under control. You will control the religious fanatics who kill in their God's name. You will educate those children you do bring into this world, and most importantly, you will end the control weapons manufacturers have on your national treasures.

"You may ask yourselves, why we would listen to some *woman*, who claims to be from the future. Am I threatening to perform the same government shake up given to the Japanese, Germans, and Soviets on, let's say, the United States and Great Britain if you don't bow down to my demands?"

Sean took all this in, and even though he didn't have the slightest idea where Alicia was going, he felt sorry for Tony that he wasn't here to hear it. It was as if she was channeling his frustrations.

Now standing next to the seated President, Alicia continued. "I don't think so. What we will do is honor an earlier agreement we made with President Roosevelt. We will continue to protect the interests of the United States as sworn servants. However, the United States Government is going to have to get used to our hammering on the issues of population control, religious fanaticism, religion meddling in government, and the dangers of an overly intrusive Federal Government.

"The good news for the rest of you is we are prepared to offer our support to any other country that wishes to conform to a paradigm shift in how you run your societies. Every country that agrees to the basic reforms I have laid out for the United States, will also share equally in our technology. We will then protect these nations fully with all of our abilities from those who wish to do them harm.

"On the other hand, the more brutal or regulated your government remains, the less we will offer. Any country that reneges on these terms, once accepted, only has to remember the fates of those who we have already dealt with.

"In closing, I will remind you that the greatest gift of a free society is the ability to give the lowest among its citizens the opportunities to rise according to their own merits. In this era, the United States Constitution provides the greatest opportunity to realize this potential. It would behoove all in this room to copy this incredible document.

"Free markets allow for the best there is in human nature to flourish. It is not a perfect system, but then again it is the best instrument to govern imperfect people. This works if societies keep a grip on their own morality and responsibilities to their communities by helping those less fortunate to be able to contribute. On the other hand, those in a free society who choose to drop out and expect a free ride from their government should suffer the negative results of their actions.

"The 21st Century began with a consolidation of wealth unseen since the turn of the previous century. Robber Barons once again walked the halls of power as they used their wealth to control the politicians. A free society cannot exist hamstrung by a heavy-handed government that legislates to the benefit of only a small fraction of its population. When it does, the historical conclusion is the demise of the society that makes this choice.

"We will give a list to every nation of their future foreign entanglements, with both the historical results of these intrusions and what we consider would be pragmatic solutions to avoid their repetition. If any one of these governments were to repudiate our suggestions, the only form of punishment we offer is to withhold the means for your country's development.

"I have one last word of warning. Every one of you should be concerned with resolving the religious disposition of Jerusalem. Zealots from around the world will use the city as a symbol of their own religious persecution if there isn't an equitable solution. Whether it was the Jews, Christians, or Muslims who controlled it, the Temple Mount is responsible for a modern era of religious terrorism. Get control of your religious institutions or you might as well accept a return to the Dark Ages in the name of your loving God.

"Our ships are headed to the American base at Guantanamo Bay, Cuba, which the United States Government has allowed us to use as our home port. Thank you for your time, *gentlemen*, as I see there isn't a single woman represented here today."

With this final statement, accompanied by the SEAL squad, Alicia and Sean slowly walked out of the lavish room and headed to the waiting Seahawks. The buzz surrounding them was much different from Alicia's last appearance in front of a government body. No one knew how to react to what they had heard.

Though it was difficult for Sean to do so, he kept his thoughts to himself until they took off in the Seahawk. He couldn't hold back the laughter that had been building up since the moment her speech hit the floor.

"I don't think you're going to be seeing silk on me for a while if you don't stop laughing at me."

Sean could tell by the tone in her voice he better get control. "I'm sorry, but what got into you? Did you say we're going to restrict our influence to the United States?"

"Think about it for a minute. Cuba is the perfect location to control the Western Hemisphere without having to deploy on long voyages that would quickly wear out both the ships and crew. Besides, if we can't convince our own government to take us seriously, how long do you think it will take them to make alliances with the intention to overwhelm us? I don't know about you, but I don't want to spend the rest of my life watching my back. Even if nothing changes, at least I got it off my chest and told it like it was. It felt good."

"I can't say that I'm in any way disappointed. Revolutionizing the world lost its appeal to me the minute Renée stopped breathing." As Sean finished, he looked out to see they were approaching the Enterprise. "Let's finish this conversation later tonight."

Tony was on the flight deck to greet them as they exited the Seahawk. When they reached the Admirals Ready Room, Sean filled him in on what happened. "I brought my camera with me and recorded her speech. You would have been proud; Alicia channeled you perfectly. I can't wait to see how it was received."

A now confused Tony asked Alicia, "What do you mean? You didn't give the speech I read?"

Alicia answered with a smile. "Let's just say, upon further reflection I thought it was hubris. Unbelievably, you were the one

New World

who was right. The only thing we would have accomplished by forcing our views down their throats would have been years of frustration."

Tony looked at Alicia in mock disbelief. "Are you telling me you've turned to the dark side – and Sean agrees?"

"No. I'm telling you Renée's loss showed me, over time, they would demonize us for anything that went wrong. I don't have any interest in becoming a martyr to the cause. We haven't let go of the whole idea. The deal with Roosevelt will stay in place, and we will continue to push our agenda in the United States."

Tony noticed some tension between the two. "You didn't know she was going to do it?"

"Not that it matters," Sean answered. "But no, I didn't. I trust her instincts. After all, it is her responsibility to make these decisions. However, I'm still digesting the repercussions of her actions."

"Personally speaking," Tony added, "if she had followed the original plan, eventually we would have been ground into dust. I'm glad to see at least one of you two finally came to their senses."

Tony's dig at Sean didn't help. "So I'm not as flexible as I once was? Alicia made a mockery out of everything I thought we were trying to achieve."

Then to Alicia, Sean added, "A heads up would have been nice."

"How could I give you a heads up about something I didn't know was going to happen before I did? What, did you want me to pardon myself, walk over to where you sat, and give you a complete rundown before I continued? At least you got a wink and a kiss."

"Besides," Tony added, "look how well things turned out when you followed the script in Washington."

Tony's comment froze both Sean and Alicia.

Sean recovered first. "You think it was our fault Renée died?"

Tony turned to pour another drink without saying a word.

"Answer me." Sean moved across the room to where Tony stood.

Alicia recognized how angry Sean was and again rushed to put herself between them. "He's just upset. You didn't mean it, did you Tony?"

Tony downed the drink, put the glass down, plopped forlorn into a chair, and sighed, "I don't know what to believe."

Before anything else could be said, Lt. Layworth called to inform Sean several world leaders urgently requested a conversation with Alicia, none more persistently than Roosevelt and Churchill. Alicia and Sean had agreed before their visit to Versailles that they would cut off all communication with the outside world. In other words, they wanted to see if all of the other children could learn to play well together without pressure from them.

"We're taking no calls," Sean answered. "Unless it's critical to the task force, please make sure we are not disturbed for the next hour."

Though still morose, Tony brought up another complication. "Do either of you have a plan to deal with our new guest who is still sitting in the Enterprise brig? Why don't we turn him over to the Polish government and let them have their way with him."

Alicia could see Sean was still angry so she answered. "Though he made an agreement with Hitler to partition Poland, it's not an option to send him there. There isn't a government in the world that could take the political fallout dealing with him would create. The only choice I can see is to keep him locked up with us and not allow anyone the opportunity to visit him. Anyway, he's best left for another day."

Then in an attempt to ratchet down the tension in the room, she changed the subject. "All I want to do for now is relax and enjoy the voyage to Cuba. However, we should take some time to figure out the details about how we are going to acclimate into this era. That is if Dr. Cutler can't find a way back home."

Tony had an idea of his own. "If you don't have any objections, I'd like to head over to the Missouri for the trip back. I can see how Commander Eddington is coming along."

Tony's request caught Sean off guard. He looked at his friend and knew that some time away from command responsibilities might be what he needed. "I think it's a great idea. Barring any further attempts to separate us from our ships, it looks like we have finished all offensive operations."

"I'll inform Commander Eddington he's going to have some company on the bridge tonight." Tony said goodbye and left.

Alicia was angry the two men didn't talk. "It's not a good idea. If all he does on the Missouri is mope, he won't be any use when we need him. Besides, you should have pushed through his anger."

"That would have been well and fine if we were still in high school, where you could let it all hang out. Unfortunately, we are responsible for this task force, and it would have had horrible consequences on our ability to control the sailors if they found out the Admiral and his Chief of Staff had thrown punches at each other. What Tony needs is a sleazy waterfront bar where he could get the shit beat out of him for a couple of weeks. We'll find those in Cuba."

Alicia got up to get ready for bed. On the way out, she mumbled under her breath, "*Men!*"

Back onboard the Missouri, Tony went immediately to the bridge, concerned about Eddington's lack of experience commanding a capital ship through rough seas. Throughout the rest of the night, they headed southwest out of the English Channel into the North Atlantic as the weather became increasingly violent.

The next morning, Sean was the first to wake, and he felt bad for the way he had reacted to Alicia's speech. It was his turn to look down on her, and as he admired the curves of her body, an awareness of her unique beauty and wisdom made him realize everything she had said was true. He lay back down and wrapped his arms around her sleeping body.

One of her eyes attempted to open, as a smile appeared. "So, am

I off the hook yet?" His answer came in a passionate kiss that led them to blow off the rest of the morning in entangled limbs.

When they finally sat down to a late breakfast, they realized there wasn't anyone who needed their attention. With nothing else left to do, Alicia convinced Sean to let others handle the responsibilities for a while. Though they checked in periodically with Captain Folger, there was nothing to do but repeat their earlier activities.

Afterward, with a glass of wine in hand, Sean took a leap off the cliff. "What do you think about the possibility of me making an honest woman of you?"

It took a moment for his comment to register, and Alicia went through several facial contortions before she gave him a gentle kiss. "I think I'd have to give the idea some thought. Both of us have spent too many years alone. We would probably drive each other crazy if we lived together and I don't want to spoil what we already have."

"I've thought about it, and the way I see it, we've already spent the last two months under those very conditions and I've grown closer to you from the experience. Besides, if it worries you so much, we'll keep two houses, and any time either one of us needs to get away, we'll have the means to do it. No one says we have to conform to the usual norms."

"Then why get married at all? Why not continue to enjoy what we have without the traditional trappings that take the passion out of most relationships anyway?" She pulled him close to her body and they rolled onto the floor, the thought of marriage put aside for the moment.

On the third day out, now in the middle of the North Atlantic, the weather turned typical for late February. They were fighting forty mile an hour winds that whipped up thirty to forty-foot waves. Rebecca was in her cabin, contemplating throwing herself overboard. The violence of the weather had forced her into a series of dashes to the head that began to feel like all she had left to expel were pieces of her stomach.

The phone rang, and after the realization it wouldn't stop ringing until she picked it up, Rebecca staggered to answer it. The voice on the other end was talking too fast and erratic to make sense. "Slow down and take a breath Forrest."

"There isn't any time. Specter's operating systems have begun to sequence a series of anomalies that don't make any sense considering we've got the systems shut down! You need to come down here now!"

Rebecca continued to talk while she dressed. "What exactly is it trying to do?"

"I'm not sure, but it looks like the program is trying to find a way to initialize startup and I don't want to be the person responsible for crashing Specter."

Rebecca didn't hear the last part, she had already charged out of her room; her misery overwhelmed by an adrenaline rush. All the way to the hangar, Rebecca ran a series of scenarios through her mind. "Was there someone they were unaware of who had access or was there a way for Specter to turn itself on?" Out of breath, she reached the hangar and shouted, "Crash the damn system, Forrest! It's probably trying to load one of Strangelove's phantom programs."

On the Princeton, the same Harpoon launcher that fired on the Decatur came to life, only this time it wasn't the only weapon energized which caused Alpha Whiskey to immediately issued the *Scatter* order to the task force.

Each ship made predetermined course changes at flank speed relative to their positions to put as much distance as possible between the ships. Onboard the Chancellorsville, Enterprise, and the damaged Decatur, the personnel in the CICs watched as their monitors suddenly showed incoming threats their weapons were beginning to track.

Rebecca saw on her monitors that the John Paul Jones had launched depth charges, with the Seawolf as the target. One hundred feet below, Captain Mark Daily had already ordered emergency dive at flank speed to maneuver away from the threat. He then yelled out to the radio operator, "Find out what the hell is going on topside!"

On the John Paul Jones, a Harpoon missile left the ship and raced toward the Enterprise, now three miles to the south. Her Phalanx guns spit out thousands of rounds a minute, which fortunately impacted the Harpoon's warhead and blew it out of the air two hundred yards from the ship's midsection.

The Chancellorsville wasn't so lucky, when moments later another missile from the Princeton exploded on the port side forward of its own launcher that left a gaping hole in the ship's hull. She began to ship water in the heavy seas and took on a twenty-degree list. Captain Johnson ordered speed cut to ten knots until damage control parties could plug and shore up the hole. However, this left his ship exposed to further missile strikes.

Just then, the John Paul Jones launched another missile, with the now vulnerable Chancellorsville as the target. The Missouri dramatically appeared out of nowhere and roared up along the port side of the Chancellorsville just as the missile exploded against the Missouri's twenty-four inches of armor protection without penetrating it. Then to act as a shield from further attacks Tony ordered the Missouri's speed reduced to match the damaged cruiser. He then contacted the Enterprise. "I'll give assistance to the Chancellorsville until the Princeton and John Paul Jones can gain control of their weapons."

At this moment, a missile crashed through the bow of the Enterprise and exploded, knocking everyone on the bridge off their feet. Captain Folger ordered speed reduced to 15 knots.

Their earlier bliss all but forgotten, Sean and Alicia arrived in the

New World

Enterprise CIC as all of the electrical equipment suddenly surged and the entire room went dark.

Through the chaos raging around her, Rebecca noticed another crisis. She called the bridge to warn Tony. "The Chancellorsville and Decatur have Specter activating, and from the looks of my readings they are going into overload again."

"Can you disengage Specter before the damn thing blows us all to hell?" Tony yelled.

"We are trying!" Rebecca yelled back.

Tony was ready to go aft and take a sledgehammer to all of Specter's computers when he looked out through the storm and saw the sight that began their sojourn. Once again, he witnessed the green mist climbing up the sides of the Enterprise, now in front of the Missouri, and around the Chancellorsville to his starboard. The difference this time was there wasn't any glow emanating along the Missouri.

Tony stood mesmerized, as the green mist intensified in brightness until it was impossible to keep his eyes open. Then suddenly a massive electrical charge raced through the glow and engulfed the ships. He couldn't tell whether it was a lightning strike or a side effect of the electromagnetic field.

Then as quickly as the light show began, both the electrical charge and the ships vanished, which left Tony chilled to the bone. He reached down and picked up the phone while the rest of the sailors on the bridge stood in stunned silence. "This is Captain Knox, anybody who hears this please respond at once."

A long fifteen seconds later came back a response. "This is Captain Turner on the Hampton. Is it safe to get near you guys again?" Following that, the ship Captains of the Princeton, John Paul Jones, Amelia Earhart, and Laramie reported in with no casualties, no damage, and no problems with Specter or their electrical systems.

—◆—

The storm was still raging when Sean and Alicia reached the flight deck, as the Enterprise lost headway. Her nuclear reactors had once again scrammed. They stared out at a sight as crazy as the one they had witnessed a lifetime ago back in January 2014, or was that December 1941. Though visibility was terrible, off in the distance the aircraft carrier Ronald Reagan was where the Missouri should have been. As they scanned to port, only half a mile away wallowing in the heavy seas was the Chancellorsville. About two miles aft and barely visible in the storm was the Decatur.

"It looks like either the Reagan has joined us or we are back home," Sean yelled to be heard above the storm.

"Where are the Missouri, Princeton, John Paul Jones, and our supply ships? And are the Hampton and Seawolf still..." Interrupting Alicia, the USS Seawolf, after an emergency blow, exploded through the rough seas to the surface a half mile to port.

"That was weird." This gave Sean a thought. "Maybe the rest of the ships are still on their way back."

He kept looking until Alicia had her own idea. "With the Enterprise's electrical systems fried, and the radio dead, why don't I get our cell phones?"

"Funny how soon we forgot about them," Sean replied.

On the bridge, Captain Folger ordered Commander Osaka, "Go forward and report back to me with damages and casualties." There was smoke drifting from where the missile punctured her hull, and Charles was worried about the fire getting out of control without power to her pumps.

It was then Sean saw a Seahawk lift off from the Reagan and head their way through the storm. It only took a minute to reach the Enterprise, landing amidships. Three figures jumped out and headed straight toward Sean and Alicia.

After they saluted, the Commander had to yell over the roar of the storm. "Admiral Van Holland sends his regards Sir, but urgently needs to know if there are hostiles in the area." The Commander stood in nervous silence for a moment, but had to ask, "I don't mean to sound disrespectful Admiral, but what the hell happened?"

"First off, there are no hostile forces, and second, it's a long story that I don't think you're ever going to hear Commander. However, I can tell you all of our electrical systems are down. The use of the radio on your Seahawk would be very helpful."

"Yes Sir."

When he reached the Seahawk, Sean contacted Admiral Van Holland and without getting into specifics, requested the Reagan's support ships come alongside to offer emergency assistance. He also asked that naval tugboats come from San Francisco to bring his damaged ships into the safety of the bay.

Over the next hour, they ferried generators and Corpsmen from the Reagan Task Force and transferred the dead and the wounded to the Reagan. Commander Osaka relayed reports from the damage control party of a scene straight out of hell in the starboard forward section where the missile penetrated, with twenty-two sailors dead in the catapult spaces. With the rough seas making the rescue difficult, it took the next four hours to bring the fires under control on the Enterprise.

When the situation stabilized, Sean decided it would be a good idea to gather the remaining members of his senior staff and have a quick discussion about how they would explain the loss of half his task force. He radioed Captains Daily, Johnson, and Commander Barrish to come to the Admirals Ready Room aboard the Enterprise immediately.

Alicia moved close to Sean. "What do you have in mind?"

"We've got to keep a lid on what we can control until we find out how Washington is going to spin what happened, and we don't have much time. They are going to know what we did as soon as they start interviewing the crew, so we can't help that.

"What Washington doesn't have, is the main Specter command center on the Missouri and the brains behind it. They also don't have the Specter command center on the Princeton. The longer we can keep them in the dark about how it helped transport us, the better deal we can work out for those who came back with us. We need the senior officers to back us up."

Alicia was confused. "How does this help us? We still don't have a clue what happened."

Sean smiled. "They don't know that. We have to sell the idea and the only way we share the information is if the government makes full disclosure to the public."

Alicia had one more thought to add to the chaos. "Do you think Stalin is still in our brig?"

"Good point. Remind me to find out after I talk to the senior officers."

Sean's mind was racing through their limited options. "Head over to that Seahawk and convince Admiral Van Holland the fires in the hangar could ignite stored ordinance and we don't want to risk extra casualties. And remember, you *are* the Secretary of Defense in 2014. This will also give us the cover we need to explain the movement of personnel to the Enterprise."

Alicia hurried off to contact Van Holland. A half an hour later, Sean and Alicia found Captains Mark Daily of the Seawolf, Frederick Johnson of the Chancellorsville, Commander Logan Barrish of the Decatur, and Captain Charles Folger of the Enterprise seated in the Admirals Ready Room.

Captain Johnson was first to speak his mind. "Our careers are over, so what's to be gained by holding anything back?"

Captain Daily shook his head in violent disagreement. "Oh, I don't know, like maybe spending the rest of our lives in an internment camp specially set up for us. Do you really think the government is going to want what happened to become public knowledge?"

Alicia picked up a communique and waved it. "I have to agree with Captain Daily. According to these orders we received ten minutes ago, Admiral Van Holland has made it clear to me that regardless of the risk, we are to turn command of our ships over to him within the next hour. A special force will be arriving soon to escort Sean and me to a debriefing. He's also received orders to assist them if we resist, and from the tone of his voice, the Admiral has already made plans to take us by force if necessary."

Sean smiled and chuckled. "I think he is still upset about the thumping we gave him in the exercise."

Sean then had to think fast. "Here it is in a nutshell. If we don't present a united front and let Alicia handle negotiations, they will make our lives a living hell. They will use whatever means they deem necessary, including threats to your families if you don't cooperate. If you do decide to cooperate, there's a good chance once you give them what they want, they'll simply make everyone, including our crews disappear." It suddenly dawned on Sean this wasn't all the government was capable of making disappear. "As a matter fact, wait to see where they take our ships."

Captain Johnson didn't notice the importance of this. "Where else would they bring us for temporary repairs?"

Commander Barrish understood. "Do the math. If the loss of an entire task force without a trace would be impossible to explain, how do you think it would sound if only half of the ships returned while the other half is traveling around in another dimension? Right now, the muckety-mucks are tripping all over themselves to find out if this was a one shot deal or something they can control for political gain. The last thing they want is for any of what happened to become public knowledge."

The phone rang and Alicia picked it up. "It's Osaka. He reports six inbound Black Hawk helicopters from the northeast and the

Reagan has launched her Seahawks. Are we in agreement?"

A quick nod in the affirmative coincided with another call from the bridge confirming the choppers had all arrived on the flight deck.

"Direct our guests to the Admirals Ready Room Commander."

Admiral Van Holland was the first one through the door. Sean and Alicia were on the couch sipping a glass of wine and didn't bother to get up.

"What the hell happened to your task force Admiral Phillips?"

Sean replied in a matter of fact manner. "I think it would be better if you didn't have a clue Don. Trust me when I warn you that the less you know about what is happening, the better off you're going to be."

"Happening? Are you telling me we can expect another attack?"

"Who said anything about an attack? I'm just warning you that whatever you think you want to know, you really don't."

Sean's attitude irritated Van Holland. "Whatever. I guess this cluster fuck is going to be way above my pay grade anyway. Admiral Phillips, I am officially relieving Captains Brewster, Johnson, Daily, Holmes, and you of command. There is a commando unit from the Army here to escort you and the Secretary off the Enterprise. Apparently, the folks in Washington don't trust the Navy right now. You are not the only ones who are being isolated. I've been ordered to maintain strict radio silence."

"First off, Commander Holmes is dead. Commander Logan Barrish over there," Sean waved in his direction, "is the one you want in his place. Further, I transferred Captain Brewster to the Missouri and Captain Folger to the Enterprise. By the way, where exactly are we being ordered to?"

"You and Secretary Calhoun will be delivered to the naval station at Hunters Point. The rest of you will wait aboard the Enterprise. After that, I can't say." The Admiral gave Sean a look and shook his head. "I'm glad I'm not in your shoes."

This was ominous news to Sean because he knew the Navy had closed the base in 1998.

Alicia noticed Sean's concern. "Hunters Point?"

"Apparently we're being placed incognito while they debrief us."

They put their drinks down, grabbed their coats, and followed Van Holland into the waiting arms of their escorts.

They never made it to Hunters Point. Their Black Hawk diverted to San Francisco International Airport where within ten minutes they were flying east in an unmarked Gulfstream, still in the company of the silent commandos.

Five hours later, they arrived at Bolling Air Force base off the Potomac where their guards escorted Alicia and Sean into a room. After a wait of fifteen minutes, in walked Vice President Clayton Rushmore, along with the National Security adviser, Harold Helms, a woman neither of them recognized, and Federica Barrett who was Alicia's replacement.

The Vice President spoke first. "What happened to your command Admiral Phillips?"

"Seems to me you should be directing that question to Mr. Mulligan at Comstock, and to tell you the truth, by the way we're being treated, I'm not sure if I feel inclined to give you an answer even if I had one."

Frederica Barrett continued the tag team of the two. "If we are to believe what junior officers and crew have told us so far, your task force, within a span of three months, engaged and destroyed the Axis forces in the beginning of 1942. So far, your senior officers refuse to say a word to either confirm or deny this. Then there is the fact half of your ships with their crews are still missing, and what is here has serious battle damage. According to further reports from Admiral Van Holland, there were also over seventy casualties aboard those ships as well.

"We're sorry for the way you were brought here, but you should know both of you, your ships, and crews will stay quarantined until we make some sense of what happened."

"So just out of curiosity," Sean asked, "where have you quarantined them?"

The Vice President was quick to answer. "To be honest Sean, I'm not at liberty to tell you."

"Well then *Clayton*, I guess I'm not at liberty to say anything, except what time will dinner be served? I'm sure Secretary Calhoun is as hungry as I am. We haven't eaten a thing since yesterday."

Sean turned to Alicia and smiled. "I guess we were right. Our ships never made it to San Francisco."

Vice President Rushmore had enough of Sean's smug responses. "What are you trying to hide? We could lock you and your girlfriend up for the rest of your lives with a list of offenses ranging from the destruction of government property to the murder of every dead and missing sailor. Is this what you want?"

"What I want *Clayton*, is for you to understand that we will not offer up the slightest bit of information to you, or anyone else, until I am assured the truth is available to the public. If there's nothing for the government to hide, then there isn't any need to keep my sailors from returning home to their families."

The Vice President started to answer Sean, when the unknown woman interrupted him. "I assure you Admiral Phillips, once we are given a reasonable explanation for what happened, an arrangement can be worked out to address your concerns."

Sean rebuffed her overture. "Nothing you've said or done so far exactly gives us confidence that we can trust any assurances you give us."

Alicia wanted to know what her role was in all of this. "I'm sorry but no one has been polite enough to introduce you."

"You are right. I am Dr. Harriet Fleishman, the President's Science Advisor. The reason I am here is to help the President understand what happened from a scientific perspective."

"While you're probably correct about your role Dr. Fleishman, it's definitely not the agenda of the men you came here with. Am I correct Mr. Helms?" Alicia had worked with Harold Helms, the former Director of the CIA and now the President's National Security Advisor, during her service to the President.

Alicia's comment made the Vice President angry. "All I know is over fifteen hundred members of the United States Navy and their ships are missing. Though there is little in the way of criminal charges the government can levy against Miss Calhoun, barring any information you supply to the contrary, we can throw the book at you Admiral Phillips. So cut the crap and tell us what happened."

"The only thing I'm willing to tell you *Clayton*," Sean answered with contempt, "is until you release the officers and sailors of the Enterprise Task Force, nothing happened except a major malfunction of the Comstock Technologies Specter program, which had our ship's weapons targeting and launching missiles against each other. This is also why half of my command is still missing, and it's too bad you don't have Dr. Safire around to ask him how this happened. Why don't you ask Mr. Mulligan if he'd care to offer an explanation?"

Without the time for an alternative if they failed to cooperate, the Vice President threw up his hands in frustration. "This is just great. You two can rot in this room until you give us the answers we need."

With that said, they left Sean and Alicia alone, which surprised Sean.

Alicia was about to say something when he gave her a look that warned her to stay quiet. Sean knew they would be recording everything they said and did.

Alicia understood, leaned forward, and whispered in Sean's ear. "So, do you want a large or a small wedding?"

Sean lost it and laughed. Sitting in this ridiculous situation, after having spent the last three months living in a bad movie, he realized God truly had a strange sense of humor.

Even without an explanation from Sean about what was so funny, his laughter became infectious, and soon Alicia was on the floor.

The people monitoring them were not amused.

An hour later, their commando escorts took them to a room on the base where no one came to see them until the next morning.

At 0730, the commandos knocked on the door. "Admiral Phillips, we need you to come with us."

Sean opened the door and asked, "Miss Calhoun too?"

"No Sir. Our orders are for only you."

"It looks like divide and conquer time." With a wink Sean joked, "Remember what I told you, if I'm not back in an hour, contact our alien friends. They'll know what to do."

Alicia laughed. "Do you want the glowing gold or silver light beam to ride out on?"

The guards were not amused. After a short walk, Sean entered a room without windows. The room also lacked any creature comforts; two chairs and a table were the only furniture. Seated in one of the chairs was the President of the United States.

"Good morning Admiral. I trust you didn't have a very restful sleep last night."

"Considering the government I've spent over twenty years serving is treating me and the sailors under my command so cavalierly, you bet your ass I didn't. Have you come here with a solution to our problem Mr. President? Or have you come to drive home the point that if we don't cooperate you'll have no choice but to make everybody's life miserable."

"That depends on whether or not you want to give your version of what happened to your command. As far as our scientists can ascertain, in the blink of an eye your entire task force disappeared. We need you to tell us what happened."

"I've had all night to think about it Mr. President, and there is nothing to be gained by explaining what happened that will allow you to restore the over six thousand men and women who shared in this event, back to their normal lives. I choose instead to let you come up with your own explanation." Sean knew regardless of what promises the President made, as soon as he got what he wanted there was a good chance they would all disappear.

"Whether you decide to cooperate or not, we will find out what we need to know, and the longer you refuse to cooperate the tougher it will be for the people you claim to care so much about. Besides, how do you know we haven't learned everything we need to know from your officers?"

"Then why are you bothering Secretary of Defense Calhoun and me? I'll tell you why. You're clueless without Dr. Safire and the scientists to understand what happened to Specter, and they aren't here. I don't see how you can acquire any useful information from any of the officers, though I'm inclined to believe they haven't cooperated for the same reasons we haven't.

"I'll repeat what we said to the Vice President. Until you release my officers and crew, you will get nothing from us. Therefore, you either allow Miss Calhoun and me to be together and find a way to convince us you won't sweep us all under the carpet, or nothing is going to change."

Sean had boxed the President in. "Why don't we focus on just one incident?"

"Which one would that be Mr. President?"

"Can you explain to me how Joseph Stalin wound up in the Enterprise's brig?"

"I can, and I will, if you release my crew."

Exasperated, the President leaned back in his chair, and pulled a pack of cigarettes out of his pocket. Unfortunately for him, he knew Sean was right. After interviewing the junior officers and enlisted personnel, the FBI was able to piece together a narrative of some of the surreal three months spent in the alternate reality. However, none of them could offer an explanation about how it happened.

With the operating system and the personnel responsible for Specter unavailable, the President and his advisors were still mystified. Those who operated the subsystems on the ships that returned were not privy to the actions Dr. Safire, Dr. Cutler, and Dr. Phelps took throughout the adventure.

When the President finally conceded to the negotiations that eventually led to the release of all involved, it took another day to arrange the press conference to announce to a shocked world where the Enterprise Task Force had been. After the President finished, Sean and Alicia met him in the Oval Office.

The President asked Sean, "When they cleared Enterprise of her personnel, one of the teams searching the ship for stragglers entered a cabin and discovered Senator Boyle asleep. When they woke him up, he didn't have any recollection of what everyone else had witnessed. Why do you suppose that is?"

Sean only laughed in response to the question.

"You're killing me Admiral."

The whirlwind Sean and Alicia's lives became after the President announced to the world how the country lost four of its warships and two supply ships, along with over 1,500 officers and crew, forced the President to assign a Secret Service detail to escort them wherever they went.

As the Commander of the Task Force, a relentless Congress forced Sean to spend a week justifying his actions under circumstances none of its self-absorbed grandstanding members could understand. After a week of questions that varied from suggesting he had an anti-Christian bias, to comparing his ego to Napoleon, Sean had enough of the self-serving morons. When he showed up for his seventh day of grilling, instead of answering any questions, he read from a prepared statement.

"I have gone through a week of listening to some of the most fictional drivel I've ever had to suffer in my life. The infantile nature every one of you operates under astounds me. Not one of you has shown the least bit of intellectual curiosity about the scientific consequences our experience signifies. Instead of discussing what this means to humanity and how we could benefit from the knowledge, you choose to wrap yourselves in the flag I have dedicated my life to and disgrace it. It isn't any wonder our nation has lost the ability to resolve even the smallest of issues."

Before Sean could continue, the committee Chairman interrupted. "How dare you question our motives Admiral Phillips? If you persist in mocking this committee, I will hold you in Contempt of Congress."

Sean smiled at the Chairman. "That's okay. I'm not the only one who has contempt for this committee. From the poll numbers I've read, not many of you will occupy your seats after the next election."

With the Chairman banging his gavel, Sean rose from his chair and turned his back on the committee to address the media cameras in the back of the room. "Since I was old enough to understand, I've witnessed Federal Politicians ignore the problems of the real world while consolidating power alongside their corporate masters. The Spirit of America, as I understood it, meant the sky was the limit, and for the first one hundred and seventy-five years of our existence this proved to be the case as we became the most powerful nation in the world." Sean paused for a moment, a look of bewilderment on his face. "What happened?"

Then his voice rose in anger. "I'll tell you what happened. Human nature happened. Politicians promised us they had all the answers and even as evidence to the contrary stacked up, we forgot the lessons of Abraham Lincoln. Our government was supposed to be of the people, by the people, and for the people, not a select few of the people.

"When the Local, State, and Federal Governments are all in lockstep against what is in the best interests of the people, it's way past time for another revolution. The only way for us to regain our freedom and liberty is to band together to vote every one of these obstructionists out of *our* government. Then we as a people need to replace them with representatives who will strip away the decades of corruption that has passed for legislation over the last seventy plus years."

Sean looked back at the committee members who clearly were not happy about the takeover of their clubhouse, but knew there was little they could do with the cameras rolling. "We only have ourselves to blame for the failures committed in our name by these second rate used-car salesmen."

Sean prepared to leave, but added one final thought. "The contempt I feel for this body is only surpassed by the disappointment I have of you, the American public. We used to be a nation of overachievers who took the example of other's success as a roadmap to follow. I don't know where we lost this as an ideal, but now all anyone wants to do is blame everyone else for their failures. When did we decide as a nation to look to government for our answers?"

To the protests of the committee, Sean found Alicia and they strolled out of the Capitol, this time to cheers instead of gunshots.

The next month blew past without a moment to themselves. Political groups bombarded Sean and Alicia with requests to lead a new coalition to challenge the status quo. Neither of them wanted to remain in the public glare. While they didn't mind the focus of this newfound awareness among the nation's citizens, both Sean and Alicia refused calls to enter the public arena of politics. They preferred instead to lend their support in other ways, like giving their voice to boycotts and massive rallies.

⋅—◈—⋅

Back in 1942, four days after the Enterprise, Decatur, Chancellorsville, and Seawolf disappeared, the Missouri, Princeton,

John Paul Jones, Hampton, Amelia Earhart, and Laramie arrived at Guantanamo Bay. Throughout the voyage to Cuba, Tony not only continued to struggle with the violent death of Renée, but also the loss of Sean, the only person in the world who could harness his talents and keep him from self-destructing.

Regardless of his emotional state of mind, for the sake of his command Tony had to choke down his pain. With the disappearance of the Enterprise, the only ship capable of projecting intimidation through its air wing, his ability to maintain a strong bearing was vital. From here on out, Tony had to learn quickly how to think like Sean and Alicia if they were to bluff their way through.

On the bridge, Dr. Rebecca Cutler had to repeat her question a second time. "I said I have Specter up and running again Tony. Are you all right? Is it okay to still call you Tony, or are you some kind of Admiral now? And why are you wearing a side arm?"

"As before, Rebecca, you know when the situation calls for formality. Please continue your report," Tony answered dryly.

Rebecca missed the old flirtatious Tony, who first would have complimented her on what she wore. This Tony was a real stick in the mud. Considering their comrades had teleported out, and more than likely still alive, she didn't see any reason to go into mourning. So, she dug deep into her wardrobe and picked out a bright yellow soda fountain mini dress, complete with a front bow. She accented this with her black knee-high leather boots, black choke collar, black gloves and topped it all off with a black wide brimmed hat. She was especially miffed he didn't notice the extra-long eyelashes it took her half an hour to glue on. Determined, she struck an overtly sexy pose and added, "Maybe I should show up naked next time."

"I'm still right here Rebecca." Tony was only half-paying attention, still consumed with how he was going to take Sean and Alicia's place as the face of the task force, and how he could sell the idea of their disappearance. As he looked at his XO, Commander Carl Eddington, and then back to Rebecca, an idea slowly began to take shape in his overtaxed mind.

Disappointed, Rebecca continued in a faux serious tone. "Yes, we've got Specter operational again, but we still don't know what happened when the other ships disappeared. Dr. Safire initiated the subroutines we have dealt with so far. This time it was more like half an event when you think about it, and I know he couldn't have so many independent programs running at once without us knowing about them."

This made Tony impatient. "I understand your fascination with all of this, but does anything you're telling me get us any closer to understanding why the Enterprise and the other ships are gone and we're still here?"

"I was getting to it, oh impatient one. What I am trying to tell you is I don't think Specter had anything to do with the time travel stuff. This time there isn't any evidence the commands came from the Missouri or the Princeton. It's like the ships that launched the attacks acted independently, which should have been impossible. Like I said, I don't think Specter was responsible for the missile launches this time." When she finished Rebecca did a quick pirouette and waited.

There was a reason Tony didn't like to make existential decisions; it gave him a headache. "So where does that leave us? If it isn't our technology sending us down the rabbit hole, what is?"

"To tell you the truth, I haven't a clue. But whatever is responsible is way beyond anything our technology has to offer. You can be sure I'll do whatever I can to figure it out now that I know Specter isn't the issue. I feel like the whole thing is some perverse way to make us dance like puppets on strings and it really pisses me off."

"Thank you Dr. Cutler. And by the way, I'm tired of being a puppet on a string."

"Excuse me?"

"You asked why I am wearing my side arm. We don't know who or what we are up against, or what will happen, so next time I will be prepared."

Unsure about what to do, Tony decided their only option was to stay with Sean's original plan. "I've got to go meet with the port officials in the morning. Commander Eddington, I need you to contact Captain Turner for me."

"Yes Sir." He picked up the phone to contact the Hampton, and then hesitated in embarrassment. "Sir, what would you like me to ask the Captain?"

"I'm sorry Commander. I thought it would be obvious to you I need Captain Turner, who is second in seniority now, to take over command while I'm gone. Send him to my quarters when he gets here. You have the bridge."

"Yes Sir."

"Captain's off the Bridge." The bridge personnel snapped to attention as Tony disappeared.

Carl Eddington turned to Rebecca with a smile and acknowledged her attire. "I've got to say this outfit is in my top three so far, Dr. Cutler."

"Only your top three Commander Eddington?" Then to give him something to remember, in her best imitation of a vamp whispered in his ear. "I guess next time I'll have to work harder – Carl."

Commander Eddington looked around the bridge to see if anyone else heard her, and satisfied no one was paying attention, mysteriously whispered back, "If you only knew – if you only knew."

It wasn't what he said that stopped Rebecca cold, it was the way it resonated somewhere deep in her subconscious, like Carl was someone she shared a deep connection too in some long ago past. "If I only knew what?"

"If you only knew how special you really are."

Rebecca could read that this wasn't what he meant, but figured her reaction was just some fluke of shorted out emotions so she let it go. "Okay Carl, I'll see you around." Rebecca spun on her heels and sashayed out the door.

"Rebecca's off the bridge!"

"*Mister* Porter!"

"Yes Sir, never again Sir," the Officer of the Watch sheepishly acknowledged, to a background of chuckles from others on the bridge.

After she disappeared, Carl silently admonished himself. "Rein it in boy. The last thing either one of us needs right now is to get sloppy."

Later on after meeting with Tony, Captain Marlowe Turner arrived on the bridge. "Commander Eddington, Captain Knox would like to see both you and Dr. Cutler in his quarters. I'm here to relieve you."

"Yes Sir," Commander Eddington replied. "Have you informed the Doctor?"

"She's on her way."

When Carl Eddington entered the Captains Cabin, he found Rebecca already seated on the couch.

Tony didn't waste any time getting to the point. "How would you two like to spend some time on shore?" Then with his attention fixed squarely on Rebecca, he continued. "It has occurred to me that with both Sean and Alicia gone we are in need of someone to act on our behalf when dealing with the snakes and alligators."

Rebecca jumped up from the couch. "In other words you want *me* to act as the fleet's ambassador? Have you lost your mind?"

Tony ignored her protest. "Not just you. Commander Eddington will accompany you as our military representative, and I am not really giving you a choice. You need to get your things in order."

Rebecca paced the room looking like a caged Tiger. "I haven't any qualifications. Besides there isn't anyone who can run Specter. You guys will be in a world of hurt if it goes down at the wrong time. Besides, I'm a scientist who seeks out facts, not some charlatan who speaks out of both sides of her mouth. I hate the idea."

"And that is why you are perfect. If I wanted someone who could spin bullshit, I would send some kiss ass ensign."

Tony paused to think about her argument about Specter, and swallowed hard. "Dr. Phelps has been by your side throughout, so bring him up to speed on anything you might have held back. With your help, he can handle Specter when you are dealing with your new duties."

"Not possible. Forrest is smart, but..." was as far as Rebecca got before Tony cut her off.

"Have him ready by day after tomorrow, Doctor."

"There is no..."

"Your ride takes you to Washington day after tomorrow at 1000 hours sharp. Be ready."

Throughout their exchange, Carl sat on the couch smiling, which Rebecca now noticed. "Why are you looking so happy?"

"I can't think of anyone else I would rather spend my time ashore with."

"Not hardly," Rebecca rebuked.

Carl's smile grew wider as his gaze locked with hers.

When Tony informed a surprised President Roosevelt that Sean and Alicia wanted out of the spotlight, and Dr. Rebecca Cutler and Commander Carl Eddington would represent the Enterprise Task Force, the President didn't have any choice but to accept the change.

While this played out, the rest of the personnel aboard the ships acclimated as best they could to their new world. Their presence in Cuban society triggered cultural changes that allowed most of them to live rather comfortable lives while ashore. Tony decided early on, every sailor would be required to serve at least five years before released from his or her naval obligations. Surprisingly, there were few desertions.

Tony spent most of his free time alone, and didn't share with anyone what he was planning. Commander Carl Eddington found out a year after their arrival in Cuba when Tony handed him a thick folder.

"What's this?"

"Go over it with Rebecca, and let me know what you think," was all he said.

What Tony turned over to Carl was an idea that had worked for centuries and should have never ended. It suggested a return of Trade Guilds to self-regulate their industries instead of governmental bureaucracies would serve society better. Throughout the Middle Ages the growth of these guilds led to self-regulating trades that demanded members focus on the quality and honesty of their work. Most of the architecture and engineering that came out of this system is the foundation of modern construction. Masters trained journeymen who trained apprentices, and there were no short cuts. For the first time in a century, the experts with the training and skills were the ones who certified contractors, not an over bloated bureaucracy that gave anyone with a pulse and five hundred dollars, a license.

Another issue Tony addressed was the suffocating influence of religion over civil rights. Most of what he gave to Carl on this was a direct result of conversations with Sean and Alicia. Fortunately, Alicia had compiled most of the information and had laid out clearly the idea that underpinned the arguments. Even without all of the modern problems of *in vitro* fertilization, Stem Cells, and DNA to complicate the argument, monotheistic religion would always be the most difficult monster to put back in a box.

The third issue was the US Supreme Court decision in 2010 that made corporations and unions no longer subject to campaign finance laws, which allowed them to spend freely in elections. This had started with an 1886 Supreme Court decision that held railroad corporations are persons with the intent of the Fourteenth Amendment to the US Constitution. Tony's solution was to work out a federal definition of a corporation that did not include the elements of personhood, such as voting or influencing voting through free speech and at the same time did not violate the 14th Amendment.

Tony maintained overall command of the truncated task force, but it wasn't long before he acquiesced to most of the suggestions Rebecca and Carl offered. The ships and crews were his, and the couple dealt with everything else. They had become for Tony, Sean and Alicia, minus the camaraderie. With his political masterpiece completed and turned over to the kids, he had nothing important to do and no one to confide in. Tony's emotional turmoil became a constant. He spent most of his time secluded from the day-to-day operations of his task force.

One day, alone in his quarters, his frustrations broke through into a vocal rage. "Once again, here I am, left alone to rot. I need something to do! *I need some action!*" As he fingered his Model 1911 Smith and Wesson, he thought, "Maybe I should jump ship and head to the jungles of the Amazon."

The years sped by with a series of deployments that reshaped the social fabric throughout the world. In April 1945, by special order and in commemoration of Captain Renée Aslan, killed in the line of duty, President Franklin Delano Roosevelt promoted Commander Carl Eddington to Captain of the USS Missouri. Dr. Rebecca Cutler and now Captain Carl Eddington grew into their new roles as diplomats, though Rebecca had to learn to reign in some of her eclectic tendencies.

They parceled out technologies to international trade consortiums created specifically to reverse engineer them for commercial applications. Washington grew to learn that it was in

Imagine A New World

their best interests to listen to their advice about the direction the era's scientists and entrepreneurs should focus their attention. In this way, the United States retained the edge over the rest of the nations of the world, both militarily and economically.

The United States Government, aided by Ambassadors-at-Large Cutler and Eddington, entered into negotiations with international representatives to set up standardized trade agreements so everyone labored under the same rules. With coherent distribution plans in place that laid out how to utilize fairly the earth's finite resources, fish stocks flourished, and wildlife and plant species rebounded. With regard to environmental law, they turned to the only culture that practiced sound environmental practices for centuries, the Indigenous Nations Americas. Sweet vindication indeed.

Fortunately, Rebecca convinced Democratic members of Congress of the Christian Right's success in poisoning the body politic. This led Congress to pass a bill that forbids all tax-exempt entities from political campaign contributions. The new law threatened any religious group who actively supported a political campaign or ongoing legislation, with a loss of their tax-exempt status. It became a win-win when Republicans added an amendment to the bill that banned Unions from the use of dues for the same purpose. Further, the bill created a legal description for corporations that made sure they were treated as separate legal entities other than as persons in Federal and State law. In September 1943, President Roosevelt signed the comprehensive bill into law. With religious organizations, unions, and corporations out of the picture, politics would hopefully land where it belonged – in the hands of the people.

This wasn't to say there were not concerns that this would leave the nation vulnerable to some demagogue rising up to create a fascist movement, but they had to take that chance.

Stuck together as they were in such constant close proximity, Carl and Rebecca soon fell in love and married in June of 1944. In

May of 1945, Rebecca delivered a healthy baby boy the named Sean Anthony Eddington.

In early 1951, the Missouri Task Force left port to support the United States response to the latest regional conflict. Six weeks later off the coast of Lebanon, Captain Carl Eddington scanned the horizon from the bridge of the USS Missouri. His eyes swept past the battleship USS North Carolina to the rest of the international fleet that was about to break up and set a course back to their home ports.

After Captain Eddington repeated this action six times over the last fifteen minutes, it finally got Tony's attention. "Put down the damn binoculars, sit down, and chill. What is the matter with you today?"

"I'm sorry, Captain Knox. I'm looking forward to our return to Cuba. I didn't realize how difficult it is to spend so much time away from my family." He slowly walked over and sat down in the Captain's Chair.

Tony thought it strange after four deployments away from Rebecca that all of a sudden this should distract him. "You better start worrying about paying attention to your duties or the only thing you'll see when we get back to Cuba is extra duty to improve your attention span."

"Yes Sir."

Even though he remained seated, Tony could see nothing had changed. Eddington still intently focused his attention on the ships off their port.

Tony started to walk over to him, when the phone rang.

Carl quickly picked it up, and after a moment turned so Tony could see his face drop. "What is it?" Tony demanded.

"There's a green mist emanating from the Princeton." He then turned away so Tony couldn't see the smile of satisfaction plastered on his face.

Dr. Rebecca Cutler Eddington had just left the office of the Senate Majority Leader and was about to ask her attaché if they had time for lunch when she noticed the look of surprise on the young woman's face. "What is it?"

"Look at your legs!"

When Rebecca looked down, the unmistakable green mist was working its way past her knees. "Oh sh…" was all her assistant heard before Rebecca vanished. It took the Capitol Police five minutes to revive the aide and another hour to get anything coherent out of her.

"…it!" As the green mist faded, Rebecca realized she now stood on the bridge of the battleship USS Missouri. She slowly turned her head when the sound of footsteps on the metal deck behind her broke the silence. "Welcome home honey."

Her joy at hearing her husband, Captain Carl Eddington, suddenly turned to fear. "Please tell me we're still in 1951." Then in a panic, she scanned the bridge and asked, "Where's Captain Knox?"

Before Carl could tell her Tony had vanished off the bridge moments before her arrival, she rushed to the window just as the green mist rose above the bow of the Missouri. She glared back at her husband. "What about our son?"

"Don't worry about Sean Anthony, he's fine." Carl walked over and wrapped his arms around her. "You're not going to like what happens next, so let me get that out of the way first. As much as I would like to prepare you for what is coming, unfortunately I cannot. Just know that you are the love of my life and we will be back together as a family if everything goes the way I planned it." Carl then gave her a quick kiss and broke their embrace.

"What are you talking about? Where are you going, and more importantly, where exactly am I going if not with you?"

The green mist had made its way to the front window, which brought Rebecca back into her husband's arms. He grabbed her shoulders to get her full attention. "Everything should work out fine. Don't worry about me, and don't worry about our son."

At that moment, Carl began to fade as Rebecca frantically tried to keep her arms around him, only to fall right through his disappearing image.

As he faded from view Rebecca heard, "All will be made clear in due time. Don't wait up for me.

Hidden in the bushes, a young boy crouched quietly watching two beautiful Red Macaws perform their mating dance. He had tracked them for the last half hour in the hope the pair would lead him to the rest of their flock. This was the next test of many given by his tribal elders as part of his transformation into manhood. His tribe had learned hundreds of years ago that the best way to survive in their environment was to understand how it worked. This is why little had changed in their way of life for over five centuries; they truly lived in harmony with the universe.

Suddenly there was a loud, cracking boom, accompanied by a bright green flash that startled the boy and sent the Macaws off screaming in protest. It took a minute for his eyes to clear and another to get control of his rapidly beating heart. When he did, he looked back at the clearing to see a strangely dressed man standing in the middle who uttered words the youth could not understand. However, the boy could tell the stranger was not happy.

"God damn it, now where the hell am I?"

Both Captain Anthony Knox and the young boy heard a rather jovial voice that came from all around them. "You wanted action – action you'll get."

Excerpt • Book III

From the Judgement In Time Series
Another Fine Mess

An F-35 pilot from the USS Enterprise reported in to the CIC. "Radar shows a land mass to the west."The pilot banked to those coordinates and five minutes later, a series of islands began to dot the ocean. "I recognize where we are. I trained in these waters."

Another F-35 pilot flying to the south reported. "I am pretty sure I am approaching... Yes, I recognize it as the Windward Passage. I am cloaking to fly lower for a closer look." After ten minutes of silence, she reported from her new position. "I see small villages with thatched roofs, but nothing that resembles anything modern."

The pilot, a highly educated, sensible woman of 32, but new to the task force, continued to circle the island village amazed at how it could exist at all. "What have I got myself into?"

www.ingramcontent.com/pod-product-compliance
Lightning Source LLC
Chambersburg PA
CBHW020627110726
47899CB00002B/687